THE
GILDED CAGE

THE
GILDED CAGE

TROY SOOS

KENSINGTON BOOKS
http://www.kensingtonbooks.com

KENSINGTON BOOKS are published by

Kensington Publishing Corp.
850 Third Avenue
New York, NY 10022

Library of Congress Card Catalogue Number: 2002101737
ISBN: 1-57566-769-X

First Printing: October 2002
10 9 8 7 6 5 4 3 2 1

Printed in the United States of America

THE
GILDED CAGE

CHAPTER 1

When the top button of her shirtwaist was slipped free, Sarah's drooping eyelids also snapped open, and a sparkle of light flared in eyes that had previously been as dull and lifeless as a faded sepia photograph. That brief flash was due to fear, Rebecca Davies could tell, but she was relieved to see it, reassured to know that the girl still had some spark of life in her. Besides, Rebecca also knew that Sarah Zietlow was perfectly safe in the hands of old Doc Abraham.

With a deft, gentle touch, the aged physician methodically continued unbuttoning the frail young woman's shirtwaist. Sarah, who had been lying tense and rigid on his lumpy examination bed, sighed softly, and Rebecca thought she detected a whimper of willing surrender at the end of the breath. By the time the doctor finished with the stubborn buttons, Sarah's entire body had perceptibly relaxed.

Dr. Marcus Abraham's reassuring bedside manner was one of his strongest qualities, and the main reason Rebecca brought her young women to him as patients. Many of the unfortunate girls who came to Colden House for Rebecca's help had endured abuses that left them with a fear of men, and Abraham was one of the few doctors Rebecca found who could examine them without adding to their distress. Even the doctor's appearance was reassuring: Garbed in a stained black frock coat that might have dated back to the Lincoln administration, and with white chin whiskers and a clean-shaven upper lip, the slightly built Doc Abraham looked more like an Amish elder than a New York City physician.

Once he'd opened her plain cotton blouse, the doctor carefully positioned the narrow end of his old-fashioned stethoscope—a hollow cedar cone shaped like the horn of an Edison talking machine—against Sarah's breastbone. Although there remained a couple of layers of woolen undergarments between her skin and the instrument, the young woman flinched at the contact and her eyes widened a bit further.

What was probably once a pretty face now appeared sepulchral, as sunken and drawn as the rest of her emaciated body. Sarah's cheeks were so hollow that Rebecca thought she could see the impression of teeth behind the taut skin. And her big brown eyes, especially in her present state of fear, seemed to be popping out of their deep-set sockets.

The severity of her gauntness was most alarming, but her thin face also showed the more common scars of a life spent on the harsh streets of lower Manhattan. There were visible wounds— her chin had once been split and failed to properly heal, and she had scabs over one eye and on the side of her neck—as well as internal ones that must have led her to adopt her callused expression that served to mask any trace of emotion. With no home, Sarah Zietlow had suffered the same afflictions as all those who try to survive without proper nutrition and hygiene and have to fend off the onslaughts of disease and violence. Right now, though, she was also clearly suffering from something that was even more immediately threatening.

Leaning over, Doc Abraham tilted his head and placed his ear against the broad end of the stethoscope. "Heart sounds strong," he quietly announced in a soothing voice.

Rebecca coughed, not for the first time since she'd entered the examination room, and shot an annoyed glance at the coal-burning stove in the corner. Tendrils of smoke worked their way around the stove's feed door, polluting the thick air with soot and cinders.

As much as Rebecca admired Doc Abraham's manner, she deplored the unsanitary condition of his office. Instead of smelling of disinfectant, the prevailing odors were of soft coal and Cavendish tobacco. And, although some objects in the cluttered room might have once been painted antiseptic white, gray was now the dominant color; a thick layer of dust and ash coated everything from the medical instruments in their open trays to the bottles of pills and liniment on the shelves. A lack of sunlight made the room appear even hazier; the small window that overlooked wintry Mott Street had steamed up and appeared to be sweating mud as the water mixed with soot and ran down the panes in dun-colored rivulets. Doc Abraham clearly didn't put much stock in modern notions about hygiene; in fact, it was only at Rebecca's insistence that he made use of the washbowl before beginning an examination.

Removing the stethoscope, the old doctor reached out to Sarah's forehead and tenderly pushed back a few locks of her lank brown hair. She had told Rebecca that she was twenty-two years of age, but the bald patches on her head, along with her haggard features and sallow skin the color of old newspaper, made her appear more like eighty-two. After running his fingertips along her temples, Abraham peered into her eyes; they weren't jaundiced like her skin, but had once again gone dull, like an ember that briefly flares before turning to ash. He then moved down to Sarah's hands, which were as bony and wrinkled as his own; lifting one, then the other, he examined them thoroughly from the palms to the fingernails.

Rebecca understood what the doctor could determine merely by looking at the woman's hands. Abraham hadn't even bothered to take her temperature. But then, she came to him largely for his demeanor; as to his medical acumen, she doubted that it was any better than that of others in his profession, who were all too ready to prescribe nerve tonics and liver pills after the most cursory of examinations.

Still holding her hand, the doctor asked, "How long have you been sick, Miss Zietlow?"

Sarah shook her head with bewilderment, as if she hadn't even been aware that she was sick. Rebecca wondered if Sarah's condition had been of such long duration that she couldn't recall being otherwise.

The doctor reached toward her abdomen, but she raised an arm to block him. In a weak voice, she uttered her first words to the man: "I have an awful bad pain in my belly."

"Female pain?" he asked.

Sarah flushed, and red mottled the yellow color that tinged her skin. Her jaw clenched and she didn't reply.

Rebecca answered for her, "No. It's not that."

Still addressing the young woman, Doc Abraham asked, "What have you been eating?"

Sarah turned to face the wall, as if she hadn't heard the question, and uttered only a groan.

Rebecca beckoned to the doctor with a nod, and they excused themselves to step into the anteroom.

In a low voice, Rebecca explained, "Miss Zietlow showed up at Colden House for the first time last night, and I don't know much about her history. All she would tell me at first was her name and age—twenty-two." In answer to the doctor's surprised lift of his brow, she added, "I assumed she was older, too." Rebecca bit her lip. "I'd hate to imagine what it was that aged her so. In any event, some girls do take some time before they're comfortable enough to reveal anything about themselves, so I didn't press her. After Miss Zietlow had a bath, some sleep, and a change of clean clothes, she told me a little more, including the fact that she's been suffering from almost constant stomach pain for some time. She seems to have only a vague concept of time—poor girl's probably just trying to survive from one hour to the next—but she thinks she's been sick for at least a couple of months."

"So she came to you for help."

"Not because she was sick, no. She came because it was so bitter cold last night. Miss Zietlow's been sleeping in an abandoned streetcar outside the Chatham Square station, on the Sixth Avenue line. Yesterday she found that the trolley had been moved away— it must have been taken back to the car barn. She couldn't find any other shelter for the night, so she came to me." Rebecca recalled the shivering girl's hopeless expression and lifeless demeanor when she showed up at the door of Colden House. "I don't think she was looking for help, though. It was more like she just wanted a warm place to die."

"Well, we're certainly not going to let that happen," said the doctor. "She's a precious child, and we'll try to see that she has many more years—better years—left to her." Rebecca smiled. Another reason she came to Doc Abraham was that he was willing to help the poor and the outcasts. He even genuinely cared about them.

Rebecca continued to describe the girl's ailments. "I tried to feed Sarah some broth last night, but she wasn't able to keep it down. This morning, the same thing. I tried giving her oatmeal, bread, broth . . . everything she ate came back up. She didn't seem to care; she said her stomach hurts too much to take in food anyway. That's why I brought her to you. Do you have any idea what's the matter with her?"

Abraham answered thoughtfully, "Judging by her symptoms, she appears to have gastric fever."

"What can be done to treat it?"

The doctor hesitated. "I said it *appears* to be gastric fever. But with the hair loss, the jaundice, and that skin rash on the backs of her hands, I suspect it might be something else." He paused again and knitted his wiry gray eyebrows. "Is there anybody who might want to poison her?"

"Poison? No, why?" Sarah had told Rebecca that she'd been living alone on the streets for several years. What kind of enemies could such a poor young woman have? Why would anyone want to kill a girl like Sarah Zietlow? "Are you sure she's been poisoned?"

The doctor shook his head. "No, I can't be certain. But her symptoms do suggest it's a possibility." He tugged at his bearded chin. "I could be mistaken; perhaps it is only gastric fever, after all, and there's another explanation for the hair loss and jaundice."

Rebecca had certainly seen a variety of problems afflicting girls who came to Colden House, but this was a new one, and she was at a loss to solve it. "What should we do?"

"Put Miss Zietlow in the hospital for a couple of days." The doctor cleared his throat. "But . . . that would entail some expense. The hospital will want to be paid."

Of course they will, thought Rebecca. The only questions were how much and how soon. The brutally cold winter was costing a fortune in coal heating fuel, and Colden House had almost no funds left to pay any of its bills. There was barely enough money for tomorrow's groceries. More than once lately, usually in the dead of night while trying in vain to get some sleep, Rebecca had grimly wondered which would be the worse fate for her girls: to starve or to freeze.

Abraham cleared his throat again, and Rebecca caught on that it wasn't due to the smoky air. "I will need to be paid, too," he said. "I hate to mention this, Miss Davies, but I haven't received payment for the last several patients you brought me. It's three dollars for the visit today—and twelve still owed from the last ones."

Rebecca promptly reached for her purse and dug a finger through the small variety store contained therein, looking in vain for a gold piece or a wadded bank note.

"Normally, I wouldn't bring it up," the doctor went on apologetically, "but with so many people being out of work these days, I have many patients not paying."

I know, thought Rebecca, *and I have more than the usual number of women needing shelter at Colden House.* With the economy getting worse, she was currently providing a home for more than thirty, in a home designed to hold no more than twenty.

After emptying the contents of the purse into her palm, Rebecca was embarrassed to find that she had only a dollar-twenty in nickels and dimes. There was the coal delivery yesterday, and she had to pay the milkman this morning. She held out the coins in her palm. "I'm sorry. This is all I have." Her hand began to tremble, and she wanted to cry with frustration.

Doc Abraham reached for her hand and softly closed her fingers over the coins. "You'll need streetcar fare to take Miss Zietlow to the hospital. We'll work out payment later." He patted her hand. "Take her to Columbus Hospital on Twentieth Street; I'll see that she's admitted and I'll check in on her at least once a day. If she doesn't get any worse, the main thing will be to feed her; we'll find something she can digest."

"Thank you." Rebecca could barely hear her own voice.

"First thing we'll try to give her is milk. That's the best thing for somebody who might have been poisoned."

At the word "poisoned," Rebecca's concern immediately shifted from her own difficulties to the fragile girl lying on the doctor's examination bed. The reason she was running Colden House in the first place was to help women like Sarah Zietlow, women who had nowhere else to go and no one else to assist them.

"I'll get her right to the hospital," Rebecca said. And after that, she would make sure that there was a bed and food available for Miss Zietlow at Colden House. She also vowed that, if somebody had indeed been trying to poison the young woman, there would be no more attempts on her life. At least not a successful one.

CHAPTER 2

Marshall Webb kept his eyes directed downward as he stepped along Jackson Street's broken, narrow sidewalk. His long legs usually carried him along as quickly as some hansom cabs, but he had to tread cautiously today. An icy drizzle was making much of the pavement precariously slick, while other parts of it were covered by a thick gray muck of slush mixed with stove ash from overflowing trash barrels that hadn't been emptied in weeks. With the brutal cold snap that New York had been enduring lately, it might be some time before the city's sanitation workers would venture outdoors to perform their duties—at least here in Corlear's Hook, an East Side neighborhood far too poor to be of any concern to City Hall. Residents had to be thankful that the cold weather at least kept the uncollected refuse from smelling as bad as it did in summer.

When he reached the pier at the foot of Jackson Street, Webb lifted his face into the biting sleet and looked ahead. As far as he could see, it appeared as if all color had been washed out of the world. The leaden sky was so low over the choppy gray waters of the East River, and the air so thick with mist and ice particles, that he could barely make out the Brooklyn Navy Yard on the opposite shore.

Webb walked around to the side of the pier and ducked his head to go underneath it. He failed to duck quite enough, and grimaced when his new stiff fur derby scraped one of the supporting timbers. With the pier sheltering him from the sleet, he took a handkerchief from the pocket of his caped mackintosh and brushed off the ice that had accumulated in small chunks on his thick mustache.

Although he was entering another world now, the waterfront's hidden netherworld, Webb saw that it, too, had only gray in its color palette. He had to step more carefully in the relative darkness, treading over piles of empty bean tins, broken oyster shells, shattered whiskey bottles, and discarded beer buckets left by "dock rats," the gangs of ruffians who roamed the riverfront and hid under the piers to split their loot and plan their next crimes. From the occasional rustling of the cans, it was apparent that the docks were home to more than just the two-legged variety of rat.

Webb found only one gaunt old man currently hiding under this pier. Huddled in a soiled overcoat that was worn through at the elbows, the man sat cross-legged in a nest that had been dug into a pile of rubbish and lined with tattered newspapers. A ragged tartan cloth was draped over his head like an old woman's kerchief and kept in place by a shapeless fedora that was missing half its brim.

"Colin McGah?" Webb called.

The old man scrambled to rise. Unlike Webb, he was easily able to stand upright without hitting his head on the rough planks above. "Whaddya want him for?" he growled. He tensed slightly, ready to dart away if he didn't like the answer.

Webb tried to sound nonthreatening. "I just need to speak with him. He has some important information that I'd like to ask him about."

It obviously wasn't often that this derelict was thought to know something of importance. He puffed himself up proudly and cocked his head, giving the appearance of a geriatric banty rooster. "Well, I'm the man you're looking for," he said. "But call me 'Kid'; everybody does." Webb thought Colin McGah was at least fifty years past the age when he should be called "Kid." The man's shaggy side-whiskers and loose, wrinkled skin were the same gray as everything else in this bleak place. The only color in his face was provided by the purple gin blossoms that bloomed on his nose.

"It's about your release, Mr. McGah," Webb said. "You had a year and a half left on your sentence, but you were released from the Tombs on November seventh." That was the day before Grover Cleveland won the 1892 presidential election, making him the only president to be elected to two nonconsecutive terms.

"No way in hell yer gonna put me back there!" McGah appeared ready to bolt again.

Webb quickly reassured him. "No, no. It was our mistake. You're a free man—if you help us out."

McGah squinted with suspicion. "Help you out how?"

"Well, somebody along the line wasn't taken care of, if you know what I mean. Freedom isn't exactly free in this city."

McGah knew exactly what Webb meant. "Hey, it was all on the up-and-up," he insisted. "The warden must have got his payoff, same as always. The guards, too." His toothless mouth began chewing nervously.

"Oh, you know how it is," Webb said, trying to give the impression that his visit here was purely routine. "We got a new mayor in the election; it's a new administration, and everybody just wants to make sure they're getting their due rewards. I'm with the Department of Corrections, and I've been sent to see if there are any holes in the system."

McGah stopped chewing long enough to ask, "Say, how'd you know where to find me?"

"It wasn't difficult. You're a well-known man in this part of the city." *Well known for getting tossed out of saloons,* Webb added silently to himself. "The bartender at the Billy Goat Tavern told me you'd likely be down here." The Billy Goat was a stale beer dive on Cherry Street; it was one of the many illicit cellar saloons that specialized in selling the watered-down dregs of beer kegs stolen from other taverns. Its customers were the dregs of the East Side's drinking class who could only afford two cents for an unwashed glass of flat, adulterated beer.

"That lousy bastard cut me off just cause I got no money." McGah whined like a real kid. "A man gotta keep warm somehow." He looked at Webb hopefully and took a step closer to him—close enough that Webb could smell the urine and vomit that saturated his ragged clothes. "You don't happen to have a bottle, do ya?"

"No, I don't. Sorry. Anyway, you were convicted of aggravated assault on one Andrew Cayce in the summer of 'ninety-one, isn't that right?" Although Webb had dates and names recorded in his notebook, he didn't refer to it; he'd found that people felt less free to talk when they thought their words might be written down.

"Yer damn right I was aggravated." McGah snorted. "That goddamn Cayce is nuthin' but a bum."

Webb almost laughed at McGah's understanding of what the

aggravated in *aggravated assault* meant. And what Webb found even funnier was when he tried to imagine who could possibly be so low on the social scale as to be rated a "bum" in this derelict's estimation. "What happened between you and Cayce?" he asked.

"Oh, a few years ago, Cayce lost a leg under the Third Avenue trolley. He'd been riding one of the cars all day and drinking from a bottle of gin he'd stole." McGah chortled. "Stupid bastard got so drunk, he ended up fallin' off the car. The one behind it ran over him and took off his leg. Turned out to be a blessin' for him, though."

"How so?" Webb was curious, and mildly amused by McGah's ready determinations of "bums" and "blessings."

"Well, Cayce, that clever bastard, made it pay off for him. From then on, he hardly ever had to worry 'bout his next drink." McGah shook his head with a touch of admiration. "Ol' Cayce came up with a dozen stories how he lost that leg, and he was always able to beg a nickel whenever he needed." He then grinned a grotesque smile that was all barren, black gum line. "Leastways, till I put a stop to it."

"Why did you want to put a stop to it?"

McGah's grin twisted into a sneer of contempt. "Cayce got hisself an old Union greatcoat—stole it off another fellah one night when he was stayin' at the Five Points Mission. Then he came up with a story. Cayce started telling folks he was a crippled war vet who lost his leg to a rebel cannonball at Gettysburg."

Webb wondered why that so offended McGah. "You didn't approve of his deceit?"

"His wha'?"

"His fraud."

McGah snorted. "Hell, what do I care about fraud? What put a bug up my ass was seein' that *uniform.*" He lifted his chin proudly. "*I'm* a veteran myself—of the draft riots of 'sixty-three." His tone became resentful. "Damn federal government thought they could draft hardworkin' white men to get themselves killed for the sake of Southern coons. Well, we sure showed them damn politicians in Washington: lynched more'n a dozen niggers here in the city and burned down that Colored Orphan Asylum—and I'm proud to say *I* helped set that fire." He paused as if expecting to hear words of admiration from Webb. On getting no response, he went on, "Anyways, ever since then, I always hated the sight of a Union uniform. And when I saw Cayce wearin' one, I took his crutch and beat him over the head till he was senseless." McGah shook his head with bewilderment. "Still don't see why I got pinched for beatin' that bum."

Webb wasn't about to debate the politics of a war that had been over for almost thirty years, and he no longer found Colin McGah to be an amusing man. "Very well, so that's what got you *into* the Tombs. What—or who—got you out?"

McGah licked his lips and shivered, burrowing deeper into his coat. "I really need a bottle. It's gonna be another cold one to-night."

Webb briefly debated giving the man a few coins in exchange for information but decided against it. No real city bureaucrat would pay a man like McGah, and Webb wanted to maintain the pretense that he was with the Department of Corrections. He did offer some incentive, though—an exchange of favors. "According to your record, you've been arrested quite a few times," he said.

"What the hell do you expect?" McGah snapped. "I'm sixty-two years old. A man lives that long, it's just natural that some of those years are gonna be spent behind bars."

"Yes, well, what I'm getting at is that it's a safe bet you might find yourself in jail again some time. And if you help me, maybe your sentence can be shortened again."

"And can you make sure that any time I do got to do is gonna be in the Tombs? I hate the Island."

Webb knew that, despite its name, the city jail known as the Tombs was an easier place to serve a sentence than the prison on Blackwell's Island. "I'm sure that can be arranged."

McGah again grinned, as if he'd won a major negotiation. "All righty then. It was Rabbit Doyle who got me out; and it was him who made sure I did my time in the Tombs—on the fourth floor, with the debtors, not down with the tough boys." He paused to make sure Webb got the hint about his housing preference.

"Fourth floor," said Webb agreeably. "And Doyle was the one who told you how to vote?"

"That was the deal." McGah added wistfully, "I liked it better in the old days when Tammany would pay a buck a vote. But this is cheaper for them—they let me out early and I vote for whoever they tell me to."

Webb knew how the racket worked, and Rabbit Doyle was a name he'd heard before. "You and others."

"Yeah, there were about twenty that I know of who got out early."

"Thirty-five, according to our records. I suppose that could certainly help in a tight election."

"Thirty-five *men*," said McGah slyly. "That can add up to *hundreds* of votes. I was six votes just by myself."

"They move you to six different wards?" Webb knew that sending voters to more than one polling place was one of the methods by which Tammany Hall padded the vote counts.

"Only two. See, I got a system." Once again McGah smiled in a manner that was intended to be sly but looked more pained than intelligent. "I been a repeater every election since 'fifty-six. What I do is I start growing a beard early in the summer. When November comes, I vote once under whatever name they tell me in whatever wards they tell me. Then I shave the beard, leaving the mustache on, and make a second round to vote again. After that, I get rid of the mustache and go back clean-shaven for the third vote."

Webb thought he'd got enough information from McGah, and it corroborated the stories he heard from the other early releases he'd spoken with. "Rabbit Doyle . . . is he still working out of . . ."

"Lucky Star Saloon on Delancey." McGah shivered again. "Sure wish I had the scratch to be there myself."

A hoarse voice called from beyond the pier, "Hey, Kid! We got us some supper!"

Another shabbily dressed man, about as old but a little taller than McGah, approached them, carrying a dead seagull by its neck.

McGah brightened at the sight and noisily started to work his mouth in anticipation of the meal.

Marshall Webb found the sight revolting. He looked from the dead, dangling bird that would be McGah's dinner to the pile of reeking refuse that would be his bed. The leaders of Tammany Hall certainly didn't live in such quarters, and they certainly dined on better than seagull for dinner, but this was the source of their power. The entire corrupt operation of Tammany Hall, which controlled all of the city government and much of the state, had men like Kid McGah serving as its roots.

It was time, Webb decided, to take the next step up the Tammany Hall hierarchy. He intended eventually to reach the top—and to bring it all down.

CHAPTER 3

Rebecca was well aware that she was about to violate one of the long-standing traditions of her parents' Fifth Avenue home—an affluent home, which functioned strictly according to tradition, order, and social propriety. Nevertheless, she pushed through the elaborately carved double doors to the library. From the startled expressions she garnered, she might as well have walked into the room stark naked.

Her father looked up from the chessboard with surprise. As his wide mouth went slightly agape, his long Cuban cigar suddenly tilted downward, the lit end coming precariously close to the starched white shirt of his black dress suit. Jacob Updegraff, her brother-in-law and the only other man in the room, appeared utterly perplexed at her entry. He dug into his vest pocket for his watch and jerked it out so quickly that he almost upset the pieces on his side of the board.

Ignoring her brother-in-law, Rebecca said, "May I have a word with you, Father?"

"Of course, my dear." There was concern on his usually placid pink face. "There is nothing the matter, I trust?" He scratched at the fringe of cottony hair above his ear.

Updegraff loudly snapped his watch closed. "Twenty minutes after four," he said with some irritation. From the scowl on his aristocratic face, he clearly disapproved of this impertinent invasion of the men's sanctuary.

"Thank you," Rebecca snapped at him in return. "I can see that on the clock." She knew that her brother-in-law's announcement of the time was his way of pointing out that she was in violation of accepted practice—a major affront in his social circle.

Her parents lived their lives in that same circle, among the old-moneyed New York families who had already been established as the social elite back when John Jacob Astor was still just the son of a German butcher. Among the traditions that developed in the Davies household was that after Sunday dinner—a stiflingly proper affair in a stiflingly proper brownstone—the gentlemen retired to the library, where there were books that no one read, while the ladies went to the "music room," where there was a grand piano that no one played. This segregation of the sexes always lasted until precisely five o'clock, when Rebecca claimed to have a headache and returned to Colden House, a weekly routine that had rarely varied for the past several years.

"Tell me," her father prodded. "What's on your mind, my dear?"

She glanced again at Updegraff. His long nose was tilted up expectantly, and his dark eyes were fixed upon her, as if warning her that there had better be some good reason for this intrusion. "I was hoping we could speak alone," she said.

Her father shook his head. "No need for that, child. Mr. Updegraff is your sister's husband. He is family."

Rebecca noticed the slight smirk that twitched her brother-in-law's mouth, but she chose not to let her irritation with him get the better of her. Looking into her father's anxious eyes, she said, "I'm afraid there *is* something the matter. I am having money problems at Colden House. And the problem is, there *is* no money. I can't buy—"

Her father visibly pulled back into his leather armchair like a turtle retreating into its protective shell. He cut off her appeal. "We've maintained our commitments to Colden House."

"Yes, I know, Father. And I am grateful. Truly, I am. But in the last few months, so many more people have been put out of work that I'm overwhelmed. You have made the same contributions as always, but the expenses have become so much greater."

"You don't have to tell me about the economy," he grumbled. "The stock market has been terrible. Railroad dividends are down, gold reserves are low, and Europe's in the middle of a depression—no market for our goods there." He shook his head. "It was almost a panic on Wall Street last month. Call loans went up to thirty percent."

"Forty percent," corrected Updegraff.

"Forty," repeated her father. "These are uncertain times, my dear. That means it's no time to be giving money away." He took a healthy sip of cognac from his snifter and pursed his lips tightly.

"But . . . Papa." Rebecca had seldom called her father by that name since she'd grown to adulthood. "Don't you understand? With things being so bad, there are so many more women out on the streets—no jobs, no homes, and for many of them no families. They need food and clothes, and a warm bed." She rested her hand on his shoulder. "Papa, I don't have the money to pay for one more coal delivery."

He stiffened with resolve. "It is impossible to do more than we have. Perhaps in a couple of months, if the economy turns around. If it doesn't, I stand to lose a small fortune." With that, he clamped his cigar between his teeth to show that he had said all he would on the matter.

Rebecca wanted to argue, "But even if you lost a small fortune, you'd still have a large fortune left." She let the thought die in her mind, though, and looked away from him in frustration. Seeing the priceless tapestries and rugs that adorned the plush library, she realized that her father simply didn't comprehend what it was to lose a home or to go hungry.

The library walls were decorated with English hunting prints and a collection of medieval broadswords, Italian daggers, and flintlock firearms. But the only thing her father or Jacob Updegraff ever killed were bottles of brandy, most often in the comfort of this room, seated in expensive leather wing chairs and bathed in the warm glow from the marble fireplace. The only hardships they ever encountered were occasional traffic jams when their broughams—driven by liveried servants—transported them to the exclusive Union Club, or when the club's wine steward ran out of a preferred vintage.

"I believe it's your move, Mr. Davies," said Updegraff.

"Yes, yes. Just mulling the situation over." He looked over the chess pieces thoughtfully before moving an ivory pawn.

"Ah, I didn't see that coming," said Updegraff. He then leaned back, drew on his cigar, and looked up at Rebecca. "I believe I know how you can solve your financial problem."

Rebecca wasn't much interested in advice from her brother-in-law. It was a sign of her desperation that she asked, "How?"

"You need to make some investments that will provide a regular income. Put your money into some sound stocks that pay dividends, and use the dividends for your operating expenses." He tapped his cigar over a gold-rimmed porcelain ashtray. "If you had done that years ago, you wouldn't be in your present difficulty."

Rebecca found his suggestion ridiculous on several grounds. For one thing, what was the point of telling her she should have invested years ago? Was she somehow to go back in time to rectify that mistake? And if she didn't have money to pay for the next coal delivery, with what funds could she possibly buy stocks. She decided to make only one obvious objection, however: "If these are such 'uncertain times' and the stock market is so 'terrible' right now, then this would be a rather poor time to make investments, wouldn't it?" Try as she might—and she didn't try very hard—Rebecca couldn't conceal the disdain she felt for Updegraff.

He chuckled. "On the contrary, this is a *good* time to invest—if you choose your investments wisely. While the timid are waiting to see what happens in the market, the smart money men are *making* things happen. Of course, I don't expect a woman to understand the world of finance." Updegraff paused to move one of his bishops, clacking it loudly into position on the board. "You know who you should talk to," he said, glancing up at Rebecca again, "is Lyman Sinclair. He's one of the top investment bankers in my firm." To Rebecca's father, he added, "You remember Mr. Sinclair. You met him at the club last week."

Mr. Davies was still studying Updegraff's last move with some bewilderment in his eyes. "Oh, yes," he said absently. "A rather young fellow, as I recall."

"Young and smart," replied Updegraff. "He's been doing quite well for us." To Rebecca, he said, "You talk to Mr. Sinclair and let him choose your investments. That will take care of your problem."

Rebecca was out of patience. "My *problem* is that I presently have thirty girls to feed and shelter, and no money with which to do it." Looking at her father, she made one final appeal. "*Please,* Papa. I don't know what to do to keep Colden House going."

He appeared to consider her predicament. "Thirty girls," he repeated. "Seems to me that would make quite a workforce. Why should you—or I—have to pay to support them at all? Set them up doing some kind of work—sewing, perhaps. Yes, that's the thing: Put them to work, and then they can pay their own way."

Sarah Zietlow, lying sick in Columbus Hospital, immediately came to Rebecca's mind. That unfortunate girl was barely able to sit up under her own power. What kind of work could she possibly do? Then frustration gave way to sadness—sadness at her father's indifference to girls like Sarah. The Davies family had helped establish Colden House as a shelter for women back in the 1820s, when public aid to the poor was cut off in the belief that charity only encouraged pauperism. Her father obviously didn't have the compassion or empathy that his grandparents did. Rebecca realized with sorrow that any further pleading would fall on deaf ears.

With his cigar in one hand, and his empty snifter in the other, Jacob Updegraff stood up. "I think I'll have one more." He went to the sideboard and reached for a crystal decanter. "Will you be returning to the ladies, Miss Davies?" It sounded more like a suggestion than a question.

Ignoring her brother-in-law, Rebecca leaned over and kissed her father on the cheek. As she did, she grabbed a couple of chess pieces and hid them in her fist. It was a childish, peevish thing to do, she knew, but she had an urge to upset this comfortable little world in some way. Besides, gripping the piece tightly helped her restrain her other impulses, which were to slap Updegraff and scream at her father.

From the sideboard, Updegraff called, "How about you, Mr. Davies? Another brandy? Nothing like good cognac on a winter evening."

"Another whiskey?"

Marshall Webb considered the question only briefly before saying yes. On a cold winter night like this one, a second shot of rye was a most welcome prospect. Besides, bartenders were more willing to talk to paying customers, and Webb was here for information.

The Lucky Star Saloon was in one of the East Side's toughest neighborhoods, not far from where Webb had met with Kid McGah. Just off Delancey Street, with its entrance actually on cobblestoned Marion Alley, the bar was close enough to the waterfront that the horns and whistles of barges and steamboats could occasionally be heard above the conversations and the clinking of beer and whiskey glasses.

Unlike most of the saloons in the area, the Lucky Star was no dive, but instead a clean, simply furnished place where men could safely gather to drink beer that wasn't watered down, play cards that weren't marked, and swap stories without being held to account for their veracity. It wasn't large—ten men could stand comfortably at the bar, and perhaps another twenty could be seated at the small tables—but it was comfortable, with a potbellied stove to keep the place warm and jars of pickled eggs to fend off hunger. The all-male clientele, mostly manual laborers and dock workers judging by their plain, rough clothes, were well mannered, meaning that they spit their tobacco juice into brass cuspidors instead of on the sawdust-covered floor.

The burly bartender put the freshly filled whiskey glass in front of Webb, and Webb slapped another dime next to it. "There's something else I need," he said.

"Whazzat?"

"I'm looking for a fellow named Rabbit Doyle. I was told he's usually here."

"Whatcha want him for?"

"I need him to fix a problem for me."

The bartender chuckled. "Well, that's what he does—fixes problems. He is here most nights, but he could be at the clubhouse right now." He began rubbing down the bar with a wet rag; thousands of bottles and glasses had scraped away every bit of varnish over the years, but this barkeep was doing his best to keep the bare oak surface clean.

"Tammany Hall?"

"Nah, I mean the local clubhouse. Tammany opened one in this district last summer, and Rabbit stops in there at least once a day." He brushed away a small pile of empty peanut shells from the bar, letting them fall to the floor.

"My boss is going to give me hell if I don't talk with Doyle," said Webb. "You expect he'll be coming here tonight?"

"Hey, Brick!" The bartender yelled toward a table where two young bruisers were huddled in conversation. From their physiques, they could have stepped out of one of the numerous boxing prints that hung on the walls. "Rabbit coming in tonight?"

The larger of the two men, with dull reddish hair that had no doubt earned him his nickname, lifted his head and answered, "Better be. He was supposed to be here half an hour ago."

The bartender looked back to Webb and shrugged as if to say, "That's your answer." He then answered a call from the end of the bar for another beer and went to the tap.

Another ten minutes passed before the door to the Lucky Star opened, letting in a gust of wintry air. The bartender came over to Webb. "There's your man."

Webb was already staring at the powerfully built six-footer who'd swaggered through the door as if he owned the place. "Doesn't look anything like a rabbit," he commented quietly.

The bartender chuckled. "Hell, he didn't get his name for how he *looks*. Doyle used to run with the Dead Rabbit gang back before the war—was one of their toughest brawlers, from what I hear."

Webb had the urge to laugh himself. Rabbit Doyle, he knew, was a ward heeler. That was the lowest form of political hack, and the job generally involved doing any dirty work that the party bosses wanted done but didn't dare do themselves—everything from bringing in illicit voters to stealing ballot boxes to beating up supporters of opposing candidates. Those of Doyle's profession came to be called "heelers" because they would heel at their master's commands, the same as an obedient dog. What Webb was amused to see was that Doyle in fact resembled a dog—a bull-mastiff, to be specific. He had a muscular build, which couldn't be concealed by his flapping greatcoat, and a large square head topped by a black derby that was a size too small. Webb put his age at mid-fifties.

Doyle walked over to join the two younger men at their table. As the ward heeler took off his hat and coat, the bartender called to him, "Man here's been waitin' to see you, Rabbit!"

Doyle scowled slightly but jerked his head as an invitation for Webb to join them at the table.

Before he did, Webb said thanks to the bartender and added, "Give them a round on me—and pour one for yourself, too."

When Webb reached the table, Doyle said in a voice like a growling dog, "What can I do for you, Mr. . . . ?"

"Marshall Webb." Webb offered his hand and Doyle returned the grip hard. "I appreciate your time."

"Can't give you much of it." Doyle nodded at the two younger men but didn't introduce them. "We got some work we got to be doin'."

Webb eased into a slat-back chair. "This shouldn't take long." He hesitated, not sure about the best approach with the ward heeler. Webb figured the further up the Tammany power structure he went, the more suspicious they would be of any inquiries, and the more cautious he would have to be to avoid arousing those suspicions. For now, he decided, he would stick with the story he'd given Kid McGah. "I was sent here from the Tombs," Webb said. "About payment."

"Payment for what?"

"The early releases in November." Webb quickly added, "Understand, I'm just a messenger here, so I don't know exactly what happened. But my boss is complaining that he wasn't taken care of, and he's sent me to find out when he can expect payment."

Doyle ran a meaty hand over his close-cropped salt-and-pepper beard. His pale, cold eyes appeared genuinely puzzled. "Who's your boss?"

"Richard Jolta." The name was an invention Webb made up on the spot. "New assistant warden."

"I don't know him. But you can tell Jolta this: everybody got what was due them."

"You sure? He seems to think he's still owed money. I told him it's probably just going to take a while for the new administration to get caught up with everything." Webb shrugged. "But he never does listen to me."

Doyle shook his head with amusement. "Maybe that's because you're wrong—there *is* no new administration. Sure, there's a new mayor—Tom Gilroy instead of Hugh Grant—and some new aldermen, but they're just names and bodies. The administration is the same: New York is 'administered' by Boss Croker and Tammany Hall."

Webb was somewhat taken aback by Doyle's openness about the corrupt system. "But I thought—"

With a wave of his hand, Doyle cut him off. "Every public job in New York is doled out by Tammany Hall. Tammany giveth, and Tammany can taketh away. So you go back and tell this Richard Jolta that he needs to be grateful for what he has—there are a lot of men out of work right now and he's gonna join them if he tries to get something that ain't due him."

Webb nodded, partly to indicate that he would do as Doyle said, and partly with new understanding. He finally realized why this ward heeler didn't feel any need to be cautious in what he said.

Everyone knew that Tammany Hall ran the city, and they knew that patronage was what kept the political machine running. Everyone from the mayor down to the patrolman on the beat was a functionary of Boss Croker and his lieutenants in Tammany Hall. It was a system so thoroughly entwined in the city's workings that there was no honest authority left to answer to. In Rabbit Doyle's mind, they were invincible.

CHAPTER 4

Men certainly are a peculiar sex, thought Rebecca Davies. As she tugged up the velvet-trimmed hem of her heavy wool skirt and stuck out her leg, she was immediately aware that dozens of pairs of male eyes were targeted in the direction of her ankle. Since her side-button boots went almost up to her calf, and the hems of her skirt and winter coat extended far below that point, they weren't getting much of a view; yet they continued to stare, much to Rebecca's amusement.

Not all the looks Rebecca garnered were leers. Some were glances of surprise—not at a lifted skirt, but at the mere presence of a skirt. The men and boys skating on this part of Central Park's lake rarely had a woman among them. Most women did their ice-skating at the north end of the lake, in the section reserved for their gender. Rebecca, however, wasn't like most women, and she tended to go wherever she pleased.

Marshall Webb, kneeling at her feet, said, "This buckle's a bit rusted." He pulled off his kid gloves with his teeth and began to work the stubborn buckle, trying to attach the straps of the skates to her feet.

Rebecca shifted on the bench and hoisted her skirt another inch to make it easier for him. "I haven't used them in years," she said. "It's been a long time since I've gone skating." But she was happy to be here, and glad that she'd accepted Webb's invitation. Both of them had been busy with their work lately, and she had sorely missed his company.

"Got it!" With one skate secured, Webb moved to her other foot, cradling it in his strong hands.

As he worked, Rebecca noticed that steam from his breath was condensing and freezing on his impeccably groomed mustache. The resulting ice crystals looked like silver streaks in the dark-brown hair, much the same color as the gray strands that were beginning to lighten his temples—and had, thankfully, provided her with something to tease him about. She had also lately been suggesting that he change his style of facial hair; Webb's Franz Josef whiskers, with the mustache that swooped around a clean-shaven chin to merge with the side-whiskers, were a bit old-fashioned and a bit too dignified. Although he certainly made a handsome appearance, Rebecca wished sometimes that he would look a bit less stiff. Formality reminded her too much of the regimented social world inhabited by families like the Davieses and Updegraffs.

Rebecca shivered suddenly as a cold shadow began to creep upon her. The afternoon sun was beginning to dip down behind the gables and turrets of the Dakota Apartments. The odd nine-story structure, which looked to Rebecca like a cross between a Swiss chalet and a Renaissance French palace, towered above the other structures in the largely undeveloped area of Manhattan. From its corner at 72nd Street and Central Park West, the massive apartment house loomed over the lake and dominated the western skyline.

"There we are," said Webb. He stood, drawing himself up to his full six feet, and held out a hand to help her up before putting his gloves back on. "Do they feel tight enough?"

Rebecca took a few cautious strides. "Yes, thank you." On an impish impulse, she then began to skate away from him. Looking back, she saw Webb give his Dunlap derby a tap to secure it more firmly to his head; then he came after her, the cape of his mackintosh fluttering as he tried to make up the distance between them.

Rebecca's own progress wasn't very fast. The ice was rough, chewed up by more than a month of skating. Winter had settled on Manhattan so early and so thoroughly this year that the red ball that signaled that the ice was sufficiently thick for safe skating had been hoisted in early December. Since then, it had never been lowered, and remained in view atop the bell tower of Belvedere Castle on Vista Rock, the highest point in Central Park.

Breathing in deep lungfuls of the brisk air, Rebecca had the sudden urge to skate faster, to propel herself far beyond the lake and keep going until she was free from the problems of Manhattan's streets and far from the cares of Colden House. It was such a relief for her to be outdoors, and a badly needed respite from her work. As the cold air numbed her face, she began to feel that she had indeed left the confines of the city.

She suddenly realized that she'd closed her eyes, and nearly stumbled on a badly chipped patch of ice. At the same moment that she opened her eyes, Rebecca felt a hand on her elbow. It kept her from falling, and once she'd regained her balance, she turned to see Webb at her side; he must have raced to catch up with her.

With a sheepish smile, Rebecca said, "I feel like a puppy who's been kept in a cage all day and finally allowed out."

That brought a smile to Webb's lips. "The way you were skating, I thought I noticed something wagging."

Rebecca gave him a playful poke to the ribs; Webb's manners were usually so gentlemanly that it still took her by surprise that he could make such ungentlemanly quips. Of course, since she had an unfortunate habit of uttering similar comments, she didn't really mind.

Webb then offered his arm. She promptly put her hand in the crook of his elbow, and the two of them began skating together slowly, and as closely as their bulky clothing would permit. The two of them slid along, negotiating their way past male skaters, most of them dressed the same: in somber dark overcoats and black derbies. A few children, heavily bundled in bright shades of red and green, skittered along on sleds or tottered on double-bladed learning skates. A group of older men, in shoes instead of skates, were engaged in the odd game of curling, sliding heavy round stones over the ice.

Rebecca looked around the lake shore, where the benches were crowded with onlookers, many of them men stopping by for a few minutes of fresh air before continuing home from their shops and offices. She realized that there was no escaping the city for her; she couldn't even skate her way out of the park, never mind Manhattan. But then, to her surprise, she found she no longer had the urge to escape.

"What are you thinking?" Webb asked.

She slipped her hand more securely onto his arm. "That things are starting to look up." Rebecca had gotten used to the fact that Webb could read her so easily; he seemed to know when she had something on her mind. "We had a young lady come to Colden House who was in terrible shape—starving, weak, and in constant pain. The doctor said she might have been poisoned."

"Poisoned?"

"Yes. But I took her to the hospital, and she's been doing much better. She'll be released tomorrow."

"That *is* good news."

Rebecca generally didn't like to talk about the problems of Colden House, but it seemed easy to speak here, removed from immediacy of situation. "I'm also making plans to alleviate our financial difficulties. We've had a terrible time lately, with hardly enough money for bread and coal." Frowning at the memory of her conversation with her father, she added, "And my family won't increase their contributions one cent."

"What's your plan?"

"Investing. My brother-in-law has suggested that I purchase some stocks that will pay out regular dividends. I'm going to scrape together whatever I can to buy them."

"I don't follow the market," said Webb, "but I know it's a risky time to be getting into it."

Rebecca knew that, too; most of the daily newspaper headlines had to do with the nation's deepening financial crisis. She also realized that this was a long-term approach and would do nothing to alleviate the current problems—in fact, tying up money in stocks might make them worse. But with no other options, she had settled on this course of action and was determined to be positive about it. "I don't mind risk," she said. "There's no payoff without risk, and if I have any hope of keeping the shelter going, I have to see that it's financially secure in the long run."

"Your family won't help at all?"

"My father says no, but I'll keep working on him." She had some hope that he might contribute to the stock investment, since she was following the advice that Updegraff had given her. "Whether he does or not, I have a little money of my own and I'll be investing all of it." Doing so would leave her totally dependent on her family if she failed to secure a stable income for Colden House. Rebecca tried to joke away the hardship in which she might be placing herself. "I'll be as poor as the women who come to my door—and I won't be much of a catch for a gentleman, I'm afraid."

She had actually never worried about being "a catch for a gentleman" and was embarrassed that those words popped out of her mouth. Rebecca suddenly pulled away from Webb and skated off in fast strides. The phrase seemed to echo in her head, and she wished she could take it back. She'd heard it often enough from her mother's lips when her mother chided her about her strong will, her indifference to hair style, or her disdain for society events. Echoing once again, they now had the sound of her mother's voice: *If you don't act more like a lady, you'll be no catch for a gentleman.*

"Rebecca!" Webb called to her.

She glanced back to see him making fast, clumsy strides of his own. As he began to close the gap between them, a small sled that had lost his rider shot in front of him. Webb stumbled over it, going down in a pile.

Rebecca skated back to him. "Are you hurt?"

He stood and brushed off a few flakes of snow and ice. "Fine, thank you." His face was flushed, and she could see that he was embarrassed about the tumble.

Rebecca fought the urge to laugh. Webb was sometimes a bit too dignified, and she enjoyed seeing him like this. More than that, she was happy that he'd been trying to catch her—maybe it was an attempt to show that she'd been wrong about being "no catch."

They skated together a little while longer, and Rebecca found herself wishing they could spend more days like this. In spring, she thought, they could take a ride in one of the gondolas that cruised this same lake. She could almost see the trees and flowers in bloom, and found herself feeling hopeful about the future.

It wasn't long before they worked up an appetite, so the two of them coasted to a bench to remove their skates. As Webb again knelt at her feet, Rebecca said, "You haven't told me about this new story you've been working on lately. Why the mystery?"

"No mystery. It's just that I'm in the early stages of research right now, so there isn't much to tell."

"Research about what?"

"Tammany Hall." He smiled. "I'm going to expose every one of their crooked schemes and everyone who's involved in them, from the fraudulent voters at the bottom to the bosses and politicians at the top."

She wasn't quite sure if he was kidding. "Are you serious? Do you know what kind of danger that would put you in?"

"I am serious. And so is *Harper's*. My editor thinks this is the time to go after Tammany."

"And what if they go after *you*?"

Webb unfastened the buckle of the first skate. "I'm not worried. I think I've discovered their weakness. And I have a plan." His smile turned mischievous.

Rebecca looked at his eyes. They always had the light of intelligence in them, but now they were positively sparkling. She wished she could tell what he was thinking; they'd been keeping company for a year, but she still had difficulty reading this man. Was he really feeling that cocky about some plan to bring down Tammany Hall? she wondered.

As Webb began working on the second foot, she thought with some hope that perhaps there was a different reason for that smile. Perhaps he had some other mischief in mind that had nothing to do with politics.

CHAPTER 5

Sarah Zietlow's young face looked so peaceful as she slept that Rebecca took her appearance as one more hopeful sign that everything would turn out all right—for everyone. Although Sarah's sallow skin still bore the harsh signs of injuries that would probably never fully heal, her expression had softened in sleep, and she nestled her head in the pillow as if she had never felt anything more comfortable.

Rebecca stood in the second-floor hallway of Colden House, holding the door to the small bedroom slightly ajar and looking in at her new guest. After three days in Columbus Hospital, Sarah Zietlow had finally been able to keep down solid food and was showing signs of regaining some of her strength. Although the hospital doctors dismissed out of hand Doc Abraham's notion of poison, favoring the gastric fever theory instead, one of them did admit to Rebecca that Miss Zietlow's symptoms were consistent with arsenic poisoning. Whatever the cause, the girl was feeling better and appeared to be out of immediate danger. And Rebecca was determined to keep her out of future danger as well.

"Miss Davies?"

Rebecca was startled by the soft voice behind her. She turned to face Miss Hummel, a short gray-haired woman who looked like a cross between a nurse and a maid. She wore a starched simple dress the same color as her hair, and a more heavily starched white apron. As much as Rebecca valued her assistant's help in the house, she wished the woman would make some sound when she walked; the way she crept around like a cat was unnerving. "Yes, Miss Hummel?" she asked sharply.

The woman had a small smile on her usually humorless face,

which Rebecca thought might be from seeing her reaction. "Forgive me, ma'am. I can't help but smile seeing you standing there like a mother looking in on her sleeping child."

Rebecca didn't know what to say. "It's Miss Zietlow. She appears to be recovering nicely."

"All thanks to you, ma'am." The older woman ran a hand over her apron, brushing away some imagined bit of dirt. "I came to tell you there's a gentleman at the door, Miss Davies."

"Another delivery?" There had been several this morning already, of coal, bread, milk, and cheese. According to the delivery men, they had all been paid for by an "anonymous" benefactor, but Rebecca had no doubt that Marshall Webb was behind it. He had made such donations in the past, always anonymous, but somehow always after she had mentioned some need in the house. She was grateful, but she was going to have to make it clear to him that she couldn't continue to accept his generosity. Rebecca wanted to be able to speak with him openly and honestly, and she didn't feel she could do that if she thought he might interpret what she said about the state of affairs at Colden House to be hints for assistance.

"No, ma'am. It's a *gentle*man, not a delivery man." With another amused twitch of her lips, she added, "It's not your Mr. Webb, either."

Turnabout being fair play, Rebecca asked with mock innocence, "Oh, is it *your* Mr. Sehlinger, then?"

Upon hearing the name of her own gentleman friend, Miss Hummel blushed slightly, giving Rebecca a small victory. She stammered, then regained her composure, and said, "It's a Mr. Lyman Sinclair, from the New Amsterdam Trust Company."

That was Jacob Updegraff's's bank. Rebecca had told her brother-in-law that she was ready to follow his advice—which was something that she never thought she could bring herself to say. "Thank you. Please tell him that I'll be right down."

While Miss Hummel glided silently down the narrow staircase of the old Federal-style row house to relay that message, Rebecca found herself struck with sudden doubt. Was it really wise to put all the money she had to her name into some venture about which she knew nothing? Yes, she tried to convince herself, whatever she might think of Jacob Updegraff or her father in other respects, they *were* smart businessmen. She couldn't imagine them encouraging her to make an investment that they didn't think would succeed. Besides, what other options did she have? How else could she ensure that Colden House could continue to operate?

After another minute of internal debate—during which she forced herself to argue in favor of making the investment—Rebecca descended the stairs to see a slim, soft-featured young man in a pinstriped brown suit standing in the foyer. He had already been relieved of his hat and coat by Miss Hummel and was running a graceful hand over short, painstakingly groomed blond hair that glistened with pomade. At first sight, his appearance caused Rebecca's confidence to waver again. "Mr. Sinclair?" she ventured, hoping that he might answer in the negative.

"Lyman Sinclair at your service, ma'am." He made a slight bow. "Miss Davies, I presume?"

Rebecca nodded and bit her lip. Mr. Sinclair was so *young*, probably not yet twenty-five and certainly not thirty. She didn't like the idea of entrusting her limited finances to someone who was several years younger than she. He was obviously making efforts to appear more mature, but they had precisely the opposite effect. Sinclair's drooping handlebar mustache was long but sparse and thin; it made him look like an adolescent who didn't want to shave off the first sign of manhood. His impeccably tailored suit was of a fine weave, and Rebecca was pretty certain the material was cashmere; but the stodgy style was more appropriate on a older man and gave the impression of a boy dressing up in his father's clothes.

"If I may say so," Sinclair ventured with a ready smile that Rebecca imagined was probably quite appealing to some young ladies, "you are every bit as lovely as your sister. I've had the pleasure of dining at the Updegraff home a number of times, and Mrs. Updegraff is a most charming hostess."

"Thank you." Rebecca had absolutely no interest in being compared to her younger sister, Alice. She actually found Sinclair's statement to be more insulting than flattering. "Yes, my sister is indeed a fine hostess." Remembering her own manners, she invited Sinclair into a small, plainly furnished sitting room. She could see why Jacob Updegraff liked this fellow; he was young enough that he could readily be ordered around, and obsequious enough to be constantly flattering his boss.

Once they were seated, Rebecca said, "It's very kind of you to come, Mr. Sinclair. But it really wasn't necessary; I could just as easily have stopped by the bank."

He waved a hand, flashing a large gold ring on one finger and a signet ring on another. "No trouble at all, Miss Davies. Considering your relation to Mr. Updegraff, I intend to handle the entire transaction personally."

No doubt to ingratiate his boss, Rebecca thought. Then she silently chastised herself for being so ungracious. Perhaps Mr. Sinclair was simply an eager young man putting forth some extra effort. His age and manners shouldn't be held against him as long as his financial acumen was sound. "Tell me, Mr. Sinclair," she said, "what particular investments are you recommending?"

His smile faltered and he frowned slightly. "Mr. Updegraff led me to believe that you didn't want to be troubled with the particulars." The smile then returned, a little too readily to be convincing. "Investments are a complicated matter, Miss Davies, and I wouldn't care to distress you with financial terms and legal language."

Rebecca knew that her brother-in-law believed her incapable of understanding such things, and he had probably said as much to Sinclair. She only wished Updegraff were here for her to vent her irritation at him. But he wasn't, so Mr. Sinclair would have to be the one to be straightened out. "There are things that distress me far more than 'terms' and 'language,'" she said to the young banker. "And being treated with condescension is high on that list. So please answer my question."

Sinclair stammered so much that Rebecca almost felt bad about making her point. "My apologies," he finally said. "I suppose Mr. Updegraff must have been mistaken."

"That happens more than he allows himself to believe."

As a loyal employee, Sinclair didn't allow himself to smile at that, but the corners of his mouth twitched upward. "To answer your question, your money will be invested in the Western Continental Railroad."

Rebecca recalled her father's saying that railroad dividends had been down. "Is that wise?" she asked. "Railroads haven't been very profitable of late."

Sinclair was obviously surprised that she knew anything about the market. It was almost the extent of what she knew, but it was enough to encourage him to be more forthcoming. "You're quite correct, Miss Davies. In *general*, railroad stocks have fared rather poorly—in fact, some are on the verge of bankruptcy. But that's because of too many rail companies building their lines in the same territory." He leaned forward and began to speak more confidently. "You see, the key to investing in uncertain times—and I admit these *are* uncertain times—is to avoid being scared into inaction by bad news. This is the time to search for those companies that have the prospect for growth."

He sounded convincing, but Rebecca wanted to know more. "What leads you to believe Western Continental is such a company?"

"They're putting their rail lines where there is little competition and a growing market—primarily in the West, where the timber industry is booming and new mines are being opened every month. Quite simply, those industries need to transport their goods, and Western Continental will provide that transportation."

That sounded sensible to Rebecca. "How has the company been faring lately?"

Lyman Sinclair then went on at length about shares, profitability, and growth rates. He spoke with the flair of a snake oil salesman, but he had numbers to support every statement he made.

Rebecca nodded occasionally as he spoke, although she didn't understand all of it. It was for her enough that what she did comprehend sounded sensible. It also helped to hear from him that the stocks had already doubled in value over the past twelve months.

When he'd finished, Rebecca said, "Thank you, Mr. Sinclair. I appreciate you taking the time to explain this to me. I feel my investment will be safe in your hands."

Sinclair beamed at her reaction. "As I said, I will handle everything for you personally."

Rebecca then excused herself to get the money and went upstairs to her bedroom. From a jewelry box that had once contained quite a few rings and brooches but now held only a few of sentimental value, she took a small sheaf of bills. Once again she hesitated. There were so many things that Colden House needed *now*—even if the money did double in a year, how would she get through that year? She peeled off a few twenty-dollar silver certificates and put them back in the box.

Back in the sitting room, Rebecca tried to hand the money to Lyman Sinclair. "This is one thousand, six hundred and twenty dollars. I'd like you to put it all in Western Continental Railroad stocks."

Sinclair hesitated. "Excuse me, ma'am—sixteen *hundred* dollars?" he stammered.

"Yes." Rebecca was puzzled by his reaction. "In cash."

"I'm sorry. I was assuming . . . considering your family . . ."

Rebecca now understood. The young man had assumed it would be more like sixteen *thousand* dollars. She pushed the money toward him.

Sinclair couldn't hide his disappointment, but he took the money. "As you wish, Miss Davies. But I was expecting a more substantial—"

Feeling both embarrassed and angry, Rebecca cut him off. "If all you've told me is true, then I expect you to *make* it more substantial."

CHAPTER 6

Ten minutes after his appointed time, Marshall Webb was finally permitted entry into the elegantly furnished office of his boss, *Harper's Weekly* associate editor Harry M. Hargis. Hargis thought it was elegant, anyway; in Webb's view, "arrogant" or "ostentatious" would more accurately describe the decor. Most of the furnishings had been purchased by Hargis during his frequent vacations abroad, and should a visitor to his office make any comment on a piece, or simply eye one for more than a few seconds, he would be treated to a lengthy discourse on Hargis's entire trip. A glance down at the brilliantly colored Oriental rug was sure to elicit a story about the editor's journey to Persia; an admiring look at the French oil paintings on the walls or the marble reproduction of *David* on a wrought-iron pedestal would trigger endless recollections of Paris or Florence.

As Webb walked in, he noticed a bronze figurine of Hermes atop Hargis's carved mahogany desk. Immediately, he averted his eye, not wanting to give Hargis the excuse to regale him with a story about his recent trip to the Greek Islands.

The dapper editor, whose personal appearance was in keeping with his surroundings, waved a hand. "Have a seat, Webb." He sounded as if there could be no more benevolent offer.

"Thank you." Webb eased into a green leather armchair that was as soft as a kid glove. He studied Hargis's expression to see if he could determine why he'd been summoned to the *Harpers* office. Nothing appeared amiss in the editor's appearance. The waxed tips of his dainty mustache were curled up to exactly the same height, and not a strand of his thinning, wavy silver hair was out of place. His celluloid wing collar, high enough to serve as a chin rest, was brilliantly white, and a green silk cravat was around his neck. A fresh red carnation bloomed from the lapel of his tailored alpaca coat, and his yellow silk vest shimmered as if it were made of hammered gold.

Hargis began, "Before I left town . . ." He then paused to run a manicured fingertip over one of Hermes' winged sandals. When Webb failed to take the opportunity to ask about the small statue, Hargis coughed and continued. "In November, we discussed doing a story on Tammany Hall, perhaps a series of stories. How are you progressing with that?"

"Quite well, as a matter of fact. I've been turning up a lot of useful material in my investigations." Webb looked away from the bronze figurine and directed his attention to the gold-trimmed ivory candlestick telephone at the other end of the desk. From his experience, it, too, might be purely ornamental. Hargis never telephoned to ask him to come to the office; instead, he sent a messenger to Webb's apartment when he wanted to see him—and he always kept Webb waiting a full ten minutes after their appointed meeting times. The fact that Hargis treated others the same way made his behavior no less irritating.

"Is this 'material' on paper yet?"

"Only in my notes," Webb answered. "And in my head. I have a lot more work to do before I can put it all together in a story."

There was disappointment in Hargis's narrowed eyes. "I've been gone some time—six weeks." He paused again. "I expected you to have something to show me."

Passing up the obvious invitation to ask where the editor had been for those six weeks, Webb said, "I've been working all that time. I've spoken with dozens of people, gone through hundreds of documents—"

Hargis slapped his hand on the desk. "That's very nice, but what I need is *words*—on *paper*—that I can publish. You came here with nothing at all for me to read?"

"No, but—"

"Let me explain something to you: the *Weekly* in *Harper's Weekly* means that we have to publish every week. That's twenty-four pages we need to fill fifty-two times a year."

Webb suddenly thought of a practical use for the Hermes statue: it would make a fine bludgeon with which to put an end to

Hargis's arrogance. Keeping his anger in check, he explained calmly, "With the information I've been gathering, there will be enough dirt on Tammany Hall to fill all of those pages for *months.*"

Hargis began drumming his fingers, but there was a glint of curiosity in his narrow eyes. "Specifics. I need specifics."

"I'm building a case against Tammany from the bottom up, starting with the source of its power: votes." Webb leaned back in the seat. "At least thirty-five inmates were given early releases from the Tombs in exchange for voting the way the Tammany bosses wanted them to. Many of them had been convicted of felonies and had lost their voting privileges. There were others from other jails, too; I've gone through prison records, talked to a number of the convicts, and have the names of Tammany ward heelers, prison officials, and judges who collaborated in the early releases."

"And . . . ?"

"I've talked to one of the ward heelers—Rabbit Doyle, in the Thirteenth District—and I have a few more that I plan to visit on the West Side and in the Bowery."

"And then? When do you get to Boss Croker and that stooge of his, the Honorable Thomas F. Gilroy?" Hargis said the word "honorable" with utter derision in referring to the city's new mayor.

"It may be some time," Webb admitted. "I intend to be thorough. And you know Tammany has its tentacles in every municipal and state office—it's not going to be easy."

Hargis idly began stroking the statue again. "I'm not sure we can wait for you to be that thorough. Why don't you set your sights directly at the top?" He paused thoughtfully. "Yes, that's it," he decided. "Go after Croker or Gilroy, and the rest will tumble with them."

"No."

The editor appeared startled at Webb's emphatic response. He wasn't accustomed to being contradicted.

Webb explained. "Boss Tweed and his ring were brought down in 'seventy-one. Did it stop the organization?"

Hargis gave his head a small, reluctant shake "no."

"And even then," Webb went on, "the only reason Tweed and his henchmen were put in jail was because one of his bookkeepers turned against him—he was able to provide facts and figures on all the money that Tammany Hall was embezzling. I intend to have facts and figures, too—on the entire organization."

After a few moments of thoughtful silence, Hargis said, "Very well. Continue your work. But I must tell you that not all of the editors here are enthusiastic about publishing articles on Tammany Hall." He turned the figure of Hermes and watched the light catch it from different angles.

"Why not?" Were they afraid of repercussions? Webb wondered. Or were some of them friends of the political leaders?

"For one thing," Hargis replied, "the newspapers are always running stories about Tammany Hall. They never achieve any results. So why waste the newsprint?"

"What they usually publish," Webb said, "are editorials preaching against political corruption. They rarely provide any specific information, much less hard evidence of wrongdoing."

"Still, the operations of Tammany Hall aren't exactly *news*. They've been the same for decades; we can do a story on them anytime."

If Hargis was being "enthusiastic," Webb would have hated to hear what the other editors thought of the proposed series. "The operations *haven't* remained the same, actually," he said.

Webb received a sharp look from his editor, who clearly didn't like all the corrections.

Webb explained, "Boss Croker is more sophisticated than his predecessors, and he has his political machine running better than ever. The new clubhouses, for example—every assembly district has one now, so local organizing is much stronger. Tammany's influence is only growing."

"That may be," Hargis conceded. "But some of our editors feel the country's worsening financial crisis is far more newsworthy. The stock market is floundering; railroads are going bankrupt; banks are closing. In fact"—he picked up a sheet of paper from his mail tray—"some banker named Lyman Sinclair committed suicide yesterday. Rumors are flying that it's because his bank is about to fail. This panic is only going to get worse."

Webb couldn't disagree about the importance of the current financial situation, but he didn't see why *Harper's Weekly* had to limit itself to only one of the stories. "Why not report on both matters?"

"Because that would make for some awfully dreary reading. We need to have room for sports, illustrations, and fiction. I'm afraid our readers will only tolerate one serious story per issue." He leaned back and folded his hands over his vest. "I suggest you do this: start with the beginning—some background on Tammany's history. Then, as you get information, write a few installments so we can see where the story might be going. Once I'm sure that you've got the goods, I'll try to convince the other editors to publish."

"Thank you." Webb was optimistic that he *would* "get the goods." He believed his conversation with Rabbit Doyle may have revealed a weakness in the Tammany system. That weakness was the fact that they believed themselves to be untouchable—and their arrogance could make them reckless and leave them exposed.

Hargis said, "I am one of the few here who have faith in your abilities, Webb. Soon, you may even be on staff. But I do have to convince the others." He again toyed with the statue.

Webb didn't particularly care if he ever became a regular writer for *Harper's*—especially since he had another source of income about which Hargis knew nothing. But he did want his investigations into Tammany Hall to bear some fruit, and to do that his findings would have to appear in print. As much as it went against his nature, he would have to keep Harry M. Hargis mollified.

"Very handsome sculpture," Webb said, indicating the bronze Hermes. "Is it new?" He then settled back to endure a lecture on Greek mythology.

CHAPTER 7

There was probably no such thing as a "pleasant" funeral, Nicholas Bostwick thought, but he was finding this one especially uncomfortable. So many things struck him as wrong that he almost regretted his decision to pay his respects to his former coworker at the New Amsterdam Trust Company—especially since he had never particularly liked the late Lyman Sinclair when he was still alive.

One thing that seemed wrong was the church itself, the Church of the Most Holy Redeemer, on East Third Street. Built by German Catholic immigrants, the massive stone edifice, with a bell tower that rose two hundred, fifty feet above street level, was considered to be the city's most important cathedral by the large German population south of Tompkins Square. It had come as a surprise to Bostwick to learn that Lyman Sinclair was Catholic; although religion was never a major topic of conversation at the bank, he knew that Sinclair claimed to be an Episcopalian. Bostwick had rarely been in a Roman Catholic church himself, and he found the elaborately decorated interior rather garish, with its statues of saints, stained glass windows, and tiers of burning candles. Although he no longer attended any church regularly, it made him think back with fondness to the simple wood-frame Baptist church he had gone to as a boy growing up in Pennsylvania.

Another reason for Bostwick's discomfort was that the pews were so sparsely filled. It made him feel conspicuous, and Nicholas Bostwick was a man who preferred to go unnoticed.

In the front rows, dressed in mourning black, were half a dozen people whom Bostwick assumed to be Sinclair's family. Their cries and wails frequently rang through the high-ceiling church, so much so that the words of the priest often couldn't be heard. Bostwick knew that the young banker had no wife or children, so he figured the relatives in attendance must be his parents, as well as brothers and sisters, perhaps.

As the funeral mass, replete with peculiar ceremonies, went on, Bostwick almost wished that he could pretend to cry over his dead colleague himself; at least then he could then raise a handkerchief to his face and shield his nose from the awful smell of incense that wafted through the air. Despite his unease, however, Bostwick managed to sit stiffly and politely throughout the service. He considered it his duty to be here—an obligation that no one else at the bank seemed to share.

After the mass, the weeping family members in the front pew slowly filed back up the aisle to the rear of the sanctuary and out the door. Maintaining a respectful distance from them, Bostwick soon followed. His sense of duty concluded with the funeral, and he intended to proceed to the office instead of the cemetery.

When Bostwick stepped out of the church's large carved doors, it was into a light snowfall. The snow was light as far as quantity, at least, but each flake was fat and several of them promptly stuck to his spectacles. As he put his hat on and pulled his muffler up around his throat, he saw Sinclair's family huddled together at the foot of the steps, waiting for the hearse that would carry their loved one to the cemetery.

Did he need to say something to them? Bostwick wondered. Perhaps a tip of his hat would be sufficient. As usual, he would prefer to avoid speaking to strangers if it could be helped.

The decision was taken from him before he reached the sidewalk. One of the younger women among the mourners detached herself from the rest of the family and stepped toward him. "Excuse me, sir," she said in a controlled voice that betrayed no evidence of weeping.

Bostwick immediately removed his hat again and made a slight bow. "Yes, ma'am?" Trying to look around the water spots on his glasses, he saw the woman had a stern but handsome face behind her dark veil. Locks of blond hair had escaped the confines of her black bonnet, and the skin of her neck was milky white.

"I don't believe we've met before," she said. "May I ask if you were a friend of my brother's?"

Bostwick hesitated. He never lied, but he couldn't very well tell a dead man's sister that her brother probably had no friends. "I worked with Mr. Sinclair at the bank." He was aware of melting snowflakes on his thinning hair, and cold water was soon trickling down behind his ears. "I am so sorry for your loss, Miss Sinclair." Bostwick immediately hoped that he hadn't erred; perhaps she had a married name.

"It's Miss Schulmerich," she corrected, then explained, "My brother was born Ludwig Schulmerich. He changed it to Lyman Sinclair some years ago."

Momentarily speechless with surprise, Bostwick mumbled an apology for the mistake.

"There's no reason for you to have known," she said calmly. "My brother was determined to make a good life for himself, and he said a more American name would help. I understood, and I didn't mind calling him Lyman." She glanced back at her family. "I'm afraid it caused a rift with my parents, however, and we haven't seen much of him in the last couple of years." Facing Bostwick again, she added, "That's why I wondered if you were a friend. I don't believe I've ever met any of his friends."

Bostwick decided he could at least imply that he and Sinclair were more than mere coworkers; implying wasn't the same as lying. "Your brother and I were indeed on friendly terms." He almost said "cordial" instead of "friendly," but once he saw the pleased look on Miss Schulmerich's face, he didn't regret the exaggeration.

"I am happy to hear that my brother had friends," she said. "I only wish we could have met while he was alive, Mr. . . . ."

"Nicholas Bostwick at your service, ma'am." He had just about reached his conversational limit, but added, "I, too, wish we could have met under happier circumstances, Miss Schulmerich." A silly thing to say, he immediately realized; *any* circumstance would have to be happier than the funeral of her brother. "I mean, not like this—although I am happy that we finally did meet." Bostwick realized he was talking nonsense and began to panic. There *had* to be a polite way to avoid any further discussion, and he frantically tried to think what it might be.

To Bostwick's relief, he heard the approaching clop of horses' hooves, and a hearse with mourning draperies inside its glass windows pulled to a stop at the curb. He escorted Miss Schulmerich back to her family and repeated to them all that he was sorry for their loss.

Before catching a streetcar back to Exchange Place, Bostwick craned his neck to look up at the church's tall bell tower. At least now he thought he understood why Lyman Sinclair's plunge from his fourth-floor apartment had been officially ruled an accident instead of suicide as the rumors had it: the "accident" determination had probably been given in deference to the family, so that they could still bury him in consecrated ground.

Nicholas Bostwick had been inside the warm bank for so few minutes that there was still steam on the lenses of his spectacles. He had just seated himself at his desk, planning to get promptly to work to make up for his absence this morning, when Jacob Updegraff—looking rather fuzzy through Bostwick's misted spectacles—approached him. That was a sure sign that something was amiss; ordinarily, Updegraff would send his secretary with a summons to appear in Updegraff's office. Not that Bostwick was often summoned there; in fact, he rarely received any attention from the bank president.

"Where have you been?" Updegraff demanded. "I've been looking for you for more than an hour."

"At the Church of the Most Holy Redeemer," Bostwick replied calmly. "I attended Mr. Sinclair's funeral."

A frown creased the banker's strong brow. "Why would you do that? We have business to attend to here."

Yes, and business was certainly being done, Bostwick could see. Several dozen high oak desks, all illuminated by identical green-shaded brass lamps, and all staffed by serious young men in stiff dark suits, were arrayed in three rows in the center of the New Amsterdam Trust Company's main room. These clerks, accountants, and bookkeepers worked in virtual silence, with a partition to keep them isolated from the public area of the bank, a perimeter around this inner sanctum where customers made their transactions with the tellers. Around the high Romanesque marble walls ran a wide balcony, where additional clerks labored over forms, slips, and ledgers. All of them worked quietly, speaking only in hushed tones when it was necessary to speak at all, giving the place the impression of a library; but it was money that garnered such respectful quietude here, not books or knowledge.

"Yes, sir," Bostwick said. "I apologize for my absence. I assumed the firm would wish to be represented at Mr. Sinclair's service."

Updegraff's response was an indifferent grunt. He placed two duck-bound ledgers and a bulging accordion folder on Bostwick's desk. Lowering his own voice—which Updegraff rarely did in the bank since, as its president, he believed himself to be the equal of money and therefore didn't have to be respectful toward it—he said, "These are Sinclair's records. At least the ones I've found so far." He leaned closer to Bostwick's ear and said in little more than a whisper, "Although Mr. Sinclair had a golden touch when it came to investing, his accounting skills were obviously somewhat lacking. I haven't been able to make heads or tails of his entries."

Bostwick nodded in a way that he hoped would look sympathetic. In truth, he assumed the difficulty could be his boss's own lack of accounting skills. During the seven years that Bostwick had done accounting work for the man, it had become clear to him that Jacob Updegraff was interested only in bottom lines and not the details that led to the final tallies.

"So I am assigning this to you," Updegraff continued. "You are to give me a complete report on Sinclair's accounts. I want to know everything about every single transaction."

Bostwick found the assignment attractive on several levels. One was that he loved to go through numbers and make sense of the indecipherable; turning confusion into order appealed to his meticulous nature. He also liked the idea of learning what Lyman Sinclair actually had been up to; the deceased banker had been so arrogant that it would be a pleasure to uncover some errors. And, if he succeeded to Mr. Updegraff's satisfaction, perhaps there could be a raise in it for him; Bostwick's salary had been stalled at eleven dollars a week for the past three years. "When do you need the report, sir?"

"I need it *now.*"

Suddenly, the project had somewhat less appeal. "I'll begin on it immediately, Mr. Updegraff."

His boss didn't say "thank you"; instead, he nodded as if to say, "Of course you will."

As Bostwick reached for the top ledger, the banker moved away from his desk. Then he turned back to look at him again. "Church of the Most Holy Redeemer, did you say?"

"Yes, sir. On Third Street. That's why it took me so long to—"

"Isn't that Catholic?" Updegraff said the name of the denomination with obvious distaste.

"It is indeed, sir. Mr. Sinclair apparently was of that faith."

"Hmph. He'd told me he was Episcopalian." Updegraff shook his thick head as if disillusioned; Bostwick couldn't tell which came as the bigger blow: learning that Sinclair had poor record-keeping skills or that he was Roman Catholic. Bostwick decided not to further upset his boss with the information that "Lyman Sinclair" wasn't even the man's real name.

CHAPTER 8

Rebecca Davies clutched her skirt, keeping it hoisted above her boot tops and thereby free of the wet snow accumulating on Fifth Avenue's broad sidewalk. The city's most fashionable street, lined with brownstones, mansions, private clubs, and quaint churches, included the residences of both the Davies and Updegraff families. Yet each time Rebecca came to this affluent neighborhood, it felt less and less like home.

The Updegraff mansion, a stately three-story structure with marble facing, was between Thirty-second and Thirty-third Streets, only a couple of blocks from the magnificent Astor and Stewart homes. Jacob Updegraff, Rebecca knew, considered the proximity to mean that he was also close to the status of the city's social elite. The Davies home was ten blocks south, and therefore further down the social scale.

Although Rebecca wasn't expected, a liveried English footman consented to allow this poorer relation of the Updegraffs inside. Once Rebecca was in the tiled reception hall, one starched maid helped her with her coat and bonnet while a second, identically attired maid went to see if Alice was available to receive a visitor. Although the Updegraff home wasn't the largest on the avenue, their staff of servants very well might be.

Rebecca was kept waiting fifteen minutes before the maid returned to tell her that Mrs. Updegraff would see her in the drawing room. Alice wasn't putting on airs, Rebecca knew; her sister was simply obeying social decorum. The two of them had been trained in the social customs and graces from an early age. Alice was the only one to master them, however, and she obeyed those strictures without fail. Alice was always the obedient one—an obedient daughter, a docile wife, and a faithful adherent of good manners.

The drawing room looked like a tropical arboretum. The upholstery and wallpaper both had floral patterns, and fresh-cut flowers filled a dozen crystal vases about the spacious room. The bright colors were a welcome change from the grays and browns that dominated the winter scenes in the streets.

Alice Updegraff, elegantly dressed in a sapphire blue brocade silk gown that accented her fair skin and blond hair, reclined on a plush velvet bed lounge. "Rebecca!" she said with surprised delight, as if she hadn't already been informed that her sister had come to visit. "It is so good to see you!" She gracefully rose from the lounge, and the two of them embraced and kissed each other's cheeks.

Rebecca did love her younger sister, even though they didn't share many interests. And she knew that Alice had a kinder heart and brighter mind than the rest of their family gave her credit for. In addition to maintaining a respectable household and attending all the proper social functions, she shared Rebecca's concern about the girls at Colden House. Alice even helped fund the home in her own way.

As a condition of the Davies family's support for the home, Rebecca's father had long ago insisted that she agree not to ask any of her family's society friends for donations. No such restriction had been placed on Alice, however, and she would occasionally mention Colden House to her friends as a worthy charity. She even alerted Rebecca when their father was in a generous mood, although such alerts had been rare this past year.

"You're looking lovely, Alice," Rebecca said. And it was certainly true; her younger sister had always been the prettier one, and now she was the one who always looked the happiest. Having achieved the greatest accomplishment that a young lady of a good family could aspire to—that is, to marry well—Alice had become quite proficient at enjoying the lifestyle to which she was so well suited.

"As are you, Rebecca." The reply was a matter of her sister's good manners rather than an accurate assessment, Rebecca knew.

The two of them sat down in a pair of matching exquisite Queen Anne armchairs; between them was a small mahogany table, which held a porcelain tea service.

As Alice poured the tea—which was the closest she ever came to doing household labor—Rebecca said, "I am sorry to trouble you, but I have a matter of some delicacy, and I need your advice."

"Does it involve your Mr. Webb?" Alice smiled like a teenaged girl eager to talk about boys.

"No." Considering whom Alice had ended up marrying, Rebecca would never seek her advice on a romantic matter. "It's about an investment I made with Mr. Sinclair."

Alice handed Rebecca her teacup. "I don't know anything about investments. Mr. Updegraff takes care of all our finances." Alice always referred to her husband as "Mr. Updegraff."

"That wasn't what I wanted to ask. You see, I need to get the money back, but I hesitate to speak with Mr. Updegraff about it. Mr. Sinclair has been dead less than a week, and I don't want to seem ghoulish. Were your husband and Mr. Sinclair close friends? I'd hate to bring this up with him if he's still in mourning." She took a sip of the tea.

"Why do you need the money back?" Sometimes Alice asked childlike questions, focusing on something that caught her interest and ignoring the rest of what had been said.

"We've had too many girls coming to Colden House. I can't house them all, but I never let them go without a meal, and there's barely money for groceries. It's the end of January, there's still at least a month of winter left, and more and more people are being put out of work." She placed her cup on the table. "I was hoping to establish some financial security for the future of Colden House, but I realize the immediate need is too great."

"If I had any of my own," Alice said, "I would help you."

"I know you would. Thank you. But about Mr. Updegraff: Do you think this is too soon to speak with him about the investment I made?"

Alice drank a dainty sip. "Well, I believe he did have a fondness for Mr. Sinclair. He considered himself to be something of a mentor to the young man. And Mr. Updegraff has been upset since his unfortunate"—her voice dropped to a whisper—"death." After another sip, she added, "Perhaps not 'upset,' but certainly distracted."

"I'm sorry to hear that," Rebecca said. "I'll wait a while longer before speaking with him, then."

"Oh, I don't believe that it's the loss of Mr. Sinclair that's troubling him—although I'm sure he does feel badly about it." She paused with her teacup in midair. "I believe it has something to do with money."

"Do you know what it is that's wrong?"

"No." Alice shook her head. "He doesn't discuss money with me, and I wouldn't understand it if he did. But I do hear the country is headed for a depression, so perhaps that's what has been weighing on his mind."

Rebecca would have been willing to wait to speak with Updegraff if he had been mourning the loss of Lyman Sinclair, but she didn't see that fretting over the economy was grounds for her to avoid speaking with him. She had her own financial troubles to worry about.

CHAPTER 9

Like most of the other banks that catered to an upper-class clientele, the New Amsterdam Trust Company, on Exchange Place, a short block from Wall Street, had a separate ladies' department, accessible through a private entrance. A properly robed maid was in attendance, and the plush furnishings, including colorful Kashan rugs, Japanese screens with lacquered panels, divans upholstered in silk damask, and potted ferns and areca palms, were more like those of a Fifth Avenue drawing room than a financial institution. There were as many mirrors, bordered by intricately carved gilt frames, in this heavily perfumed room as there were brass cuspidors in the bank's main business area. Many of the ladies who came to transact business probably found the luxurious accommodations to be quite an attraction. Rebecca Davies, however, was not one of them.

She didn't like being redirected to the side entrance by an armed guard when she tried to enter the bank through its main entrance. Nor, when she finally stopped arguing with the guard and consented to go to the ladies' department, did she care for being treated like a porcelain doll instead of a human being. The wizened male clerk in charge of the department fawned and hovered about the female customers seated about the plush room like a eunuch taking care of a harem.

"You don't seem to understand," Rebecca said to the slightly built old man. "I am here to see Mr. *Jacob Updegraff.*" It was the fourth time she had tried to make that simple point understood.

An insipid smile remained plastered on the clerk's face, and he bowed stiffly at the waist; Rebecca thought she heard him click his heels. "My name is August Bugge," he said. "It would be my pleasure to be of service." It was the third time that he had given his name and made that offer.

Since repetition was obviously accomplishing nothing, Rebecca paused to think of another approach. Taking a new tack, she smiled sweetly and said, "That is very kind of you, Mr. Bugge. And, yes, you can be of great service to me."

The old clerk's smile broadened with relief. "I am here to assist, ma'am."

"Would you please give Mr. Updegraff a message that Miss Rebecca Davies is here to see him?" When Bugge's smile faltered again, she quickly added, "I am his sister-in-law. He will be most grateful to you for letting him know that I am here. As will I, of course."

Bugge appeared a bit dubious about his mission, but like an obedient servant he agreed to her request. After a stiff bow, he backed away and retreated through a varnished oak door that connected the ladies' department to the rest of the bank.

After a wait of fifteen minutes, during which Rebecca twice declined offers of tea from the maid, Bugge reappeared with a towering young man in a conservative chocolate brown suit.

While Bugge went to assist another lady, the handsome younger man, who stood close to six and a half feet tall, approached Rebecca. "Miss Davies?" he asked. The high-pitched voice sounded almost girlish and wasn't at all suited to his stature.

"Yes."

"My name is Harold Nantz. I am Mr. Updegraff's personal secretary." He paused for a moment to give her a chance to realize the importance of his position. "He's asked me to show you to his office."

Harold Nantz said nothing more as he proceeded to usher Rebecca through the door into the main bank. They traversed the tiled corridors of the main floor to the rear of the building, where they stepped into a small elevator decorated with intricately engraved brasswork. It was operated by a uniformed old man, who handled the levers with the intensity of a riverboat captain negotiating a side-wheeler through treacherous waters. On the second floor, Nantz led the way past several private offices, with names painted in gold on the closed doors. He stopped at one that read *Jacob R. Updegraff, President,* and knocked politely.

"Come in!" Rebecca recognized the gruff voice as that of her brother-in-law.

Updegraff's secretary opened the door and stood aside to let Rebecca go in first.

This was her first time in Updegraff's place of business, and she was somewhat surprised at the decor. Despite her brother-in-law's fondness for creature comforts, his office was almost spartan in its furnishings. There was nothing in the room that could divert his attention from the business of making money—not a single photograph or painting adorned the walls, and the one rug was a solid dark green. The desk and chairs were of dark-stained oak, and a couple of file cabinets and bookcases of the same wood and color were along the walls. On a pedestal behind Updegraff's swivel chair was a glass-domed stock ticker, which chattered intermittently.

"What a pleasant surprise," Updegraff greeted her. Proper social rearing required that he say polite words, but his expression indicated that he was hardly pleased to see her. There was a scowl on his low brow, and a vein bulged in his thick neck.

"Thank you for seeing me," Rebecca replied. "I won't take much of your time."

Updegraff nodded, not with appreciation but as if to say, "You're darned right, you won't." He gestured for Rebecca to take a chair; after she did, he sat back down in his own. To Nantz he said, "You have some correspondence to finish, I believe."

"Yes, sir." Nantz obediently walked over to his own small desk in a windowless corner.

"Actually," Rebecca said to her brother-in-law, "I was hoping that we could speak in private." She noticed that Nantz didn't hesitate even the slightest bit at her request; he promptly sat down at his rolltop desk and began rifling through some papers.

"Mr. Nantz is my private secretary and the very sole of discretion. You may speak openly in his presence."

"Very well." Rebecca clutched her purse in her lap. "I came to see you about the investment I made with Mr. Sinclair." She hated to be bringing it up at this time; it was only two weeks ago that she had given Sinclair the money, and less than one week since the unfortunate man fell to his death. "I was so sorry to hear that he's dead."

"Yes, yes. A terrible loss." Updegraff began toying with the watch fob attached to the heavy gold chain that hung over his striped vest—a signal that he was already tracking the time until she left, perhaps. "What, specifically, is it that you want to discuss?"

"Well, you see . . ." There was no way to say it other than directly, Rebecca decided. "I need that money back. We've had some more expenses at Colden House—a broken water pipe, for one thing—and I don't see how we can make it through the winter without more money." She rummaged through her purse, pulled out a small sheet of paper, and pushed it on to Updegraff's desk. "This is what I gave to Mr. Sinclair, and I'd like it back."

Frowning, the banker picked up the paper. "You made him write you a receipt?" From his tone, she had breached some kind of social or banking etiquette. It was all the money she had, though, and she hadn't been about to hand it over to a man she'd never met without getting a receipt for it.

"I assumed that was standard practice," she said defensively, although she thought her action had been perfectly reasonable.

"Considering our family connections, it is actually rather insulting. I would almost go so far as to say *impertinent.* " Updegraff shook his head and slid the receipt back to her. "As for getting your money back, you apparently don't understand the nature of your investment." He went on as if explaining something to one of his slower-thinking maids. "You didn't make a *deposit;* you made an *investment.* Your money isn't sitting here in the bank vault; you bought something. You bought stock in the Western Continental Railroad. That makes you part owner of that company."

Rebecca didn't care for his condescending tone, but forced herself to remain civil. "Very well, then, where are my stock certificates? I'd like to sell the stock back."

Her brother-in-law hesitated while the stock ticker spit out a ribbon of paper. "The certificates themselves may be in transit. We are currently reviewing Mr. Sinclair's accounts; I hope you'll understand that his loss was totally unexpected, and it will take some time to determine the status of every account he handled."

"Of course I understand. But you know that I bought the stocks—I have the receipt. Can't I go ahead and sell them without the certificate? Don't bankers buy and sell stocks that way all the time?"

"I didn't realize you were such an expert on banking procedures, Miss Davies." Updegraff made no effort to conceal the contempt in his voice.

Rebecca wondered whatever her sister had seen in this man. Other than being of a "good family," he had no redeeming qualities that she could discern. "All I want," she said, "is to get back my money so that I can keep the women at Colden House alive through the winter. *You're* the expert, so please tell me: how do I go about selling back the stock?"

"You'd take quite a loss on broker's fees to buy and sell so quickly—unless the stock has appreciated in this time, of course."

"How much *is* the stock worth now?"

He hesitated to answer, although this time the ticker was silent. "I don't have that information at hand. The railroad in question is not one of the larger ones, so only an investor—or a banker like Mr. Sinclair, who was handling the stocks—would be likely to track their value closely. It may take some time to find out what your investment is actually worth, especially since it was such a paltry sum."

Rebecca didn't have time; there were two months more of winter and she needed the money now. "If I can't sell the stocks immediately," she said, "then I would like a loan."

Updegraff grinned. "A *loan?* With what collateral?"

She hadn't considered that her brother-in-law would demand that she put up collateral for what he himself called "a paltry sum." Trying to tally what she owned that might be used, she was discouraged to realize that she actually owned almost nothing. Colden House itself wasn't even something that she owned; it was her family's, under the control of her father. "I can give you my word that I will repay the loan as soon as I can sell back the railroad stocks I bought from Mr. Sinclair."

He shook his head, clearly amused at her naive notion that a bank would take someone's word that they would pay back a loan. "I can't simply give you money like that. Even if you intend to pay them back now, what if that Colden House of yours needs some more repairs? Undoubtedly, you would spend the money on that instead of repaying the loan." Updegraff shook his head again. "Eventually, your father would probably end up having to pay off your debt." He leaned forward. "A lady of your age really must learn to stand on her own some time."

Resisting an impulse to slap him, Rebecca gritted her teeth and replied, "I said I would pay you back from the railroad stocks. Use those for collateral; if they're worth as much as Mr. Sinclair claimed, they should more than cover the loan I'm seeking."

Updegraff pulled his watch from his vest pocket and glared at its face. Without looking up at Rebecca, he answered, "And as *I* said, we are evaluating the status of Mr. Sinclair's accounts. Until that evaluation is complete, a loan is simply out of the question." The stock ticker chattered again, and Updegraff got up to read the paper strip. He held the coiled ribbon in both hands, sliding it through his fingers to straighten it out as he studied the information it contained.

Rebecca was becoming convinced that Updegraff was trying to hide something. There was something more than the prospect of parting with some of his precious cash that was making him uneasy. "Why would it take so long to sort out Mr. Sinclair's accounts?" she asked. "Surely he kept records."

"Of course he did. That's what we're reviewing." He studiously kept his gaze directed at the ticker tape.

Rebecca decided to give her brother-in-law a good, sharp verbal poke. "I read in the newspapers that Mr. Sinclair's death might have been a suicide—and that he might have been driven to it by some banking scandal. You don't suppose there could be any truth in that, do you?"

The paper he was holding ripped as he turned to face her. "The newspapers have as little comprehension of financial matters as you," he said sharply. He then regained enough of his manners to say, "It has been good to see you, Miss Davies. I shall tell Mrs. Updegraff that you are looking well."

Harold Nantz recognized, as did Rebecca, that she was being dismissed. The secretary stood up and offered to walk her out.

She declined the offer and left the office without another word to her brother-in-law.

A long shadow fell over Nicholas Bostwick's desk. He looked up to see Harold Nantz towering next to him.

"Mr. Updegraff wishes to see you in his office." Nantz didn't lower his gaze to look at Bostwick; it was as if he refused to notice anyone who didn't come up to his own height.

Bostwick closed the ledger he'd been studying, then paused to clean an ink smudge from his thumb with his pocket handkerchief.

Nantz cleared his throat noisily to remind him that the president was waiting.

It was Nantz that Bostwick had wanted to keep waiting a moment. He didn't care for the man, because of the way Nantz interpreted his proximity to power to mean that he had power himself. The secretary was little more than an errand boy as far as Bostwick was concerned, and he wasn't about to be hurried by him. After a lengthy inspection of his thumb to be certain that no ink remained—and to aggravate Nantz—Bostwick rose from his desk. As much as he would have liked to irritate the secretary further, he wasn't about to risk annoying Mr. Updegraff. "Let's go, then," he said, lowering the pitch of his normal speaking voice a little; if Nantz liked to accentuate the difference in their heights, Bostwick would bring attention to the young man's incongruously high voice.

As Bostwick followed the secretary to Updegraff's office, Nantz carefully brushed at an imaginary piece of lint from the lapel of his expensive suit. It was another way of pointing out the difference in their ranks. As the president's personal secretary, Nantz was expected to wear more expensive attire; clerks and accountants like Bostwick wore cheaper cuts of cloth, partly because it was all their meager salaries permitted and partly because they should sport nothing finer than what those of a higher office might wear.

When they entered Jacob Updegraff's office, Bostwick could tell that the boss was not in a good mood; he worked a cigar in his mouth as if trying to turn it into chewing tobacco.

"Ah, Bostwick. It's about time."

"Yes, sir. I'm sorry for the delay."

Harold Nantz sniffed as if he'd won some kind of victory, but when he stepped toward his corner desk, he was cut off by Updegraff. "Be so good as to leave us for a few minutes," Updegraff said. "I wish to speak to Mr. Bostwick in private."

The secretary meekly said, "Yes, sir," and left the office, closing the door behind him. He looked like a puppy that had been kicked by its master, and Bostwick had to bite his tongue to keep from smiling.

Updegraff waved his tattered cigar at a chair. "Have a seat, Bostwick."

Bostwick did so; he almost had to, because of the surprise. He'd never had a private meeting with Updegraff in his office before, and the few times he had been in this room at all, he'd never been permitted to sit.

The bank president got right to the point: "What have you been able to determine from Mr. Sinclair's records?"

Bostwick shifted in the chair, savoring its comfort. He allowed himself to imagine that Updegraff might even offer him a cigar. "I hate to speak ill of the late Mr. Sinclair," he answered, "but all I can tell for certain is that he was rather shoddy at record keeping."

"How so?"

"They're incomplete, and in some cases the figures don't add up. He shows quite a profit, but I don't know how that profit was achieved."

"You've reviewed the books carefully?"

"Yes, sir. The books, the correspondence . . . I've studied every piece of paper you gave me, and I simply can't put things together in any way that makes sense." It had been a most vexing project for Bostwick; he liked things to add up and make sense.

This wasn't news that his boss wanted to hear. Updegraff angrily crushed the cigar into a brass ash tray. "We must find the money!"

"Excuse me, sir. Are there funds missing?" Bostwick had thought the only issue at hand was piecing together Sinclair's records.

It was a long moment before Updegraff answered. "I will take you into my confidence, Bostwick. As we know, Mr. Sinclair made quite a bit of money for his investors and for the bank. However, I have been unable to locate a cent of it."

"Do you suspect fraud?" Until now, Bostwick had assumed that Sinclair's worst fault was carelessness.

"The newspapers speak of fraud, and some investors are demanding an accounting." He snorted. "Even my dratted sister-in-law is asking about her investment." Updegraff swiveled to and fro in his chair for a few moments. Then he put his elbows on his desk and leaned toward Bostwick. "The bank can not afford a scandal, especially not in uncertain times like these. We *must* find that money."

Bostwick didn't know what to reply, so he simply said, "Yes, sir."

"I am assigning that task to *you*."

Too stunned even to answer "Yes, sir," Bostwick clutched the arms of the chair, suddenly feeling faint.

Updegraff went on, "I expect you to do whatever it takes to learn what Mr. Sinclair had been doing. You are to determine every transaction he made, and track down every penny he handled."

Bostwick finally was able to spit out a simple question. "How do I do that?"

"Check his home, talk to his friends, find any other papers he might have left."

That sounded simple, but it was no guarantee that it would bring about the desired results. "Wouldn't that be a job for a detective, sir?"

"It's a job for *you*. No detective would understand financial accounting the way that you do. And, more importantly, I can count on you to be discreet."

"I appreciate your confidence. I only wish I was as confident myself."

"Oh, you'll succeed. You'd better, if you expect to have any kind of future with this bank." He leaned back and folded his hands over his belly. "You see, another banker here might go to a competitor with information that we had some financial irregularities, in the hopes of gaining a better position for himself. But you won't do that—you simply don't have the ambition. All you want is the security of your job and a regular paycheck."

That was true enough, but Bostwick didn't care for the way it sounded. It made him sound lazy when in fact he simply liked stability and the comfort of routine. "I do value my position at New Amsterdam," he allowed.

"And if you want to keep it, you'll carry out this little assignment. Of course, if you succeed, I would be most grateful, and your position with us would be very secure." He bit the end of a fresh cigar. "Remember, you are to be discreet in this undertaking. You will report directly to me and to me alone. Is that understood?"

There was no way to misunderstand, so Bostwick said that he did.

"Fine. Then get started. The sooner we can quell any rumors, the better for the bank."

As he left the office, Bostwick felt overwhelmed at the task he'd been given. The only thing that brightened his load was seeing the miffed expression on Harold Nantz's face at his having been allowed a private audience with the president. But if Nantz had known the burden that Bostwick had just been given, he would have realized that he had no cause to envy the accountant.

CHAPTER 10

Marshall Webb had planned to spend the weekend alone in his apartment, working on the first installment of his Tammany Hall story for *Harper's Weekly*. The building's infernal new steam heating system did so much clanging, hissing, and belching, however, that he had the sense of being cooped up with a roommate who snored.

After once again trying to reduce the noise by bleeding some air from the radiator next to the parlor window, Webb brewed a fresh pot of coffee—which provided far more warmth than the radiator—and returned to his large rolltop desk. He skimmed over what he had already written; his prose wasn't particularly inspired, he could tell, but the first piece of his series on Tammany Hall was intended to provide the background and history of the organization and necessarily had to be a bit "dry."

He reported that the Society of St. Tammany, also known as the Columbian Order, had been founded in 1789. The name Tammany was chosen in honor of a Chief Tamamend. The chief may have been purely mythical—some said he was a Leni-Lenape who had fought against the British, others claimed he had helped Pennsylvania colonists survive in the New World, and the Delaware Indians credited him with carving out Niagara Falls—but legend or not, the chief had captured the imagination of eighteenth-century Americans. He had been canonized by Revolutionary soldiers as America's saint, and several fraternal societies named "St. Tammany" in his honor were organized.

The New York Tammany Society, like most of the others, continued the Indian imagery throughout its organizational structure. Lower chiefs were called *sagamores*, while the leaders—

thirteen of them, representing the thirteen colonies—were *sachems*. One of the latter was selected as "grand sachem," the society's head. New members were *braves*, and the society headquarters was the *wigwam*.

Webb snorted as he read over that section of his article. It made Tammany sound like any other fraternal society with a penchant for funny names and strange rituals. But it was also a political machine. From its founding, the society had been antiaristocratic, a fraternal organization for the common man. It soon became allied with the Democratic party and enormously popular with immigrants, especially the Irish.

He got up from the desk, walked to the window of his second-floor apartment, and looked out on bustling East Fourteenth Street. Just off Union Square, the street was lined with a variety of entertainment and dining places, including everything from Luchow's Restaurant and Huber's Dime Museum to Steinway Hall and the Academy of Music. And, by craning his neck a little, Webb could see the wigwam, Tammany Hall itself. The imposing three-story brick structure, which also housed Tony Pastor's variety house in a separately accessed area of its ground floor, was crowned with a statue of Chief Tamamend on its cornice.

Although Tammany supporters claimed that it was merely a benevolent social and charitable organization, one of its committees, the General Committee of Tammany Democracy, was admittedly a distinctly political operation. It was through that committee that the society flexed its political muscle and reaped the financial spoils that came with power. And it was no surprise that Tammany's sachems were the ones who fed the most from the public trough; the current grand sachem, Thomas F. Gilroy, was also the city's new mayor, and other sachems included his predecessor in the mayor's office, Hugh Grant, as well as the true leader of Tammany, Richard "Boss" Croker, who raked in millions of public dollars without holding any elected office at all.

This was what Webb wanted to expose, but before he could prove a case against Boss Croker, he would have to work his way up through the system, speaking to fraudulent voters like Kid McGah, and ward heelers like Rabbit Doyle. For now, he had to give the editors at *Harper's Weekly* enough material to get them interested in publishing his articles.

So Webb returned to his desk, picked up his gold-nibbed pen, and began scratching away on a fresh sheet of foolscap. In the dry, plodding style that his editor preferred, he continued to sketch out the history of Tammany—from the early years of the society, when Aaron Burr was its guiding force, to its later leaders such as the notorious Boss Tweed, whose ring of cronies had managed to plunder a staggering $200 million from the city treasury over a period of six years from 1865 to 1871. Tweed's insatiable greed had such a devastating effect on the city's economy that it resulted in the Panic of 1873—as well as in Tweed's eventual arrest and imprisonment.

Webb had just started to write about Tweed's successor as Tammany boss, "Honest" John Kelly, who earned his moniker by being less conspicuous in his thievery than Tweed had been, when there was a soft rap at the door. It wasn't the knock of a man, Webb thought.

After pausing at a small wall mirror to straighten the knot of a silk Windsor tie that was already perfectly centered, and to run a finger over his mustache and whiskers to make sure not a strand of hair was out of place, Webb opened the door to see that he was correct in his assumption.

Rebecca Davies stood there, looking like a spring blossom in her yellow reefer jacket and a dark-green mohair skirt. Her lace braid hat, trimmed with satin and a sprig of violets, had been unable to contain her hair from the wintry winds, and long, curly locks of honey-blond hair framed her fair face. "I hope I didn't come at a bad time," she said.

As far as Webb was concerned, there was never a bad time for Rebecca's company. "Not at all. Please come in."

While he helped her off with her coat, he tried to think of what refreshments he might be able to offer. There was little in the ice box and not much more on the one kitchen shelf that served as a pantry. "Would you like some tea?" he asked, silently hoping that she wouldn't ask for cream with it. He also hoped she wasn't hungry; most of the food in his kitchen wasn't fresh enough to serve to a guest.

"I could use something to warm me up," Rebecca said, "but I'd really like something a bit stronger than tea."

"Sherry?"

"Perfect." Rebecca glanced around the room before choosing to sit on the horsehair sofa.

As Webb went to get her drink, he was acutely aware that his apartment really wasn't presentable enough for a lady. Although Rebecca had visited him several times before, he had never been entirely comfortable about it. The main room, a combination parlor, library, and dining room, was furnished in a distinctly bachelor style. It was primarily functional, with little decoration except for some framed Civil War woodcuts on the walls. The largest piece of furniture in the room was his massive rolltop desk, on either side of which were matching glass-door bookcases. The dining section of the room was located at the window and consisted of a small oak table with a pair of bent-back chairs. The parlor area was almost as spare in its furnishings; other than the sofa, the only other seat that Rebecca might have chosen was a spacious leather easy chair that Webb favored.

He returned with her glass of sherry and one of port for himself. Upon seeing her face, Webb's concern about his decorating vanished. Rebecca's fine features were fixed and hard; her lips were a bit tight and her jaw clenched. He'd seen that look before and knew it meant that something serious was troubling her. After handing her the drink, he sat next to her on the sofa. "What's the matter?"

Rebecca turned to him. "You can tell?"

Webb nodded. They had been together often enough during the past year that Webb believed he could read her pretty well. And if it wasn't her voice or facial expressions that gave her away, it was her eyes—hazel eyes that could flash fire when she was angry or glow with soft warmth when she was happy. Right now, there was a mix of fear and anger in them.

After Webb prodded her once more to tell him what was bothering her, Rebecca took a sip of sherry, then said, "It's nothing new, really. I've had some unexpected expenses at Colden House." She smiled wryly. "Although there's really no such thing—unexpected expenses come up so often, I should have learned to expect them by now."

"Anything I can help with?"

"No, thank you." She shook a slim finger at him in warning. "And I don't want you to make any 'anonymous' donations either, or I won't tell you about this."

"Very well." But as he agreed, Webb immediately began thinking of a way to circumvent her instruction. Perhaps he could get someone else to funnel the donation for him. Although he might not be able to make as much of a contribution as he would have liked anyway—Webb's own income wasn't coming in as it once had.

Rebecca went on, "With the latest expenses, I wanted to get back the investment I'd made with my brother-in-law's bank. Colden House—and the girls who live there—simply won't be able to survive the rest of the winter with the funds I have left."

"Did you speak with Mr. Updegraff?"

"Oh yes." She shook her head tightly. "It was an entirely unsatisfactory meeting."

"He wouldn't give you back the money?"

"No." Rebecca was obviously trying to keep down her anger. After she collected herself, she asked, "You've heard about Lyman Sinclair?"

"He's the banker who died a couple of weeks ago."

"Yes. He also happens to be the banker I gave the money to—upon Mr. Updegraff's recommendation. Now Mr. Updegraff tells me that they have to review Mr. Sinclair's records before there could be any possibility of me getting the investment back."

"That sounds reasonable."

Rebecca shook her head. "I asked if there was something else he could do to get me some funds—he *knows* I gave it to Mr. Sinclair, so he knows I wasn't asking for a handout. All I wanted was a loan. But he wouldn't help at all." She took another sip of wine. "The strange thing is, when I mentioned the newspaper reports that Mr. Sinclair might have killed himself over a financial scandal, he became quite upset. It led me to believe there might be something to those stories."

Webb suggested, "Perhaps he was simply upset at the situation—the death of Sinclair or the fact that his bank might be having money problems. A lot of them are. And with one of his bankers committing suicide at a time when rumors about a coming financial panic are already running rampant, it's got to be especially difficult for your brother-in-law." Webb felt no particular sympathy for Jacob Updegraff; he simply didn't want Rebecca worrying any more than was warranted about her investment with his bank.

"I wish you were right." She shook her head again. "I've just had lunch with my sister and I talked to her about it. Alice says her husband is troubled by something, although she doesn't know what. He's been surly and short-tempered, she says." Rebecca frowned. "From my experience, Mr. Updegraff is hardly a pleasant man, but he's always been kind to Alice. She's says lately he's been snapping at her, though."

"She doesn't know why he's acting that way?"

"No. She's asked him, but all he'll say is that it's business, and nothing she would understand." Rebecca's lips tightened, and Webb could tell she was again struggling to remain calm. "He doesn't think a mere woman could understand anything about business or money—he certainly made that belief clear to me when I went to see him at the bank to ask about my money." Pausing for a sip of wine, she then said, "Alice is worried; she does love her husband—heaven knows why—and she thinks he may be in some serious trouble. *I* think Mr. Updegraff can take care of himself; *I'm* more worried about the women staying at Colden House, and being able to shelter them." Her voice dropped slightly. "And I'm hoping you can help me."

Webb didn't understand. "But you just told me you *don't* want my help. What do—"

Rebecca held up a hand. "Yes, I'm sorry. I meant I don't want you making any donations. I'm going to work on getting funds myself. Instead of hoping for large donations, I'm going to start writing letters to businesses, charities, and maybe some of the city's well-to-do, asking for small donations." She laid her hand on Webb's arm. "What I'm asking you to do is find out if there's any truth to the rumors about Mr. Updegraff's bank. I'd like to be sure that my investment is safe. And, I have to admit, I've probably caught a bit of my sister's concern for her husband—not that I'm worried about what may happen to *him*, but I'd hate for Alice to be hurt in any way."

Webb took a moment to think over Rebecca's request, still not sure that he understood her completely. "Of course I'd be happy to help, but I have to admit I'm not sure that I know how. I don't follow the financial news, and I really don't know much about Mr. Updegraff or his bank."

Rebecca said wryly, "The only thing there is to know about my brother-in-law is that his primary goal in life is to make money. He already has more than any human can spend in a lifetime, but it's not nearly enough for him. Alice once told me that he considers it his duty to grow the family fortune. The Updegraffs—and their money—have been in New York since Peter Stuyvesant's time; every generation has accumulated more wealth to pass on to their heirs, and my brother-in-law would consider himself a failure if he didn't do the same." She stopped, as if thinking to herself about something she couldn't fathom. Then she went on, "I didn't expect you to examine his accounts or anything. I just thought you might ask around at *Harper's* and see if they've gotten any reports of something amiss at the bank."

"I'll do whatever I can," Webb agreed. As he thought about it, though, it occurred to him that *Harper's Weekly* might not be the best place to start. There was another source that might be more informative.

CHAPTER 11

Sergeant O'Melia had to rap his nightstick on the door for a full minute before there was a gruff yell from inside: "Enough with the bangin', already! I'm comin', damn it!" When the door was cracked open a few cautious inches, a crescent of unshaven face came into view and the same voice asked sleepily, "Whatcha want?"

"Police business." The burly sergeant tapped the badge on his greatcoat with the tip of his nightstick. "You the super?"

"Yeah."

"You gotta open up Four-D for the gentleman here."

Nicholas Bostwick wasn't accustomed to being referred to as a gentleman, but he was certainly enjoying the police officer's solicitous behavior toward him. Ever since O'Melia had picked him up at his own apartment promptly at seven o'clock this morning, he'd made it clear that he was at Bostwick's service and willing to assist him in any way.

"Four-D?" the building superintendent repeated.

"Yeah, the Lyman Sinclair place."

"Awright." The superintendent rubbed the back of his hand across his stubbly chin. "Gimme a minute to get dressed."

The police officer gave him less than that before hurrying him with another rap on the door. "We ain't got all day, so quit yer primpin' and get the hell out here!"

The building superintendent promptly followed the order. Still tucking his flannel shirt into his trousers, he led Bostwick and O'Melia upstairs through the Langford Arms, one of New York's better apartment buildings. The halls and stairwells were clean, well lit, and free of the usual obstacles left by inconsiderate tenants—there were no toys or broken furniture to block their path.

Bostwick thought that said something about the class of people who lived in the building.

Soon, the three of them stood outside apartment 4-D. While the superintendent put the key into the lock, Bostwick found himself intensely curious about what they would find inside and what it would tell him about Lyman Sinclair—not only about his accounts but about his lifestyle. Bostwick had never liked the arrogant banker, but he had secretly envied him in a way; Sinclair had in abundance the drive and ambition that Bostwick had never felt within himself. While Bostwick yearned only for the security of a steady job and regular paycheck, Sinclair was always pressing to get to the top—and it was no secret that Sinclair's idea of making it to the top meant making himself into a millionaire.

As they stepped into the wide foyer, the superintendent grumbled to O'Melia, "You know, I'm starting to lose money on this place. Mr. Sinclair only paid through January. When can I rent it again?"

"When the captain says you can." There was no sympathy in Sergeant O'Melia's tone. "Until then, you make sure nobody gets in here unless there's an officer with him to give you the okay." He grabbed the handle of the nightstick meaningfully. "You'll have me to answer to if anybody gets inside without permission." O'Melia nodded at the open door. "We'll let you know when we leave, so you can lock up again."

The superintendent muttered a few inaudible words, but obediently left, closing the door behind him.

Bostwick was impressed, and somewhat exhilarated, by a sense of power that he rarely got to experience. It wasn't his own power, of course, but he enjoyed having it wielded on his behalf. The real influence, he knew, was Jacob Updegraff's. Like most Wall Street financiers, Updegraff enjoyed a close relationship with the police department, especially Superintendent of Police Thomas F. Byrnes, who benefited from stock tips in exchange for allowing his department to be used as a private security detail for the bankers. It was Updegraff who had Lyman Sinclair's apartment sealed soon after his death, so that not even the junior banker's family could have access to any papers or materials that might be bank property. And it was Updegraff who had arranged for Sergeant O'Melia to accompany Bostwick to the apartment and clear the way for him to search its contents.

Bostwick first took a casual look about the spacious parlor. The furnishings certainly appeared expensive, but they were sparser than he expected. It gave the impression that Sinclair had been hesitant in his decorating, perhaps fearful of including anything that wasn't quite right—anything that might result in his being accused of bad taste.

Individually, what Sinclair had put into the room was absolutely magnificent. The armchairs and side tables were Chippendale in style, although Bostwick wasn't expert enough to know if they were authentic. A tufted burgundy leather sofa faced a white marble fireplace, which had built-in bookshelves on either side of it. The books arrayed neatly on the shelves all appeared to have leather bindings stamped in gold. In one corner of the parlor was a mahogany desk polished to a mirror finish, and in another was a double-doored glass china cabinet that held exquisite figurines of porcelain and crystal. The walls, papered in a soft solid red, were bare except for the brass light fixtures and two oil paintings that looked as though they may have been painted by one of the old Dutch masters.

Despite its luxurious appointments, the room seemed oddly sterile, though—more like a furniture store's showroom than a home. There were no photographs on the walls, no magazines or newspapers on the tables, not even an empty coffee cup on the desk. An ornate silver picture frame was on the desk, but it contained no photograph. There was simply nothing personal in the place that Bostwick could see, nothing to say that the person who had lived here had been Lyman Sinclair.

Although Nicholas Bostwick's assigned task was to collect any papers and documents that he could find, he didn't begin his search immediately. Perhaps it was morbid curiosity, but he felt himself drawn across the parlor to a French door that led out to the balcony, the place from which Sinclair had plummeted to his death.

Bostwick glanced back at Sergeant O'Melia and saw that he was already actively engaged in a search of his own. The officer was quietly going through the drawers of a sideboard, examining the silverware it contained, slipping pieces of it into the pockets of his greatcoat. This was standard procedure, Bostwick knew. No one in the New York City Police Department performed his duties without getting a little something extra for his efforts. It was true all the way down the ranks: Superintendent Byrnes received lucrative stock tips for his services, precinct captains accepted weekly protection money from brothels and gambling houses, and the uniformed officers settled for whatever valuables they could fit in their pockets when they went out on a call.

With O'Melia obviously in no hurry for Bostwick to get to work, the accountant looked out through the glass door for a few moments. Then he opened it and stepped onto the broad balcony and into the bracing air.

Sinclair's apartment, on West Fourth Street, provided a marvelous view of Washington Square. It was a view made all the better by the good weather. The morning sky was crystalline, and the air so clear and the sun so bright that Bostwick thought he could make out every detail of the elegant Greek Revival row houses on Waverly Place across the Square. He could also see partway up Fifth Avenue, which originated on Washington Square's north side and graciously journeyed up through most of Manhattan.

Bostwick could easily picture Lyman Sinclair standing in this same spot, gazing toward that "Avenue of Mansions" and dreaming that he would someday amass enough wealth to take his place beside the Astors, Vanderbilts, and Updegraffs who built their homes on Fifth Avenue. Sinclair might have achieved that goal, too, Bostwick thought, if his life hadn't been cut so tragically short.

The accountant removed his hand from the balcony's wrought-iron railing and turned to go back inside. As he did, he noticed how high the railing was; Bostwick could have walked directly into it and not fallen over onto the street below. Sinclair had been about Bostwick's height, so he couldn't have accidentally fallen, either. Bostwick decided that the banker most likely did jump; never mind the "accident" verdict of city officials who may have been coaxed into sparing the Schulmerich family the additional grief of dealing with a suicide.

Getting back to his assignment, Bostwick returned to the parlor, where Sergeant O'Melia was looking over the china cabinet with a look of dismay. Either Lyman Sinclair didn't have the kind of loot O'Melia preferred, or it had already been picked clean by the police who had been first on the scene after Sinclair's death.

Bostwick first went to the desk and began searching for papers with the same diligence that he searched for arithmetic errors in accounting ledgers. There was little in the desk, mostly correspondence, but every letter and every envelope went into Bostwick's alligator valise.

Next he went to Sinclair's bedroom, which contained a large platformed sleigh bed, a washstand, dresser, and corner chair. The wood was all dark cherry, and the fixtures were all polished brass. As in the parlor, there were no photographs or personal mementos.

Bostwick looked under the bed for any boxes that might hold papers, and found there was hardly even any dust. In the closet, he found a wardrobe rich in vicuña, alpaca, and cashmere, but there was still no trace of the thing he most needed to find: an account book with a complete record of Lyman Sinclair's investment transactions.

When he returned to the parlor, Sergeant O'Melia was slouched in an armchair. "You just about done?" he asked.

Bostwick bit the inside of his lip. "Almost." He looked around for anything he might have missed. The only other paper anywhere in the room was between the leather covers of the books on the shelves. He almost decided to give up his search, but Bostwick was constitutionally incapable of leaving any loose ends. So he went to the bookshelves.

Ignoring an impatient grumble from the police officer, Bostwick quickly worked his way along one shelf and then the next, pulling each volume to check that there was nothing behind it and nothing within its pages. It was an easy task; just like most other things in the apartment, the books were largely for show. Most of the bindings were stiff, and the gilt-edged page tops were stuck together, never having been read.

Finally, in a calf-bound volume of Isaac Newton's *Principia*—a book that no one was likely ever to open—Bostwick found that a section had been torn out and replaced with several sheets from an accounting ledger. He was first delighted with his find, but after scanning the entries, he realized that Mr. Updegraff was not going to be happy at what he'd found.

CHAPTER 12

The dripping piece of rare roast beef on the tines of Lawrence Pritchard's fork seemed to glow a bright red as he drew it toward his waiting mouth. The reason, Marshall Webb could tell, was because of the stark color contrast between the bloody chunk of meat and Pritchard's pasty complexion.

Ever since Webb had known the man, Pritchard's appearance had always resembled that of a malnourished ghost, with sunken eyes, a bony jawline, and pale, drawn skin. This year's long winter had left the middle-aged man's clean-shaven face even whiter than usual. Yet Webb did notice that, despite the lack of sunshine, there must have been something that brightened up Pritchard's life recently, because there seemed to be an extra glint of life in the eyes that blinked owlishly behind his pince-nez.

"How's the beef?" Webb asked.

Pritchard swallowed and dabbed at the corners of his mouth with a napkin. "A bit overcooked, but not bad. And the rum punch is most excellent! How are your oysters?"

"A bit *under*cooked."

"Wha—? Oh, very funny."

Webb scooped another raw oyster from its shell, popped it into his mouth whole, and chewed it.

This was the first time in months that Webb had seen Pritchard, and it was one of the first times that he had been willing to be seen with him in a public place. For years their relationship had been a secret, but Webb no longer guarded their association so carefully. This Monday afternoon the two of them were dining in the rotunda lunchroom of the Astor House hotel. Situated at Park Row and Broadway, next to St. Paul's Chapel, it was the busiest restaurant in downtown New York, and a popular eating spot among the newspaper and magazine publishers who had their offices in the area known as Printing House Square. It was so crowded, and so many conversations rang about the high-ceilinged lunchroom, that it was almost like hiding in plain sight—no one was likely to notice Webb and Pritchard among the hungry horde.

Webb followed the oyster with a long swallow of dark ale. "Thank you for having lunch with me on such short notice," he said.

"My pleasure." Pritchard paused from cutting another piece of roast beef and wagged his knife dismissively. "Besides, I'm a publisher. Having lunch is a major part of my job."

Webb resisted the temptation to suggest that Pritchard put a couple more meals on his daily agenda. Pritchard's build was so slight that when he wore black suits he could almost be mistaken for the ebony walking stick that he liked to flourish. "Still, I appreciate you taking the time," he said. "I have a favor to ask of you, Lawrence."

"Of course. Anything." Pritchard then dabbed at his lips again; he did so after every bite he ate. "Unless it's about . . ." He lowered his knife and fork and glanced down at his plate. "If it's about the new book, well I'm afraid that . . ." Pritchard reached into a pocket of the overcoat draped over the back of his chair and pulled out a thin sheaf of manuscript paper. "I am giving this back to you. I simply cannot publish this book." He placed the pages in the center of the small round table.

Webb glanced down at his own handwriting on the title page:

WELCOME TO AMERICA
or
A Firing Line on Fire Island
by David A. Byrd

Webb grabbed the pages, folded them, and slipped them into his own pocket. This wasn't something he would want anyone from *Harper's Weekly* ever to see. Not even Webb's family knew that he secretly wrote novels for Pritchard's Dime Library under the Byrd pseudonym. Writing thirty-two-page action novels that appeared between lurid paper covers was not at all a respectable occupation. Although he figured he could explain away being seen with the editor—he could always simply claim that Pritchard had information that Webb needed for a *Harper's* story—he didn't want to leave hard evidence of their connection lying on the table where anyone could see it. "Why can't you publish it?" he asked calmly.

Pritchard blinked rapidly and adjusted his pince-nez so they sat higher on his beaklike nose. "I am sorry, Marshall. You have always been one of my favorite authors; I like you personally, I admire your writing skills, and your books have always been among my most profitable. Over the years, I have published everything you have ever submitted to me, and I have been proud to do so. But I cannot publish this one." He lowered his voice to a whisper. "You have diseased Russian Jews in this book, and you try to make them *sympathetic* characters!" He pursed his lips and shook his head with distaste. "My readers are not going to feel sympathy for choleric immigrants—especially not Russian Jews."

Webb was sorry to hear Pritchard say that. He *had* felt sympathy for the unfortunate immigrants when he learned what they had had to endure. Although the characters in his story were fictional, the events were all factual. Only six months ago, in August of 1892, the steamship *Normannia* arrived in New York harbor from Hamburg, Germany. A cholera outbreak in Hamburg had made all immigrants coming from the city suspect, many of them Russian Jews who had journeyed to Hamburg to begin their final passage to America. Public fears about the disease prompted the state of New York to order the passengers quarantined. The place selected for their quarantine was Fire Island, a nearly uninhabited barrier island south of Long Island. Once word of the immigrants' arrival spread, however, an armed mob of citizens from Islip and other Long Island towns prevented them from landing, forcing them to stay aboard ship, where food and water were running out. Eventually, National Guardsmen arrived, and the immigrants were herded ashore and placed in quarantine in a hotel taken over for that purpose.

"Very well," Webb simply said. He decided not to argue with the publisher. Although Webb understood the harsh reality that newcomers to America often faced, he felt that he had never been able to adequately portray that reality in his fictional writing, and he wasn't really satisfied with the final draft of *Made in America*, anyway. Perhaps it was more a subject for journalism than fiction, he thought; if so, he could always try to interest *Harper's* or one of the city's numerous competing newspapers in publishing the story of what happened at Fire Island.

Pritchard continued with his meal. "You really must get back to writing Westerns, Marshall. Readers want characters they can identify with and cheer for. It must be clear to them who the heroes are."

"The heroes would be the cowboys, not the Indians, right?" Webb asked facetiously. He had once enjoyed Westerns, reading them when he was young and writing them when he was older, but he wasn't eager to go back to the genre. "And the leading character has to wear a white hat?"

"Of course." Pritchard laughed nervously. "Please don't tell me you've forgotten how to write a Western. They were always your best novels—better even than your Civil War stories." He paused with his fork in midair. "You know, I did take a chance with you by publishing the book you did on the Homestead steel strike last fall. It hardly sold, and I am taking a loss on almost the entire print run. You tried to make the *strikers* the heroes."

"Not the heroes," Webb replied. Didn't Pritchard realize that most people were neither heroes nor villains but merely human beings? "I only wanted to make the lives of the steelworkers better understood. And whom would *you* have as the heroes: Andrew Carnegie or the army of Pinkertons he hired to gun down the strikers?"

"Look Marshall, I do not publish complex books, and I am not trying to change society. All I want—all my readers want—is a simple story; it has to have a hero and a villain, and the hero has to prevail at the end. That's all there is to it." He dabbed at his lips. "If you can go back to writing that kind of book, I would be happy to publish every manuscript you can give me. Those books have made us both a lot of money over the years, and there's no reason why we can't make a lot more."

Webb thought over that prospect. He certainly could have used the money that he had been anticipating for the Fire Island novel. Dime novels had been his major source of income, and since he hadn't been writing many lately, his bank account was dwindling rapidly.

As Pritchard continued his meal, Webb ignored his own lunch and considered his options. In the past year, while investigating the disappearance of a young girl who'd arrived at the new immigrant station on Ellis Island, he had come to realize that there were far fewer happy endings in reality than there were in rags-to-riches dime novels. He had wanted to bring that harsh reality to public attention and, hopefully, instigate some changes to better the lives of those who came to America with such hope. If he couldn't write that kind of story for Lawrence Pritchard, at least he still had another vehicle in *Harper's Weekly*. His article on Tammany Hall, for example, might really change the way the city operated. But he still needed an income, more than his infrequent pieces for *Harper's* had thus far earned him.

"I'm sure I can remember how to write a satisfactory Western," Webb said, hoping Pritchard didn't notice his complete lack of enthusiasm. "I'll start on one for you soon."

"Wonderful!" Pritchard was so excited that he uttered the word before he'd finished swallowing his last bite. After a brief coughing fit, during which some color actually came to his cheeks, he composed himself. "Excuse me." The publisher took several sips of rum punch. "Almost went down the wrong pipe."

"Are you sure you're all right?" Webb asked. For a moment, he thought New York was about to have one less publisher.

"Yes, yes." Pritchard inhaled long and loudly. "All clear." He then leaned forward. "I *am* sorry. You asked me about a favor and all I could talk about was books. Tell me, Marshall: what can I do for you?"

"I was hoping for some information—"

Pritchard blurted, "You know I never reveal sales figures. If you—"

Webb returned the rudeness, cutting off the publisher. "This has nothing to do with sales. Nor with publishing at all."

"My apologies." Pritchard smiled sheepishly. "It was reflex, I'm afraid. Some of my writers are overly inquisitive about such matters."

With a nod of understanding, Webb said, "What I'm actually interested in is bankers."

Pritchard frowned so deeply that his pince-nez almost fell onto his steak. "I don't know anything about banking."

Webb knew that Pritchard wasn't a wealthy man, although his publishing business had made him "comfortable," and as far as Webb knew, the man had no ties to the financial industry. But he also knew that Pritchard followed the society pages and exchanged gossip about the city's upper class the way that other men followed news of their favorite heavyweight fighters or base-ball players. "Not 'bank*ing*,'" Webb corrected. "Bank*ers*. No one knows more about the lives of 'The Four Hundred' than you do, Lawrence." The reference was to the number of people who could fit into Mrs. Astor's opulent ballroom; according to society wags, there were only four hundred people worth knowing in New York City, and the exclusive register had been identified by the guest list to one of Mrs. Astor's famous balls.

Pritchard beamed at the compliment. "I do have some connec-tions with that element of society."

Those "connections" didn't include any actual contact with the elite themselves, however, Webb was sure. Trying not to smile himself, he asked, "Do you know anything about Jacob Upde-graff?"

Pritchard leaned back and lifted his gaze toward the restau-rant's ceiling. The way creases formed on his high forehead, he appeared to be searching through a vast storehouse of informa-tion in his brain. "Well," he said hesitantly, as if not satisfied with the fruits of that search, "the Updegraff family is one of the oldest and wealthiest in the city, of course. To them, the Astors are nou-veau riche and not of their class."

Webb nodded; he knew that much already.

Pritchard continued, "The Updegraff women are all active in the proper society events, and the men are members of the right clubs. But they don't try to bring attention to themselves—it would be considered vulgar. As a result, there isn't much talk about them. If you ask me, the family has made itself so exclusive that they're almost not a part of society anymore."

"What about Jacob Updegraff specifically?" Webb asked. "Do you hear anything about him?"

"Nothing scandalous—and if there was, I certainly would have heard about it. I believe his only interest is making money, and that makes him a most *un*interesting fellow in my book."

"Any rumors about unscrupulous financial deals?"

"Not that I've heard." Pritchard smiled. "But then, a shady fi-nancial deal would hardly be newsworthy in this city, would it?"

"I suppose not." Webb was disappointed that he learned noth-ing about Jacob Updegraff.

"Why do you ask? Do you suspect him of something?" The publisher looked hopeful that there might indeed be a touch of scandal to the bankers.

"I have a, uh"—Webb wasn't quite sure how to refer to Rebecca—"a friend. She's invested some money with him, and I'm a bit concerned whether her investment will be safe."

Pritchard grinned broadly. "Ah, a 'friend.' I've recently begun keeping company with a 'friend' myself." The twinkle in his eyes that Webb had noticed earlier sparkled a bit brighter. "Quite a nice lady, from a very fine family. I would be happy to ask her if she is aware of anything about Jacob Updegraff. You know how women are—they gossip all the time, so perhaps she's heard something."

If Pritchard's new romantic interest was fond of gossip, then the two of them certainly had something in common, Webb thought. "Thank you. I'd appreciate that. And there's one more banker I'm interested in: Lyman Sinclair. He worked for Updegraff in the New Amsterdam Trust Company."

"I know who *he* is," Pritchard said. "He's the one who decided to do a swan dive onto the sidewalk."

"Swan dive" was the way it might have been described in one of the novels Pritchard published. Webb didn't much care for referring to the man's death so callously. "Do you know anything about him other than the fact that he died?" Webb asked.

"Oh yes. Lyman Sinclair was quite the opposite of the Updegraffs as far as his personal life. Instead of protecting his privacy, Sinclair was always trying to draw attention to himself. He was at every opening night of every show, at any party to which he could inveigle an invitation, and he was a regular at the Yacht Club and the racetrack. I've heard that he even bribed some newspaper writers to mention his name in the society pages."

"*Why?*" Webb had always been a private man himself and couldn't fathom a desire to have his life reported in the newspapers.

Pritchard thought for a few moments. "I don't know for sure why he was so eager to be known, but he seemed to come from nowhere. No one knew anything about his family or background. Although he claimed to have attended the best schools and liked to mention names of affluent classmates, none of those classmates ever remembered seeing him. The rumor was that Lyman Sinclair came from a poor family and was attempting to push his way into society."

"Other than trying to climb the social ladder, what else did he do?"

"He made money, by all accounts. One of the reasons he was tolerated by the upper class was that he seemed to have a golden touch when it came to investing. He made a lot of people a lot of money."

"All legally?"

"I don't know. But I never heard any dissatisfaction about how he handled money."

"Anything else?"

Pritchard thought for a moment, then shook his head. "All I really know about him was that he was all about appearance."

"Could you ask around—discreetly? About both Jacob Updegraff and Lyman Sinclair."

"Certainly." Pritchard then called to their waiter for the check. "You will be starting on that Western for me, won't you?"

"Yes I will." *But not immediately,* Webb thought to himself. He'd had another lead on his Tammany Hall story and he needed to pursue that first.

"Can I have it by the end of this month?"

That wouldn't be nearly enough time. "A month from today," Webb said. He doubted that he could have it by then, either, but there was nothing quite as elastic as a publishing deadline. Webb figured he could stretch it all the way until summer if need be. The reading public could wait for one more yarn about cowboys and Indians, as far as he was concerned. There were more important things that he had to do.

CHAPTER 13

Much to Nicholas Bostwick's disappointment, Jacob Updegraff had failed to make the offer for which he'd been hoping. When Bostwick had reported to the bank president that he'd acquired ledger sheets and a number of papers from Lyman Sinclair's apartment, he'd told Updegraff that some of the information might be embarrassing to the bank. He also suggested that, for the sake of secrecy, he be permitted to review the material in a less public area than at his desk in the middle of the bank's main room. What Bostwick had in mind was that he might be allowed to work in one of the offices on the second floor. Although Updegraff agreed that caution was warranted, the thought of giving Bostwick one of the prized private offices apparently hadn't occurred to him. Instead, he ordered Bostwick to take all the material home and work there until he had a complete report. He also gave the accountant a deadline for that report: two days.

So Bostwick labored away, reading of investments, payments, and profits in the tens of thousands of dollars. As he did, he thought often of Lyman Sinclair's luxurious home and its expensive furnishings. It was a far cry from the twelve-dollar-a-month third-floor Greenwich Village walk-up to which he was now confined.

Bostwick couldn't help but look around at the relative poverty of his own surroundings. The only luxuries in his one-room bachelor apartment were a secondhand upright piano and his prized possession, a new Edison talking machine. There was no carpet on the floor, and as for decorations, he didn't own oil paintings or china figurines like Sinclair had. Nicholas Bostwick made do with pasteboard studio photographs of opera singers, chorus girls, and actresses; most of these small sepia images were given away as promotional items with packages of Old Judge and Dog's Head cigarettes. Everything else in the place—the narrow bed, which had no headboard, the small pine dining table with two cane-bottom chairs, and the sideboard that served as kitchen, cupboard, and pantry—was of little better quality than what could be found in an East Side tenement.

The air quality wasn't much better, either; the potbellied iron coal stove in the center of the room was poorly ventilated, and the fish market on the first floor contributed a disagreeable odor that permeated the entire building. Bostwick had tried a number of strong German colognes to mask the smells, but none had been sufficient to do the job. He generally kept his one window partly open in winter to allow the coal smoke to escape, and in summer, when the hot street radiated its own noxious odors of horse excrement and uncollected garbage, he kept the window closed.

Bostwick's window was now half open, letting in frosty air and the angry sounds of snarled traffic on Bleeker Street. Although he didn't especially want to let a winter chill into his room, he had been cooped up in his apartment for more than a day and craved fresh air more than heat. Besides, he was adequately attired, in a neatly pressed serge business suit with a vest, starched collar, and tie. The clothing wasn't intended solely for warmth—since he was doing banking business, Bostwick automatically dressed appropriately—but it did help fend off the draft.

The presence of the piano in the apartment left no room for a desk, so Bostwick worked at the dining table, with Sinclair's correspondence, documents, and ledgers arrayed in tidy stacks. He knew that Mr. Updegraff would expect him to answer any possible question about the information they contained—Updegraff had neither the patience nor the bookkeeping acumen to evaluate the numbers himself. So Bostwick arranged and rearranged all the entries in several ways to see what he might be able to glean about Lyman Sinclair's accounts. In penmanship that a twelfth-century monk might have envied, Bostwick made a chronological record of each entry, cross-referenced to any letters or documents that related to the transaction. On a separate sheet, he made a similar list, this one alphabetical by investor, with the investor's transactions subsequently listed by date.

No matter how Bostwick tallied the numbers, however, they

didn't add up. The only thing he could tell for sure was that the entries in the ledger from Sinclair's apartment bore little relation to what had been recorded in the official ledger at the bank.

Nothing frustrated Nicholas Bostwick as much as numbers that refused to be reconciled. He liked for everything to be neat and orderly and to fall into its proper place. Here it seemed as if he had been assigned to solve a jigsaw puzzle that was missing half the pieces.

Stymied in his work, Bostwick decided that he needed to hear some music. Music was one thing that always made sense to him, its rhythm, meter, and pitch as mathematically exact as a balanced ledger sheet. It also provided one of the few passions in his life.

From a drawer in the sideboard where he kept his precious wax-cylinder recordings, Bostwick took out his latest acquisition, the U.S. Marine Band's performance of "Washington Post March." He carefully placed the fragile brown cylinder in the phonograph, cranked the handle, and placed the stylus against the rapidly spinning piece of wax. After a spoken introduction that gave the performer, song, and catalog number, music came loud and clear through the instrument's brass horn. Bostwick would have preferred that time weren't wasted on the introduction, for a recording lasted a mere two minutes, allowing only part of Sousa's composition to be captured on wax.

Bostwick replayed the music several times, listening to it attentively. This was the Marine Band's first recording without John Philip Sousa, who had recently left to form his own band. Bostwick was curious to hear how the musicians would perform without their famed leader to direct them. To his disappointment, the tubas were rushing the beat a bit and some of the cornet playing was rather ragged. Although the errors were barely noticeable, Bostwick had the urge to smash the cylinder on the floor. It seemed that nowhere today could he find the precision and balance that he yearned for.

He could do nothing about the Marine Band's performance, he decided—destroying the recording certainly wouldn't help—but perhaps he could still make sense of Lyman Sinclair's accounts.

Bostwick settled back down at the table, sifted a few papers, and glanced over the columns of numbers. He was determined to sort them out and establish order from the chaos.

* * *

Rebecca worked methodically at her writing desk in the small Colden House sitting room that she used as an office. She was following through on her plan to send out letters requesting funds to support the home.

Having started a few days earlier, Rebecca had by now refined the process to the point where she had three basic forms of appeal. One was used for women who had once been sheltered at Colden House; although she only heard from a small minority of her residents after they left, Rebecca thought they would best realize just how important it was to keep the place operating. Another basic letter went to wealthy individuals who she knew gave to charities, and the final one was tailored to businesses and asked for donations of goods or services instead of money.

The letter writing had become so routine that Rebecca frequently had to force herself to slow down. When she wrote too quickly, the words became an illegible scrawl, and she'd had to throw more than one partially written letter in the wastebasket at her feet.

It wasn't only the boredom of repetition that made her attention wander, however. St. Valentine's Day was less than a week away, and it was the first one since she and Marshall had begun—what exactly *had* they begun? she wondered. It wasn't quite "courting," but it seemed to be a bit more than "keeping company."

One problem in defining the nature of their relationship was that society had determined romance to be for the young; a woman who passed the age of twenty-five without marrying was usually considered a spinster. Rebecca was nearing thirty, as her family frequently reminded her, and Marshall was a couple of years older than she. Whatever it was they were doing, Rebecca did enjoy his company; she only wished they were together more often. Well, at least she had Valentine's Day to look forward to. It would be nice if he would let her know what he had planned, though—and he'd darn well better have something planned.

"Miss Davies?"

"Yes, what?" Rebecca answered more sharply than she intended. She had managed to work up an anger at Marshall for letting Valentine's Day pass by unnoticed—although the date hadn't yet arrived. *You're being as foolish as a schoolgirl,* she told herself. "I'm sorry," she said to Miss Hummel. "I was a bit preoccupied."

The older woman calmly answered, "Yes, ma'am." She had a

hint of a smile on her usually stolid face, and Rebecca imagined that Miss Hummel had somehow divined the subject of her preoccupation. Fortunately, she made no mention of it. "Miss Zietlow has asked if she could speak with you," she said. "I knew you were working on your correspondence, so I thought I should check with you first."

Rebecca welcomed a break from the letter writing—it wasn't really "correspondence," she thought, since that implied a two-way communication, and as yet she hadn't had a single response. "I'd be happy to speak with her. Please send her in."

Sarah Zietlow must have been waiting just outside, because she came through the door within seconds of Miss Hummel's walking out.

The young woman appeared to be a completely different person from the one who had first appeared on her doorstep almost a month earlier, Rebecca was happy to see. Her skin color was almost normal, having lost its yellow tinge, and she had put some weight on her thin frame. She was neatly dressed in a plain white shirtwaist with a charcoal gray pleated skirt.

"Come, sit down," Rebecca said. She stood and led Miss Zietlow to a tufted sofa, where she sat down next to her. "You're looking quite well." The only aspect of the young woman's appearance that hadn't returned to normal was her hair, which was still thin and bald in spots. Despite that, she was beginning to look like quite a pretty girl, with bright sparks of life in her big brown eyes.

"Thank you, Miss Davies," she answered in a small voice. "I'm feeling much better, all thanks to you. That's why I wanted to talk to you." She lowered her head slightly. "I've decided that it's time for me to leave."

Rebecca wasn't sure that was a wise idea. It might be premature. "Why do you want to go?"

"There are others who need to be here more than I do now. You already have a full house here, and there's lots of others on the streets who need your help. I'm well enough to be taking care of myself."

Rebecca appreciated the selfless offer, but she wasn't about to simply let Sarah Zietlow go back out on the street. "Where would you go, Sarah? What would you do?"

The young woman didn't answer for several moments. Finally, she simply said, "I can take care of myself."

"Do you have any family?"

"No, ma'am. My mother died when I was seven. My father left soon after that. A neighbor lady raised me until I was twelve; then she moved to California with a new husband. They didn't want me with them, so I was on my own, and been on my own ever since."

"Any aunts, uncles? Other relatives?"

"None that I know of."

"Friends?"

Sarah hesitated. "Not really."

"So you have no place to go. How would you live?"

"Same as I have for years." She looked up at Rebecca. "I was doing fine, ma'am, until I got sick. Now I'm better and I can go back."

She hadn't necessarily been "sick," Rebecca remembered. Doc Abraham had believed that Sarah Zietlow may have been poisoned, and there was no telling whether it was accidental or someone had wanted to kill her. "There's something I have to ask you, Sarah," Rebecca said.

"Yes, ma'am?"

"Is there anyone who would want to harm you?"

Sarah bit the inside of her lip, and it was some time before she answered. If a weak voice, she finally said, "A girl on the streets is bound to get hurt sometimes." She glanced up at Rebecca and eyed her earnestly. "I never sold myself, ma'am. But men are a lot stronger than I am—and meaner. Sometimes they came after me. I'd run when I could, or fight if I had to, but sometimes I did get"—her gaze dropped—"hurt."

Probably half the women at Colden House had been through similar ordeals. "I'm sorry," said Rebecca, "but I meant is there anyone who might want to"—there was no easy way to say it—"kill you?" Ever since the girl had arrived at the home, Rebecca had been primarily concerned with keeping Sarah safe and helping her recover. She hadn't tried to learn who might have poisoned her, but if the girl was planning to leave, she wanted to be sure she wouldn't be going into harm's way again.

Sarah looked up sharply, her expression puzzled. "Ma'am?"

"When I took you to the doctor, he said your symptoms were

consistent with poisoning. And it had probably been over a period of time. Is there anyone who might have given you poison?"

The young woman fidgeted uncomfortably and began to wring her hands. "That was my own doing, ma'am."

Rebecca sighed. She knew of more than one woman whose existence had become so intolerable that they had finally taken their own lives. With no job or place to live, Sarah could find herself feeling that same way again. "Listen, Sarah—"

"I learned my lesson," she interrupted. "I promise it won't happen again."

Rebecca patted her forearm. "What I'd like you to promise me is that you'll stay with us a little longer. Give me some time to see if I can find you a job so you can support yourself."

"Jobs are hard to find these days, ma'am."

"I know. But let me try. Miss Hummel tells me you do more work in the kitchen than almost anyone." It was a requirement that residents who weren't sick share the cooking and cleaning chores in Colden House; the place wasn't intended to be a hotel, but a temporary shelter for those who truly needed it. "I'll see if I can get you work as a cook or maybe a waitress. I know someone who owns a few lunchrooms."

Sarah perked up at the prospect. "I'd work very hard! Please tell them I'm a good worker."

"I will. And you'll stay until I can look into it?"

Sarah agreed and left to begin helping with the day's kitchen chores. As she went out the door, she passed Miss Hummel coming back into the room.

The older woman had several envelopes in her hand. "Afternoon mail just came, Miss Davies."

Rebecca opened them eagerly, still hoping for some response to her letters. She was sorry to find that her efforts weren't paying off financially—the three envelopes contained a total of only four dollars—but she almost cried with gratitude when she read the notes that accompanied them. They were all from women who had once stayed in the shelter and now wanted to help others as much as their meager incomes would permit.

CHAPTER 14

Marshall Webb walked slowly along squalid Broome Street toward the river, past crumbling East Side tenements that should have been razed years earlier. Lines of laundry strung from their windows, and fire escapes that sagged under the weight of those who couldn't afford indoor apartments were proof that the buildings were still inhabited, however.

As he searched for the address that he'd jotted in his notebook, Webb had to tread carefully. Not only did he have to avoid the foul piles of frozen snow that were mixed with horse excrement, and the heaps of discarded trash, but he also had to step around reeking drunkards sleeping in the gutter, and ragged children huddled over steam grates trying to keep warm. He negotiated his way around the innumerable pushcarts that clogged the street and sidewalk, and ignored the pleas of vendors who were hawking everything from secondhand clothes to sour pickles.

Near the corner of Goerck Street, three blocks from the East River and a stone's throw from the Lucky Star Saloon, where Webb had met Rabbit Doyle, he came to a three-story brick building that was in better repair than most of the buildings in the area. The first-floor window had a faded sign in it that read *J. Violano, Shoemaker*.

Webb stopped inside the shop first, where a reluctant Mr. Violano agreed to give him directions only after he'd been given a dime for his trouble.

Then Webb walked up to the second floor, where the hallway was lit by a single gas jet no brighter than a match. Since none of the doors had names or numbers on them, he counted them until he reached what he believed to be the right one. It was a flimsy door that hung unevenly on its hinges and vibrated when Webb rapped on it.

"Yeah? Who the hell is it?" called a gruff male voice from inside.

"My name is Marshall Webb."

"Whaddaya want?"

"Mr. Rettew?"

"I said whaddaya want?"

"To speak with you, if I may."

" 'Bout what?"

Webb was rapidly getting tired of talking through a closed door, even though the wood was thin enough that sound passed through it easily. "About the election, Mr. Rettew. May I come in? Or we could go out and talk over lunch, if you prefer."

"Already had my lunch!"

Webb waited a moment to see if there would be an answer to his first question; when none came he repeated it.

"What the hell are you botherin' *me* for?" was the reply. "Election's over. Winners are all decided."

Persisting, Webb said, "It's *how* they were decided that I'm interested in. You were one of the official poll watchers for this district. I'd like to know what you saw."

There were shuffling footsteps from within; then the door was cracked open and a grizzled man of about sixty peered up at Webb. "Why? What's your interest?"

"I'm a writer for *Harper's Weekly*. We plan to publish an article on how the election system works in New York—or doesn't work. I want to be sure that it's an *accurate* article."

The old man snorted. "I'll believe that when I read it. But awright, I'll do my part." He opened the door and motioned for Webb to step inside. "I'm Craig Rettew. I'll tell you what happened."

"Thank you." Webb walked into a dark, cramped one-room apartment that smelled of cooked cabbage and coal smoke. There were dark-brown water stains on the ceiling, and a threadbare rug on the sagging floor. Rettew apparently lived alone, kept company by an array of faded wood-framed photographs that hung on the walls between patches of peeling striped wallpaper. The pictures helped divert attention from the many holes in the crumbling plaster.

Two overstuffed chairs faced each other close together, one of them apparently serving as a footstool. Rettew limped a few steps and pointed to the smaller one with his heavy cane. "Sit there, if you like."

Although the seat cushion looked thoroughly filthy, Webb accepted the hospitality; he slid the chair back a bit and sat down.

Supporting himself with his cane, Craig Rettew lowered himself into the larger chair. "Damn leg hurts like a bastard in this cold weather." He reached for an open wine bottle on the floor next to him. "Only thing that helps," he said before taking a long swallow.

When Rettew offered him a tug at the bottle, Webb smiled politely and replied, "No, thank you."

The old man wiped the back of his hand over his mouth, his skin rasping against several days of gray stubble. He settled deeper into several layers of baggy clothing. A corduroy jacket that was missing its buttons was wrapped over his wool sweater, and a collarless shirt was visible underneath. "What, exactly, do you want to know?" He studied Webb through dark eyes that seemed shrouded in shadow from the bags and crows'-feet around them.

"I'd like to know if you observed any voting irregularities. I would like to write as detailed an account as possible on exactly how Tammany Hall gets its candidates into office."

Rettew chuckled. "By cheating. Voter fraud."

That was no news. "How was that fraud accomplished?" Webb asked. "What, specifically, did you witness?"

"Repeaters, for one thing. I saw dozens of men—rounded up from local saloons, I expect—who came through the polling place and voted two or three times that day. I objected, but Rabbit Doyle—he's a Tammany ward heeler—made sure they got to cast a vote every time they came through. Every time under a different name, of course." Using both hands, Rettew pulled his bad leg straight out. "Ah, that's better."

"What happened when you did object?"

"At first I was ignored. Then when I kept objectin'—and believe you me, I raised a fuss every time I spotted one of his goddamn repeaters—I was threatened."

"With what?"

Rettew took another swallow from the bottle. "Doyle's exact

words to me were, 'We're gonna break yer goddamn neck if you don't shut the hell up, old man.'" He shook his head at the memory. "Doyle's always been a mean son of a bitch."

"You've known him for some time?"

"Oh yeah, for years. We're from the same neighborhood—Five Points. Doyle was with the Dead Rabbit gang back then. As a matter of fact, he got his name because he was the one who used to carry the rabbit—the gang always carried a fresh-killed rabbit nailed to a board when they went into battle, and Doyle would hold it up like it was their flag or somethin'." He leaned back. "Now, in those days, it was the Bowery Boys who did most of the strong-arm work for Tammany Hall—beating poll watchers, intimidating voters, stealing ballot boxes, you name it. Doyle was one of the first of the Dead Rabbits to get into that line of work for them; he helped give Tammany a strong foothold in his district— it's voted Democratic every election since before the war—and in turn Doyle got to move up in the Tammany organization."

"And how long have you been a poll watcher?"

"Almost twenty years now. I'm a registered voter in the Thirteenth District, and I represent the Republican candidate at the polling place every election. Don't get me wrong—I don't care a whit about one party or another. I'd support anybody who wasn't part of the Tammany machine."

"Why?" Webb wondered what would make this man fight the system for so long.

"You saw why when you were on your way here." Rettew glanced toward the apartment's one window; there were several boards nailed across it—to prevent intruders, Webb assumed— leaving only a few gaps for sunlight to squeeze through. "This is my neighborhood. It's mostly decent people who live here; they just happen to be poor." The old man briefly clenched his jaw. "And it's Tammany Hall that keeps them poor. Every two years, a political hack like Rabbit Doyle will pay out a dollar a vote or give away beer in exchange for votes, and the rest of the time, Tammany bosses rob the city blind. With Tammany in power, nobody in the East Side—or anywhere else in this city—is ever going to get a better life."

Webb admired the man's attitude. "You mentioned repeaters were one thing you noticed. What else?"

"There were voters who shouldn't have been allowed through

even once, because they don't live in the district. The polling place was the lobby of Scott's Theatre—that's a little dance hall owned by Matt Scott. Scott's also on the city payroll as some kind of assistant deputy commissioner of public works or something—it's a no-show job that puts him in Tammany's pocket. So his theater is used for a polling place, and every customer who walks in to see a show is told to stop at the booth and vote the Tammany party line."

"What I don't understand," Webb said, "is why do they bother cheating? Tammany already has a lock on the city, and Grover Cleveland was a cinch to win the presidency anyway."

Rettew laughed. "It sure wasn't to help Cleveland. No, Tammany Hall wasn't about to do Grover Cleveland any favors even though he is a New York Democrat. Cleveland never played ball with Tammany—or with any of the upstate political machines. When he was mayor of Buffalo, he tried to get rid of corruption in that city; and as governor he totally rejected the spoils system, leaving Tammany Hall out in the cold." He laughed again. "You know what Boss Croker said after Cleveland did win the White House?"

"What?"

"Croker said, 'Our situation is not too bad. Cleveland never does anything for his friends—but we are not his friends, so he may do something for us.' No, Tammany wasn't working on Cleveland's behalf. They just want to overpower any possible opposition. And don't be so sure about them having a 'lock' on the city. Their Democratic candidate, James Southworth, did win the assembly seat for this district. But Frederick Gibbs, the Republican I was watching for, lost by only fifteen hundred votes. If it wasn't for the fraudulent voters that Doyle brought in, the margin would have been a damn sight closer than that."

Webb paused to jot down some notes. He wanted to make sure he got the names and details right. "Was there anything else peculiar about this election that you saw?"

"Sure was." Rettew took another pull at the wine bottle. "But I'm not sure *what* it was, exactly."

"What do you mean?"

"Well, I kept makin' objections to the voters Doyle was pushing through, and he was getting angrier about it as the night went on. He had a couple of his plug-uglies with him—Brick Fessler and Danny Alcock—and about an hour before the polls were to close he told them to take me outside and make sure I was in no condition to come back in."

"Did they?"

Rettew snorted. "You think I could stop them? I'm not as young as I used to be, and even then I'd have been no match for those two." He hesitated before going on. "They took me into the alley behind the theater and gave me a good thrashing. I did get one shot in with my cane—got Fessler right on the nose. Broke it, I think." Rettew paused to savor the memory of that small victory before going on. "But that just made him mad. He busted a bottle over my head and I was out like a light. They left me lying in the alley."

"Did you report them?"

"Oh, sure. I make a report every year on the voting and on any violence or threats."

"It's happened before?"

Rettew patted his right leg. "Four years ago, they broke my leg. Never did heal right."

"And you still serve as poll watcher?" Webb was impressed by the man's tenacity.

"I'm sure as hell not going to hand my district over to those bastards. And they've done more than beat me. I used to be a brakeman on the Second Avenue El, but that's a city job, and Tammany made sure I lost it. After Tammany put me on their blacklist, I couldn't even get a job with the sanitation department. I work for John Violano downstairs sometimes now, resoling boots when he gets backed up with customers; but these days there aren't many customers, so I don't work much at all."

Webb was incredulous at all that Rettew had endured. "Nothing's ever happened as a result of your reports?"

"The only thing that happens is the election commission loses them. And as for the cops, they can never seem to find any witnesses to the beatings. Hell, except for the uniforms, they're no better than the thugs working for Doyle." He lifted the wine bottle, then rested it on the arm of the chair without taking a sip. "Oh, speaking of the cops: there were police wagons at the theater. I saw 'em after I came to."

"Do you know what they were doing there?"

"I didn't get too close. I watched from around the corner. Every few minutes, a police wagon would pull up and unload a group of men. I call 'em men, but they looked more like walking ghosts—hardly any of them looked like they even knew where they were. But they were all pushed into the theater, and I'm sure they voted."

"You don't know where they came from?"

"The loony bin, more'n likely. They just had that look to 'em."

Webb asked if there was anything more Rettew could tell him. The older man searched his memory but came up with nothing else.

As Webb stood to leave, Rettew asked, "You really going to get all this in print?"

"I'm going to write it," Webb promised. "It's up to my editor whether it gets published. But I can assure you I'll do my best to convince him."

Rettew smiled. "I'd love to see Boss Croker's face when he reads all this—and realizes the rest of the city is reading about his dirty work, too."

"I'm also going to look into this further," Webb said. "May I speak with you again if I need to?"

"Any time." He looked up at Webb. "And you'll find there's more of us who'd like to see this city out of Tammany's clutches. They'll be glad to help you, too."

Webb hoped that was true, because he knew Tammany Hall was not going to relinquish its power without a fight.

Harry M. Hargis didn't require much convincing. The waxed tips of his mustache perked up at hearing Webb's report. "It sounds as if you've been making progress," he said. "You've justified my confidence in you, and I am happy to tell you that I have convinced the publisher to go ahead with your Tammany Hall series instead of the one that had been proposed on the financial crisis." He leaned back and folded his pink hands over a striped silk vest that probably cost as much as Webb's entire suit.

"Thank you," Webb said. He was so pleased at hearing the news that he glanced around the luxurious office to see if there was some new piece of art that he could make a complimentary comment about. The bronze Hermes still appeared to be the latest acquisition, however; it maintained its place of honor atop the editor's polished desk. Webb had endured a long enough discourse about that piece the last time that he was here, and he decided he'd shown sufficient gratitude by his simple thank-you.

Hargis seemed to want more. "It wasn't easy, I'll have you know. No reflection on you, but there was a strong sentiment in favor of going with the financial story instead. That subject affects the entire country and could boost our circulation outside the city." He absently twisted the diamond ring on his pinky finger.

Knowing his editor's ego, Webb thought that Hargis might have been considering it appropriate that the ring be kissed. "If I may ask," he said, "what was it then that made you decide to run my articles?"

Hargis hesitated, probably unwilling to reveal to a mere writer the thinking processes of an editor. "There were several factors," he finally answered. "One is that our core readership is in New York, and Tammany Hall is a major part of this city. Second, who knows what's going to happen to the country's economy? At present, the financial outlook is quite bleak, but what if there's a sudden turnaround? Grover Cleveland hasn't even been sworn into office yet and he's already taking steps to shore up the nation's gold reserve. If things suddenly improve, we would be left without a story—at least not one that could run for any length of time." He smiled smugly. "The nice thing about Tammany is that there's no end of material to keep a series going." Hargis leaned forward. "Speaking of which, I'll need the first installment by the end of this week. And you *will* have to make sure you get another piece in every week after that—no delays, no exceptions."

Webb was able to do better than that. "Here's the first installment," he said, handing the editor the final draft of the piece that provided the historical background of the Tammany Society. "The next article will be an account of Tammany's political activity—from Alexander Hamilton through Boss Tweed and up to the present: Richard Croker." He placed a few more pages on Hargis's desk. "This is a rough draft of that article as well as some notes for the follow-up pieces."

Hargis immediately began reading. For him, it involved a fair amount of physical activity; he kept holding the pages at various distances from his face and alternately squinted and bugged his eyes, trying to bring the handwriting into focus. Webb knew that Hargis was too vain about maintaining a youthful appearance to wear the eyeglasses that he obviously needed. The editor didn't know it, but Webb intentionally wrote in smaller print whenever he was preparing something for Hargis's perusal.

"Very good," said Hargis somewhat vaguely, as if he wasn't entirely sure what he had actually just scanned. "Get me the final draft of the second installment next week." He jerked his head toward the door, signaling that Webb was dismissed.

Before Webb did go, he asked his boss, "Incidentally, sir, whom did you have working on the financial story?"

"One of our staff writers: Mr. Hopkins." Hargis, squinting and grimacing, was already paying more attention to the papers on his desk than to the man who wrote them.

Without another word, Webb left Hargis's office.

A few doors down the hall from the editor, Webb found Keith Hopkins at his desk. The two had never formally met, but Webb had seen him in the *Harper's* offices once or twice before. Hopkins, he knew, was considered to be one of the publication's most astute writers and thorough researchers. In Webb's opinion, Hopkins's prose tended to be a bit turgid, but his articles were always informative.

Hopkins shared a room with three other writers, none of whom were presently at their matching desks. Although it housed four times as many people as Hargis's office, the room was half the size and had almost nothing in the way of decor. A calendar, telephone, and some old framed *Harper's Weekly* covers were all that adorned the beige-painted walls. Every bit of boxy oak furniture—desks, file cabinets, and bookcases—was stained exactly the same shade and was faded to the same degree. The place must have been furnished all at once, and no changes had been made since.

"Mr. Hopkins," Webb said.

Hopkins, a redheaded man of about forty with a droopy mustache so sparse that it looked like it belonged on a boy of sixteen, blew his inflamed nose into a handkerchief the size of a pillowcase. "That's me," he wheezed. "What can I do for you?"

"My name's Marshall Webb. I do some freelance writing for Harry Hargis." He approached Hopkins's desk and offered his hand. "It's good to finally meet you."

Hopkins looked up at him with watery eyes. "Oh, yes, I've

heard him mention you." He blew his nose again and waved off Webb's hand. "Got a hell of a head cold. Better keep your distance."

Webb backed up a step. "I'm sorry to hear that." He looked around at the vacant chairs nearby. "But I'm glad I caught you in. I thought you might be at lunch."

"No point in me eating. Can't taste a goddamn thing." Hopkins tugged at the back of the plaid muffler wrapped around his neck, and shuddered in his tweed suit.

"The reason I've come to see you," Webb said, "is that Mr. Hargis tells me you were doing some work on a story about the financial crisis."

"I *was*. But they killed it."

"I heard. I'm sorry."

Hopkins went into the preliminary throes of a sneeze. It never culminated, though, and he appeared frustrated. "Damn! I can't wait until this thing is over with." He brushed the handkerchief over his nostrils.

Webb said, "I hear chicken soup is good for colds."

"Maybe, but I'll keep trying bourbon—I prefer the taste." Hopkins looked as if he wished he had a bottle on his desk this very moment. "Anyway, I thought the editors actually showed some good sense in killing the financial series. With more bankruptcies every day and the stock market being so volatile, they decided that a weekly publication really couldn't cover it all in a timely manner. I have to agree with them—the daily newspapers are much more suitable for this kind of reporting." A wet sneeze suddenly exploded and Hopkins promptly went to work to mop up the spray with the handkerchief. "Ah, that felt good."

Webb took another cautious step backward and averted his gaze from the clean-up operation. "The last time I spoke with Mr. Hargis, he mentioned something about that banker Lyman Sinclair committing suicide—he said there were rumors about Sinclair's bank failing. That's the New Amsterdam Trust Company, isn't it?"

Hopkins nodded. "It wasn't really *his* bank, though. Sinclair worked under Jacob Updegraff."

"Did you learn anything about what Sinclair was involved in? Is there any truth to the rumors?"

"I learned a few things before I had to shelve the story." He glanced up at Webb with suspicion in his swollen eyes. "You're not planning to write about this yourself, are you?"

"No," Webb answered honestly. "My interest is purely personal. I have a friend who invested some money with Lyman Sinclair and I want to know if she needs to be concerned."

"*Every*body should be concerned about their investments these days—nothing is a safe bet right now."

"Is it true that the New Amsterdam is on the verge of failure?"

Hopkins thought for a moment. "I didn't look too deeply into the bank's viability, so I can't say for sure. But there were a few things that caught my attention."

"Such as?"

"The *kind* of investments Sinclair was making. He was putting a lot of money into small Western railroads that no one has ever heard of." Hopkins shook his head. "He appeared to make profits with them, but I wouldn't call them sound investments."

"Were they so shaky that he might have killed himself over the prospect of them failing?"

After another wipe of his nose, Hopkins answered thoughtfully, "I don't understand what would ever drive a man to that point. But as far as finances, I didn't find anything to indicate that there was a disaster coming—mind you, though, I didn't get beyond the point of making some preliminary inquiries."

"What about Sinclair's personal life? Do you know anything about that?"

"Yes, as a matter of fact. Something odd." Hopkins opened a desk drawer and began burrowing. "I wrote it down." He pulled out a sheet of note paper. "Here we are: Sinclair had his name changed a few years ago, before he became a banker. His real name was"—Hopkins stumbled over the pronunciation—"Ludwig Schulmerich."

Webb copied the name into his own notebook. "Anything else?"

Hopkins shook his head. "As I said, I didn't get very far."

"What about Jacob Updegraff? What do you know about him?"

"Well, everyone knows his family, of course. One of the oldest in New York, and richer than Midas."

"What about his banking practices? Anything that might get him into trouble?"

"Not that I'm aware of. Updegraff is known for his caution. He doesn't take enough risks to get himself into trouble. He goes for safe investments that give a small but predictable rate of return." Hopkins sniffled. "He's a bit of an old lady, if you ask me."

Webb, who had never liked Rebecca's arrogant brother-in-law, enjoyed hearing him described that way. He was also happy to hear that Rebecca's investment was probably safe in Updegraff's cautious "old lady" hands.

CHAPTER 15

Rebecca Davies was a bit confused by Alice's telephone call, but she readily did as her sister asked. Although Alice had failed to make it clear exactly *why* she wanted Rebecca to join her this afternoon, the tone of her voice—like that of a frightened little girl—was enough to convince Rebecca to change her plans for the day. So at eleven A.M., Rebecca was ready, dressed in her hat and coat and waiting in the Colden House foyer.

The hall clock was still ringing the hour when one of the Updegraffs' uniformed coachmen came to the door to pick her up. "Good morning, Miss Davies," was all he said before escorting her in silence to the brougham parked at the curb. Although it was the Updegraffs' "second" carriage—their better carriage was for Jacob Updegraff's exclusive use—Rebecca thought it a beautiful vehicle: dark blue with black moldings and silver lanterns, and drawn by a chestnut horse that was probably better groomed and fed than most of the passersby here on State Street.

The driver opened the carriage door and held out a protective hand, ready to support Rebecca if she should falter as she stepped up and into the cab. Upon seeing Alice, nestled under a white fur lap robe, Rebecca almost jumped inside. "How are you Alice?" she said. For all appearances, her sister showed no sign that anything was amiss.

"I'm very well, thank you. And you?" Alice patted the cushioned leather seat.

Rebecca promptly slid into it and pulled another robe over her own lap. "I'm fine. But I'm not sure I understand. Where are we going?"

"Shopping." Alice nodded at the driver, who closed the door and went to take his own seat in front of the cab.

Since Colden House was in the Battery, the southernmost part of Manhattan, and didn't have the kind of shops that women of Alice's class patronized, Rebecca knew they would be riding for a while. As the brougham traveled up Broadway, she used the time to try to find out what was on Alice's mind, but all her younger sister would say was that she wanted to go shopping.

They headed into the area that was once home to the city's finest shops. Near City Hall Park, they passed the "Marble Palace" which A. T. Stewart had built to house the department store that revolutionized retailing. A dozen blocks north of that was the strip of Broadway where Lord and Taylor, Brooks Brothers, and a dozen other shops had established themselves. Some had moved farther north to a more modern shopping district on Sixth Avenue, but a few of the old, established shops remained.

One of these was Himmer & Corey, an exclusive dress shop between Spring and Prince Streets. The carriage pulled up to the store, which had an elaborate cast-iron front that made its exterior look like a Venetian palazzo. A middle-aged porter, dressed almost like a policeman in a blue uniform with brass buttons, darted from the shop's doorway and opened the door to the carriage.

As Alice and Rebecca stepped out, the porter opened a large black umbrella and held it above their heads. There was no precipitation, nor even any sun, but the leaden air felt like snow, so the porter took no chances. After making certain that they wouldn't have to suffer the distress of so much as a single snowflake alighting on them, he held the door for them to enter the store.

Having left the protective care of their driver and the porter, Alice and Rebecca were greeted by a new team of caretakers, this one comprised of Himmer & Corey's sales staff, eager to serve them.

A pretty young blonde in a smart blue dress suit greeted Alice: "Mrs. Updegraff! It is so nice to see you again. You are well, I trust?"

"Yes," was Alice's simple answer. She nodded at Rebecca. "This is my sister, Miss Davies."

"So nice to meet you, a genuine pleasure. My name is Christina Epperly, and I will do everything I can to make your shopping a pleasant experience." To Alice she said, "What can I interest you in today?"

"Sherry."

"Of course." Miss Epperly snapped her fingers, and two handsome salesmen in similar dark suits jumped to her side. "Some sherry for these ladies," she told them. "We'll be in the salon."

Overall, the store was beautifully laid out and decorated, Rebecca thought, but once they were led to the salon, she found that private section of the shop to be positively sumptuous. The appointments were as fine as in any Fifth Avenue mansion, with plush carpets, colorful tapestries, full-length mirrors, and chairs and sofas that dripped with fringe and tassels. She and Alice were divested of their hats, coats, and gloves by Miss Epperly, then sat down side-by-side on a Turkish sofa. By that time the sherry arrived, two crystal glasses of it carried on a silver tray by one of the male clerks.

"Is there anything else I can get you?" Miss Epperly asked. Rebecca had the sense that there was nothing they could desire that she wouldn't procure for them.

When Alice shook her head, the saleslady discreetly withdrew a few paces, enough to give them some privacy but close enough to be at their beck and call. The male clerks stood like guards near the entrance of the salon, awaiting orders.

Rebecca took advantage of the relative privacy to ask Alice in a hushed voice, "What are we doing here? On the telephone, you sounded like there was some urgent matter you wanted to discuss with me. Surely, you weren't seeking my opinion in picking out dresses."

"Oh, I didn't come to shop. I've just always liked this store." Alice took a sip of sherry and smiled appreciatively at the taste. "It's such a lovely place, and the staff is so obliging."

Was that all Alice wanted—to come to a place that she found familiar and comfortable? "Is there anything the matter at home?" Rebecca asked, wondering if that was perhaps why Alice wanted to leave the luxury of her mansion for the minor amenities of a dress shop.

"Yes. I have been—" Alice choked back a small sob. "Mr.

Updegraff has—" Clearly not prepared to talk about it yet, she signaled for Miss Epperly, who quickly strode over. "Do you have anything nice?" she asked.

"Oh, yes, Mrs. Updegraff. We have some lovely new material that would be perfect for your spring gowns." She then gave instructions to the male clerks, who promptly scurried away to do her bidding.

Rebecca briefly debated prodding Alice into talking, but before she could try again, the clerks returned, accompanied by several similarly attired reinforcements, all of them cradling bolts of material in their arms. They lined up before Alice, like visiting dignitaries waiting to be presented at the court of a queen. One by one, they stepped forward, bowed, and held out their rolls of cloth while Miss Epperly described every detail of each fabric's material and weave.

While Miss Epperly discussed Spanish laces, French silks, and a choice selection of satins and velvets, Rebecca kept her eye on Alice. She saw that her sister seemed to have as little interest in the material as she did. Alice's eyes stared without appearing to focus. Now and then she would nod or utter a murmur of approval, but her thoughts were far away from the plush salon of Himmer & Corey.

Eventually, Alice said, "That will do for now, Miss Epperly. I'd like to discuss the selection with my sister."

"Very good, ma'am." The saleswoman hustled her staff away, leaving the sisters alone.

Alice then turned to Rebecca. "Tell me about your Mr. Webb. Are you in love?"

The question stunned Rebecca into silence. She hadn't thought about it, much less ever considered discussing with Alice how she felt about Webb.

Alice added wistfully, "I'd like to hear about something romantic. I read about romance in books, but sometimes I wonder if it ever happens in life."

"I thought *you'd* be the one to know about that," Rebecca said, increasingly perplexed by the direction of the conversation. "You're the one who's married."

"Yes, I have a husband." Alice's eyes began to well with tears. "But it's not a romance—it never has been. Jacob Updegraff was simply a 'good catch,' according to Mother. He was always polite, did the right things—brought me flowers and jewelry, escorted me to all the important society events—but it seemed so *arranged* between the families. I would have liked to have the chance to fall in love."

"You don't love your husband?"

Alice raised a lacy handkerchief to her eyes. "I suppose I do. . . . I don't know. I've been comfortable with him, at least. And he's always been kind to me." She hesitated. "At least until recently."

"What has he done?" Rebecca was instantly riled, ready to give Jacob Updegraff a piece of her mind—or perhaps a good kick—if he'd done anything to harm Alice.

Alice put her hand on Rebecca's arm. "He hasn't struck me. He's just been so angry lately. I know it has to do with money, but I'm not sure if it's the bank's or the family's." She looked into Rebecca's eyes. "I didn't do anything wrong—I don't know anything about money. So why is he suddenly so angry at *me* all the time?"

"I don't know," Rebecca answered. She had heard dozens of reasons why men got angry from the women at Colden House, but never really did understand them.

"I'm scared of him sometimes." Alice began to weep openly. "I've never felt afraid of anything before, but now . . ."

"Do you think Mr. Updegraff would ever harm you?"

"I don't think so. It just has become so different in house lately, so unpleasant."

It was strange, Rebecca thought. She had girls at Colden House who had survived all sorts of unimaginable cruelties from violent husbands and fathers, and here Alice was distraught over her privileged home life having become "unpleasant." But to someone who had been as pampered and sheltered as her sister, Updegraff's recent behavior probably did make her feel that her life was in turmoil.

Still weeping, Alice continued, "Becoming an Updegraff is all I've ever accomplished—it's been my life. If my husband turns against me, what do I do? Where could I go?"

Rebecca put an arm around her sister's shoulder. "You can come to me. Anytime."

CHAPTER 16

Jacob Updegraff studied the columns of numbers Nicholas Bostwick had prepared for him with a vacant expression on his face. His wide mouth began to gape so much that Bostwick worried that the lit cigar between Updegraff's teeth might fall and incinerate all his hard work.

Bostwick had never seen his boss as out of sorts as he was today. Even his suit was rumpled, as if he'd slept in it, and he'd done a shoddy job shaving his chin. When Bostwick had first walked into the office, Updegraff had been slouching in his seat, looking as if he'd just been bludgeoned into some kind of defeat. He'd rudely dismissed his personal secretary, Harold Nantz, with a grunt and a jerk of his head. Now he looked as if he was utterly perplexed by Bostwick's summaries.

It was the latter situation that troubled the accountant. He'd put so much effort into making everything as clear as possible, that even a dull schoolboy should have been able to follow Bostwick's numbers.

Not having been invited to sit, Bostwick remained standing before the desk. He cleared his throat and offered, "If I may, sir. Mr. Sinclair's records were not complete, and I found them rather confusing. I attempted to sort them as best I could, but I'm afraid it still isn't very clear."

"I can see that," Updegraff muttered.

"Perhaps I can explain." Bostwick then showed how the account totals were organized by chronology, name of investor, and amount of transaction. He pointed to the cross-referenced supporting papers—correspondence, receipts, notes. As he guided his boss through the numbers, he did so carefully to avoid pricking Updegraff's inflated pride. Updegraff asked few questions, and Bostwick was readily able to answer each one.

When he'd finished, Bostwick said, "I know this isn't complete, but it is as thorough an accounting as I could make with the information that Mr. Sinclair left us."

Updegraff grunted approvingly and used his cigar to wave Bostwick into a seat. Leaning back, he drew on the cigar and exhaled a stream of smoke. "I have only one more question for you."

"Yes, sir?"

"Where's the money?"

That, indeed, was the biggest question remaining, and Lyman Sinclair had left no clues to its answer that Bostwick could find. "Some of it has been paid to the investors," he said. "As you can see, Mr. Sinclair received a little more than five hundred, forty thousand dollars. And if you check the chronological account, two hundred, ten thousand were disbursed to the early investors. As to the later investments, perhaps the money is in a vault. Or in stock certificates. Mr. Sinclair appears to have put most of this money in the Western Continental Railroad."

"Did you find stock certificates?"

"No."

"A vault?"

"No, sir." Bostwick hadn't known he was supposed to be looking for one. "I assumed Mr. Sinclair would have put the money in one of New Amsterdam's vaults."

"What *did* you find?"

"Only these papers, sir."

"So what you're telling me is that there's . . ." Updegraff furrowed his brow.

Bostwick did the calculation for him. "Three hundred and thirty thousand dollars."

Updegraff finished as if he hadn't heard the accountant. "Three hundred and thirty thousand dollars missing."

"I'm afraid so, sir."

The bank president folded his hands over his belly and swiveled his chair around to look out the window behind him. After a few minutes, still with his back to Bostwick, he asked him, "What do you know about the Western Continental Railroad?"

"Nothing, sir. Except that I believe it's out west somewhere."

Updegraff swung his chair back to face him and gave Bostwick a withering stare. "That's not particularly helpful."

Bostwick shrugged in apology and mentally reprimanded himself for the gaffe.

"We need to find out about this railroad into which Sinclair was putting so much money," the banker murmured to himself. Then to Bostwick he said, "You'll have to take care of that. Leave my name out of it."

Bostwick agreed and resisted the impulse to ask why. He then ventured, "There are two other ways we might be able to find out about the money."

"What's that?" Updegraff sounded eager for any hope.

"If you look at the list of investors, one was Benjamin Freese. He made a rather substantial investment more than a year ago and profited quite handsomely. Perhaps you could ask him about his dealings with Mr. Sinclair."

Updegraff crushed out his cigar, and his face reddened. "The hell I will!"

Had he just made another mistake? Bostwick wondered. He knew that there was some kind of rivalry between his boss and Freese but didn't know the details—and certainly didn't know how strongly Updegraff would react to the mention of Freese's name. Bostwick quickly went on, "I also thought it might be worthwhile to look into Mr. Sinclair's personal finances. I don't know what his salary was, but his expenses were considerable—apartment, art, clothes, and I found receipts for a substantial quantity of jewelry."

"Are you suggesting he was stealing?" Updegraff sounded more disappointed than angry.

That was indeed his suspicion, but Bostwick answered, "I am merely an accountant, sir. I do not draw any conclusions until I total the numbers." He hesitated. "With your permission, I believe I should try to learn more about Mr. Sinclair's private finances."

Updegraff considered the suggestion. "That's a sound idea, Bostwick," he decided. "Do remember, though, that you are still to report only to me."

When Bostwick said that he understood, Updegraff dismissed him and told him to send Harold Nantz back in.

Bostwick was halfway to the door when Updegraff said, "You've done a good job, Bostwick. I hope you'll have more to report soon."

The accountant froze momentarily. Updegraff must really be out of sorts, he thought, for he rarely praised anyone for anything. "Thank you, sir. I will do my best."

"Your efforts have already been commendable," Updegraff said, "In fact, I feel that you deserve a raise in salary."

Bostwick was now nearly in shock. His boss gave out money even less readily than compliments. He could barely whisper another thank-you.

Updegraff waved it away. "Of course with our present financial difficulties, we're not in a position to actually give any raises at this time. But perhaps soon."

"Yes, sir. Thank you, sir." Although he would have liked the extra money, Bostwick was almost relieved at the way the situation turned out. It meant that Mr. Updegraff was still himself. Bostwick didn't like change—not even in those who would be improved by some changes.

CHAPTER 17

Rebecca didn't know why she had been so worried. Valentine's Day was turning out to be quite an enjoyable, lovely occasion. There was only thing that she wished had been different: Marshall had waited until only the day before yesterday to ask her to dinner. To Rebecca, it had seemed an interminable few days waiting to hear from him, but she did understand that time moved at a different rate for men than it did for women. And she'd learned in the past year that Marshall had a particularly short clock—he rarely made plans more than a day in advance. Fortunately, he had thought to make a reservation at Enzio's, one of the city's finest Italian restaurants and the one where they had first dined together almost a year ago.

There was one other thing that put a bit of a damper on the occasion for Rebecca: she frequently thought of Alice, whom she was certain was not having much of a Valentine's Day celebration with her husband.

When the courteous silver-haired waiter who'd brought them their champagne came back for their dinner orders, Rebecca opted for fettuccine Alfredo. Marshall chose the shrimp scampi.

As soon as the waiter left the table, Rebecca couldn't help but tease, "Not your usual—sole Florentine?" On their first visit to the restaurant, Marshall had been so distracted—by Rebecca, he later confessed—that he'd absentmindedly ordered "the usual." The waiter, at a loss for what that might be, unwittingly brought him a dish that contained two foods that Marshall detested: fish and spinach.

Marshall smiled sheepishly. "Thank you for the reminder. But no, I think I'll stick with the shrimp."

It had been months before Marshall admitted what had happened, and even then it was only after they had been served the same meal at her parents' house and he had barely touched a bite.

She looked around the restaurant. "I think this is becoming my favorite restaurant," she commented. It certainly had one of the most romantic settings, with soft candlelight, fresh flowers on every table, and a strolling violinist who played skillfully and softly enough that diners could still engage in conversation.

Marshall didn't follow her glance; instead his remarkable eyes remained directed at her. "Mine, too," he said.

Rebecca almost blushed. Marshall seldom expressed verbally what he was thinking, but she was learning to read him, she thought. His clothes, for example, were one indicator. Marshall was always fastidious about his appearance, wearing expertly tailored suits, shirts of the finest cloth, and boots made by the best shoemakers. She understood by now, though, that the chestnut brown cashmere suit he currently had on—which nearly matched the color of his sweeping mustache and whiskers—was the one he reserved for special occasions, so that was a strong sign that this evening was important to him.

"Thank you again for the brooch," she said. "It really is lovely." The delicate gold pin in the shape of a rose blossom was perfect—not too extravagant and just the right size. She had promptly pinned it to her lace-trimmed basque.

Marshall appeared to struggle for something to say. She thought perhaps he was considering a reply along the lines of "not as lovely as you," but Rebecca had come to accept that that sort of sweet talk was unlikely ever to make its way out of his mouth. He proved that she was correct, at least this time, when he simply answered, "You're welcome."

Conversation faltered a bit after that, and it was something of a relief when the food arrived.

They then talked as they ate, commenting on the food—which was excellent, but not a topic that Rebecca found terribly interesting. They also reminisced about some of the enjoyable times they'd had in the past year, but Rebecca could never get a hint from Marshall what was on his mind for the future. If Alice would ask her again about their "romance," Rebecca would be hard-pressed to give her an answer.

Somewhat frustrated, Rebecca looked around at the other couples in the restaurant; they didn't appear to be having any difficulties with conversation, and she was mildly envious.

By the time the waiter returned to clear the plates from the main course, Rebecca had given up on the hope that the evening would take more of a romantic turn for her and Marshall. "Are you making progress with your Tammany Hall story?" she asked.

"Yes!" His face lit up. "And some very good news: *Harper's* has decided they will definitely publish it. The first installment will be out some time in the next two weeks." He sounded so enthusiastic that Rebecca was mildly jealous of his work.

"Congratulations. I have some good news, too."

"Wonderful! What's that?"

"You remember that young lady I told you about who was poisoned—Sarah Zietlow?"

"Yes. How is she?"

"Fully recovered. In fact, she's doing so well that she's been insisting that she's ready to leave Colden House." Rebecca recalled her talk with Miss Zietlow. "It was quite selfless of her. She said there were too many girls who needed help more than she did."

"Do you still have so many?"

"Oh, yes." Rebecca didn't want to talk about the fact that she still had virtually no funds with which to continue the shelter. Some small donations had continued to come in from girls who had once stayed at Colden House. Rebecca was grateful for what they gave and was happy to read in their notes that their lives had improved, but there still wasn't enough money coming in to support the home. Rebecca decided to focus on one success story. "As for Miss Zietlow, though, I've found her a job working in the kitchen of a lunchroom near the Pulitzer Building."

"You've helped a lot of young women get on their feet," Marshall said with admiration in his voice. "I know you still need money, and I have been looking into your investment with your brother-in-law's bank."

Rebecca was happy to hear that; sometimes Marshall could be a bit preoccupied with his own work. "Did you learn anything?"

"Not yet. I talked with one of the writers at *Harper's*—he began looking into the New Amsterdam Trust Company after Lyman Sinclair committed suicide. There was some suspicion that he took his life because of some difficulties—or irregularities—at the bank."

"And?"

"The writer hadn't found anything amiss. But he hadn't gotten very far in looking before the story was killed. He did tell me that Jacob Updegraff is too cautious to get involved in anything dishonest, though, so hopefully, your sister won't have anything to worry about."

"She *is* worried. I spoke with her today, and she says Mr. Updegraff has been moodier than ever and will hardly even eat. There must be *something* wrong." Rebecca decided not to mention what her sister had talked about with her at the dress shop. Since Alice couldn't identify the problem exactly, Rebecca didn't think she could convey to Marshall how her sister felt—especially since she wasn't sure she understood how Alice herself felt.

"I'll keep looking," Marshall promised. "I did learn that Lyman Sinclair was really Ludwig . . . I don't remember the last name, but it started with an *S.* Anyway, I thought I would look into his background. Perhaps your brother-in-law's concern is over something that Sinclair did."

"Perhaps." Rebecca knew that Jacob Updegraff would take anything that happened at his bank personally and as a reflection upon himself and his family name, whether or not he was responsible for it. And, she worried, perhaps he would hold Alice responsible, too.

"I've also spoken with Lawrence Pritchard," Marshall said. "He has some contacts, and he's going to see if he can learn anything for us."

"He'll be discreet, won't he?" Rebecca had met and liked Marshall's dime-novel publisher, but she didn't consider the man to be terribly bright.

"I'm sure he will be." Marshall suddenly looked uncertain himself. "I'll speak with him again and stress the importance of discretion. Oh, he's asked me to write another Western, by the way. I need to get that done in a month or two."

That wasn't welcome news to Rebecca. The two of them had little enough time together without Marshall's starting another book. But she smiled gamely. "What's this one going to be about?"

Marshall looked blank. "I don't know. The same as all the others, I suppose."

The waiter came by and Marshall took care of the bill. They then went out to the brougham he'd hired for the evening, and Rebecca found that he had one more pleasant surprise for her.

"To the Metropolitan Opera House," he instructed the driver.

If Rebecca had any doubt that Marshall wanted to make this a special evening for her, that erased it. Because she knew that he hated operas as much as she loved them.

CHAPTER 18

W ebb shuddered in his camel hair overcoat as his body heat seemed to rush out of him. Surely, he thought, the highest peak in the Alps could be no colder than where he was now, on a rocking cable car crawling across the Brooklyn Bridge. The temperature had fallen to the low twenties, and the wind blew shrilly over the bridge and through the cable cars. The cars, drawn by a thick, steam-powered steel cable, seemed reluctant to move, almost paralyzed by the bitter cold. They groaned and squeaked as the cable sluggishly pulled them over to the Brooklyn side of the East River.

The slow, solitary journey gave Webb plenty of time to think. And the primary subject of his thoughts was Rebecca Davies.

Webb hoped to have more evenings like the two of them had last night. To make that possible, though, he would have to clear up some of the responsibilities he'd undertaken. His article for *Harper's Weekly* would have to continue, of course, since it was to be a weekly series. And he had promised Lawrence Pritchard a dime novel; although unenthusiastic about writing another formula Western, Webb was a man of his word and would have to fulfill that promise. The task he thought he had the best chance of concluding quickly was determining what had happened to the money Rebecca had entrusted to Lyman Sinclair—and of course, if he succeeded at that mission, it would certainly relieve Rebecca of some of her worries and perhaps permit her more leisure time, too.

By the time the car finally made the crossing onto Brooklyn soil, Webb still hadn't exhausted the scenarios in his mind of how the two of them could spend those free hours.

After switching to a Nassau Railroad streetcar, Webb still had a long journey ahead of him, first along commercial Fulton Street, where the tall buildings served to block much of the wind. Then it was down Flatbush Avenue—so far down that the area became almost rural. The single horse-drawn streetcar traveled around the fountain at Prospect Park Plaza, past Mount Prospect Reservoir, and finally along Frederick Olmsted's beautiful Prospect Park itself.

Three miles into Brooklyn, in what was once the village of Flatbush, the car reached the end of the line. After the few remaining passengers disembarked, the horse and streetcar pulled into the railroad's car barn at the corner of Vernon Avenue. The home Webb was seeking was in sight, less than a block away.

He had first checked the telephone directory and had found no "Schulmerich" listing—not much of a surprise since only a small percentage of homes were equipped with the instrument. A subsequent check of records for greater New York turned up exactly one family with that name, residing at this address on Flatbush Avenue.

The home was an old one-story frame farmhouse with a sharply sloped roof. Much of the clapboard was curling with age, but the entire house had been freshly painted a pale yellow with dark-green wood shutters. The picket fence looked new and recently painted white. In the front windows were evidence that this place was home to the family of the late Lyman Sinclair, formerly Ludwig Schulmerich: black crepe, a traditional sign of mourning, was draped around the windowpanes.

Webb stepped onto the creaking front porch and knocked on the door. A dog inside immediately began barking furiously.

A woman's voice cried, "Quiet!" and the barking diminished, but only slightly.

The door opened halfway, and a young woman in a plain dark-gray wrapper asked, "Yes? Can I help you?" She was probably about twenty, although her short stature—not quite five feet, Webb estimated—made her appear younger. The woman had blond hair so light and skin so fair that she almost looked like an albino. Her features were rather plain and sharp, but not nearly as sharp as her piercing eyes.

She was far too young to be Sinclair's mother, so Webb guessed that she might have been a sister. "Miss Schulmerich?"

"I am Liesl Schulmerich. I don't believe I know who you are." The look on her stern face was demanding.

He tipped his derby. "Marshall Webb. I was hoping I might speak with you for a few minutes." He hoped she would notice that he was shivering and invite him inside.

She gave no sign of noticing his discomfort. Keeping one hand on the collar of a growling dog that had some beagle in its mixed lineage, she asked, "What is it that you wish to speak with me about?"

Trying to keep his teeth from rattling, Webb said, "Are you related to Ludwig Schulmerich?"

She hesitated. "Ludwig was my brother."

Webb took off his hat completely. "My condolences on your loss."

"Thank you." She waited, obviously certain that this wasn't what Webb had come to say.

He went on, "Your brother worked as a banker under the name Lyman Sinclair."

"Yes, he did."

"I was hoping you might be able to tell me something about his work there."

"Why? Are you with the bank, Mr. Webb?"

"No. I'm not. I'm—" With numb fingers, he reached into a pocket and handed her his *Harper's* business card.

"You're a writer," she said with distaste.

"Yes, but I'm not planning to—"

She cut him off. "The newspapers have written some cruel things about my brother, suggesting that he was involved in scandal and saying that he committed suicide."

"I won't—"

"Ludwig would *not* commit suicide. He was raised a good Catholic boy, and he knew suicide is a terrible sin."

"I'm not writing a story about your brother," Webb finally got in. "I have a friend who invested with him, and I'm trying to help her find out what happened to her money."

"I know nothing of my brother's business," she replied, "but I do know that nothing good can come of talking to a writer. Now I will thank you to leave us in peace." With that, the door closed so hard that it rattled the windows, causing the black crepe bunting to flutter.

Nicholas Bostwick thought Miss Schulmerich was quite a fetching young woman. Her fair complexion was like porcelain, and her fine blond hair so light that it was like a mixture of platinum and gold. And she was so petite that Bostwick seemed to tower over her, which was a refreshing change for a man who was only five feet, five.

What he couldn't understand, though, was why she had such an irritated expression in her piercing eyes. And the barking dog at her feet was rather unnerving to him, as well.

His hat in his hand, Bostwick said, "You probably don't remember me, Miss Schulmerich. We met at your brother's, uh, funeral." He had hoped to avoid mentioning that unhappy occasion. "My name is—"

"Mr. Bostitch. I remember." She still looked inexplicably angry for some reason.

"Bost*wick*," he corrected in a soft voice. He had been nervous enough about coming to the Schulmerich home—and especially about speaking with this attractive young lady again—but now his confidence was shaken to the point that he felt weak in his shivering legs.

"Did you give our name to a Mr. Webb?" she asked.

Bostwick had no idea what she was talking about. "No, ma'am. I don't even know anyone by that name."

"He's a writer, for *Harper's Weekly*. He came to see us yesterday and wanted to talk about my brother." She tilted her chin up. "I sent him on his way."

Still at a loss, Bostwick said nothing for a moment. "I'm sorry, Miss Schulmerich, but I do not know who he is. I can assure you, I have given your name to no one."

She studied him while the dog growled menacingly. "I apologize," she finally said. "You were good enough to come to my brother's funeral, and here I am making you stand in the cold. Please come inside."

Bostwick stamped a smattering of snow from his wet boots before stepping into the small front hall. Miss Schulmerich let go of the dog's collar long enough to take Bostwick's hat and overcoat, then showed him into a rustic parlor that was furnished with simple oak furniture and heated by a soot-stained brick fireplace.

The dog followed close behind him, sniffing suspiciously at his trouser legs. "What kind of dog is he?" Bostwick asked.

"*She's* some kind of mix—mostly beagle, we think."

Bostwick was annoyed with himself for his error; he didn't

want her to think he couldn't even tell male from female. "She's very nice," he said, patting the dog cautiously on the head. "What's her name?"

"Sabre." Miss Schulmerich looked impressed as the dog began licking Bostwick's hand. "She likes you. She generally doesn't let strangers touch her." Pointing to the sofa, she offered a seat and a cup of tea.

Bostwick accepted both, then sat down and waited for her to come back with the tea while the dog sat at his feet. Things were taking a turn for the better, he thought.

When she returned, the two of them sipped strong, dark tea for a while, with little conversation; then Miss Schulmerich said, "It's very kind of you to call, Mr. Bostwick. *Is* this a social call?"

"No, I'm—well, yes, but not entirely." Bostwick wasn't sure how to broach the subject of her brother's finances. "As you know, your brother and I both work—worked—for the New Amsterdam Trust Company. I have been charged with putting his accounts in order, and I'm afraid the records he left weren't quite complete." Lest it sound like a criticism of her brother, he quickly added, "Of course, his loss was so sudden—and tragic—that it's perfectly understandable that he didn't have all of his records current." In fact, Bostwick's true feelings were quite the opposite; an accounting ledger should be kept up to date at all times, as far as he was concerned.

"I don't know what I could tell you," she said. "As I mentioned to you before, Ludwig has had little contact with the family since he went into banking. I know nothing about his business."

Bostwick had already tallied some of Sinclair's personal expenditures, and it was these that he hoped to learn more about. "He might have had some money in personal accounts—temporarily, of course. Do you know anything about his personal finances?"

Miss Schulmerich hesitated. "If I did know, I'm not sure that I would tell you. I didn't know my brother well in recent years, but I do believe he is entitled to his privacy, especially now that he's gone. As it is, there is no need for me to betray any confidences—I can honestly tell you that I do not know anything about his personal finances." She added sadly, "Nor about anything else in his new life. I have never even been to his home."

"I was there," Bostwick said. He quickly assured her, "Only to retrieve some bank documents, and there was a police officer present to make sure nothing was disturbed."

"You've had more access than we've had, then." Her jaw tensed. "My parents attempted to get his effects, but the police still call it a possible crime scene. My parents are in the city now, trying to get the police to release his possessions." She shook her head sadly. "All they want is something to remember him by, something to make them feel closer to him. They've missed him these last few years."

"He's had no contact with you at all?"

"Not really. He did send money once—a generous amount. Enough for us to move out of Red Hook and buy this house. But my parents didn't want money; they wanted him to be part of the family."

Bostwick looked around, trying to guess the value of the house. Probably between one thousand and fifteen hundred dollars, he estimated, depending on how much land it was on; he could find out the exact price later. Even assuming fifteen hundred, that was still a small fraction of the total amount that was missing.

"It's a lovely home," he said. Looking at the walls, he noted the photographs on the mantel, and a few facial profiles cut from black paper, like silhouettes that hung on the walls in oval frames. "One thing I noticed in your brother's apartment was that there were no pictures at all." He immediately regretted saying that, for there was a look of disappointment in Miss Schulmerich's eyes. "I mean, was there no young woman in his life?" If there was, that would explain some of Sinclair's receipts.

She shook her head. "Not that I know of. But Ludwig was quite a charming young man—when he wasn't absorbed in trying to make money. I'm sure he must have had some romantic interests, but that is not something a young man would reveal to his sister, is it?"

Bostwick said he doubted so, although he had so little experience in romance that he didn't know for sure. He did know, however, that he was starting to feel such an attraction for Miss Schulmerich.

That was the end of his questions about Lyman Sinclair, but the two of them continued to talk for some time. Bostwick was delighted to find that he and Miss Schulmerich shared a mutual interest in music.

CHAPTER 19

Marshall Webb caught the morning ferry at the Twenty-eighth Street pier, next to the Bellevue Hospital complex. As soon as he stepped aboard the crowded steamboat, he began to hope that it would turn out to be the fastest-moving ferry in New York. He didn't want to remain in its wretched confines one moment longer than necessary.

The ferry to Blackwell's Island had long ago been nicknamed "The Tub of Misery," and it soon became apparent to Webb that that name was well deserved. Most of the passengers who rode that ferry did so unwillingly; they were criminals, paupers, lunatics, hospital patients, and others who were considered undesirable by city authorities. So they were herded onto the ferry and shipped from the island of Manhattan to various detention facilities on Blackwell's Island, a long, narrow strip of land in the middle of the East River. Seven thousand of society's rejects made the island their home at any given time; for some it was temporary, but for too many it would be their final home before being taken off to be buried in Potter's Field.

This morning, Webb found himself on a journey with a large number of prisoners in striped uniforms and leg irons, a dozen who looked as if they didn't have all their faculties—some of them shrieked incoherently and clawed at their own skin—and quite a few ragged individuals who looked as though they'd been evicted from the city's worst flophouses. In addition to the necessary police officers and Correction officials, there were visitors on board who were bringing baskets of food and other comforts to friends and loved ones already in residence on the island.

The ferry progressed northward far too slowly for Webb's liking, but the southern tip of Blackwell's Island was finally off the starboard side. This was the site of the Smallpox Hospital, and the boat made no stop. They plodded on, Webb mentally keeping track of the streets on the Manhattan side of the water. Blackwell's Island stretched from Fiftieth up to Eighty-fifth Street, so there was still some distance to go.

They next came to the landing for the penitentiary, where the shackled prisoners and their guards disembarked and the prisoners shoved into police wagons known as "Black Marias" for transport to their cells.

Continuing the journey, they then passed the Workhouse, the Almshouse for Women, the Blind Asylum, the Charity Hospital, and the Hospital for Incurables before reaching the Lunatic Asylum at the northernmost end of the island.

Craig Rettew, the old poll watcher who had witnessed the voting irregularities in the Thirteenth District, had told Webb that he believed the men brought in by police wagons that night must have come from "the loony bin." A patrolman with a taste for gin but not enough money to buy it confirmed this to Webb in an unlicensed saloon near the Delancey Street station house. So Webb decided to visit the city's infamous insane asylum to see if he could learn the details of their release.

The Lunatic Asylum, which consisted of three feudal-style buildings complete with turrets and battlements, was enclosed by a high fence on twenty acres of land. From this part of Blackwell's Island, Hallett's Cove and Astoria, Queens, were visible to the east; and across the river to the west, Webb could see the buildings of Yorkville, one of Manhattan's fastest-growing German neighborhoods.

Upon landing, Webb was ushered into the main building, an octagonal structure that housed the receiving room, offices, and most of the wards. Along the way, he had to show his paperwork three times to various officials, none of whom looked pleased to have Webb in their facility.

It was city policy that no one who wasn't an inmate or an official got onto any part of the island without a permit from the commissioner of Charities and Correction. The Lunatic Asylum was especially wary about granting access ever since innovative journalist Nellie Bly had herself committed to the asylum and subsequently wrote a searing series of articles on abuses at the institution, for the *New York World*.

Webb hadn't faced much difficulty in acquiring his visitor's permit, though, since *Harper's Weekly* was a far more reputable publication than Joseph Pulitzer's *World*. The clerk Webb had spoken with at the Department of Charities and Correction assumed that *Harper's* would publish a favorable article—an impression that Webb was eager to foster—and promptly pushed through approval for the permit.

Once in the asylum's receiving room, Webb's credentials were given a final examination by a gruff blue-uniformed officer. "Let me go find Dr. Goldstein," he said, after determining that the papers were in order. "He can help you find whatever it is yer lookin' for." As the officer turned to leave Webb alone while he went for the doctor, he added a stern warning, "You wait right here. This is no kind of place to go wandering."

Webb's wait was less than ten minutes before the officer returned with a young man in starched white hospital garb. "I'm Neil Goldstein," the man said. "What can I do for you?" Goldstein was young for a doctor, in his mid-twenties at the most. He had short, curly black hair, and his fleshy, clean-shaven face had the expression of a bored basset hound. His voice carried harsh evidence of a Bronx upbringing.

"Marshall Webb. I'm with *Harper's Weekly*." The two of them shook hands. "I was hoping you could show me around the asylum." It wouldn't achieve much for Webb simply to begin asking questions about the release of inmates, so he accepted the fact that he would have to endure a standard tour of the facility.

Goldstein sighed. It clearly wasn't how he had planned to spend his morning. "Is there anything in particular you're interested in?"

"No," Webb lied. "I'd like to know about the general operations at the asylum."

"Very well," Goldstein said gamely. "Let's begin this way."

"Thank you."

They began walking down a cool, dimly lit hallway. Both Goldstein's pace and speech were sluggish. He explained that the main building was the only one Webb could be shown, since the two outlying structures, called the Lodge and the Retreat, housed the most violent cases, and visitors were strictly prohibited for safety reasons. He then went on to give a tired spiel about how well treated the patients were and how their lives were incomparably better in the asylum than they could be anyplace else.

"How large is the medical staff?" Webb asked.

"There's generally one physician, plus nurses and attendants. We all come over from Bellevue Hospital."

"So you're the only doctor here?"

Goldstein hesitated. "I'm in medical school, but I'm not quite a doctor yet—I have about a year to go." He immediately appeared to regret making the admission. "I fill in for Dr. Duchaine on occasion when his duties at Bellevue prevent him from coming."

"How often is that?"

Concern became increasingly visible in Goldstein's young face. He almost pleaded, "There won't be any need to mention our names in your article, will there?"

"I don't believe that will be necessary. I'm primarily seeking information on conditions and procedures; I don't see any reason why I should have to include names." Webb flashed his most ingratiating smile. "There have been some unfortunate stories printed in the scandal sheets about this asylum, and my publisher would like me to correct the record."

Goldstein appeared relieved. "That's good to hear. We tend to be a bit nervous whenever a reporter comes through these days."

"I understand," Webb said sympathetically. "Now, how often do you fill in for Dr. Duchaine?"

"At least three days a week. The rest of the staff call me 'Doctor' as a courtesy." He stepped to one side of the hallway, as did Webb, while a dozen or so women, dressed in identical calico frocks, were led single file by a burly attendant. "They're off to the basket-weaving room," Goldstein said. "They seem to enjoy doing that kind of work—and of course, we sell the baskets they make."

Webb tried to study the women without appearing to stare. They ranged in age from about sixteen to sixty, but even the youngest had a sad, weary gaze that didn't appear to focus on anything in particular. After they'd passed by, he asked Goldstein, "What, exactly, is wrong with them?"

"What's wrong with them is that they're lunatics," was Neil Goldstein's matter-of-fact answer.

What an astute medical diagnosis, Webb thought wryly. "Are they suffering from any particular type of lunacy?"

"Hard to tell," Goldstein replied. "Two-thirds of all the patients here are foreign, and it's hard to diagnose somebody when you can't understand a word they're saying."

Webb drew up short. He had to resist asking, "So there are probably people in here simply because you can't understand their language?" Instead, he forced himself to keep walking again. "How does someone get committed to the asylum?" he asked.

"They must have a certificate of insanity issued by a judge. That means that everyone in here—except the staff, of course"— Goldstein chuckled at what he apparently thought was a fine joke—"is here by court order."

The future doctor then led Webb through the women's wards, where groups of stony-faced women, all in the same calico uniforms, worked at mat making, basket weaving, and crocheting. "The best cure for melancholy is labor," Goldstein explained.

"Where are the men's wards?" Webb asked. He wanted to start steering the course of the tour in a direction that could lead to information on the night inmates were released to vote in the election. There was no point asking questions about the women, since they couldn't vote anyway. Tammany Hall would only have recruited from the male patients.

"This way." Goldstein led Webb to another wing of the sprawling building, all the while extolling the virtues of the asylum's facilities.

Once there, they encountered several groups of men, who were generally noisier than the women patients. Like the women, they were dressed identically, in plain blue coarse-woven shirts and trousers. Many of them also had the vacant expression that was so prevalent among the women. Others, though, looked more angry than lost. Some spoke incoherently, and Webb thought a few were enduring *delirium tremens* brought on by withdrawal from liquor. "What kind of labor do the men do?" he asked. Few that he saw appeared to be engaged in anything productive.

Goldstein scowled. "Not much. Most of them just sleep and eat, and expect us to take care of them like this is some kind of goddamn hotel." He shot a quick, scared glance at Webb.

"Don't worry. I won't quote you." He saw one patient, who was lolling on the floor, borrow a match from another to light his briar pipe. "They do seem to be a lazy bunch," Webb commented, trying to sound sympathetic to Goldstein's point of view. "It must have been a nice break for you when they were taken out for the election." He turned to look Goldstein in the eye. "By the way, did they all come back?"

Goldstein suddenly looked as if he was about to faint. "I didn't think anyone knew about that!" He began to pant, sounding short of breath. "It was supposed to be a secret. How did you know?"

Webb smiled. "I believe it's common knowledge. There are no real secrets in New York."

"It was all perfectly legal, you know."

"And rather clever, I thought. Tammany Hall does have quite a remarkable system." He smiled again. "Tell me: do they pick the men they want as voters, or do you?"

Goldstein leaned against the wall for support. "This won't be published, right? *Please* tell me you won't be writing about this."

Webb didn't want to lie to the man, so he hedged. "I can promise not to mention your name—if you're forthright with me."

The young medical student took a deep breath. "It's all done strictly according to the law—and I don't write the laws." He paused for another breath. "The way it works is, Tammany Hall sends one of their ward heelers over to see who might be suitable—that means who can be certified as sane. The test is to see if a man can hold a broom when he's told to. If they can do that, they can vote."

"What about the foreigners? You said two-thirds of the patients here are foreign."

"When election day comes, the Tammany boys come back and round up *any* man who can hold a broom. They ferry them over to the city and take 'em to the courthouse, where a judge declares them competent. And the ones who aren't citizens go to another judge for a quick naturalization. Then they're all put on the voting rolls."

"Do you think it's healthy for the patients to be away from here without medical care?" Webb asked, wondering if any thought was given to the well-being of the patients.

"Hell, just look at them," Goldstein answered. "Their lives aren't going to amount to much no matter where they are. I figure it's good for them to get a day or two on the outside. And we can sure use the break in here. No one's ever gotten hurt."

"And they've all come back?"

"Oh, yes. After voting, they're taken back to court and declared insane again. Then it's back home to the asylum." He looked at Webb. "Nobody gets hurt, and like I said, it's all legal. A judge has to certify them sane and insane."

Webb knew what his next task would have to be: he would identify those judges and check their court records.

CHAPTER 20

Harold Nantz laid down his writing pen and silently rose from his desk the moment he saw Nicholas Bostwick come into the office. Without waiting to be dismissed by Updegraff, and without so much as a word or a nod to acknowledge Bostwick's presence, the tall secretary stalked out of the room and left them alone.

The office was cloudy with acrid smoke, all produced by Jacob Updegraff, who was puffing at a fat, black cigar as intently as if he were working a bellows in a blacksmith's shop. He looked up at Bostwick. "I hope you've learned something by now."

Bostwick noted that the bank president was looking worse each time he saw him. His face was haggard, his eyes bloodshot, and his skin seemed to be turning the same color as the long ash that danced precariously at the end of his expensive cigar. "Yes, sir." Bostwick hesitated, knowing the news wasn't going to make Updegraff look any happier. "I've learned a few things about the Western Continental Railroad—its revenue, assets, miles of rail, corporate ownership . . ."

"And?"

Bostwick took as deep a breath as he could in the smoky air. "Western Continental is virtually out of business, and it has been for some time. All totaled, the railroad's assets are worth about fifty thousand dollars at the most. And Mr. Sinclair's clients put far more than that into it."

"Then how did—" The ticker machine behind him suddenly chattered, and Updegraff jumped at the sound, causing ash to fall from his cigar and scatter across his polished mahogany desk. Composing himself, the banker went on, "Then how did Mr. Sinclair's investors make money on it? You told me yourself—you showed me the numbers—some of them made quite a bit of money from their stock in the railroad." He planted the cigar between his teeth and drew heavily on it.

"I believe . . . I hate to say this without proof, Mr. Updegraff . . ." Bostwick was feeling short of breath. Between the smoke and having to tell his boss bad news, he had to struggle for air.

"Yes, yes. Just say it." The cigar burned fiercely, matching the expression in Updegraff's eyes.

"It is my belief . . . that is, according to the records I've been able to piece together, all indications are . . . that Mr. Sinclair used money from newer investors to pay dividends to earlier investors." Having got that out, Bostwick again took a gulp of air.

"That's ludicrous! There's no profit in a scheme like that—how can the bank make money?"

"The bank can't." Bostwick thought his boss should have caught on by now. "But Mr. Sinclair could." He produced a sheet of paper with neat columns of numbers. "I have investigated Mr. Sinclair's personal expenditures, and they far exceeded his income." There were figures for rent, clothes, jewelry, artwork, and the $1,250 Sinclair had given to his family for the house in Flatbush—it had pleased Bostwick to learn that he had been so accurate in his assessment of the place's value.

Jacob Updegraff stared at the paper, but Bostwick sensed that he wasn't focusing on the numbers. "This is terrible," was all his boss finally said, mostly to himself. "And if word gets out, it could be a disaster for the bank." He looked up at Bostwick. "You will continue to keep everything you've learned strictly confidential."

"Of course, sir."

"I'll have to figure out what to do about this situation." Updegraff swiveled his leather chair to face the window and leaned back against the headrest. "There must be something that can be done," he muttered to himself, rubbing his hand over his jaw. His voice dropped almost to a sigh when he added, "But how did it all ever come to this, anyway?"

Bostwick remained standing, silent, for several minutes. Updegraff was so clearly talking only to himself that Bostwick was uncertain whether or not he had been dismissed. Finally, he ventured, "Have you spoken with Benjamin Freese, sir? He was one of Mr. Sinclair's first investors, and surely a man like Mr.

Freese wouldn't put his money into something unless he believed it to be a sound investment. Perhaps he can tell you what it was that convinced him to trust Mr. Sinclair."

Updegraff didn't turn around but addressed Bostwick in no uncertain terms. "Whatever conversations I may or may not have with Mr. Freese are between Mr. Freese and myself. Your job is to provide me with information, Bostwick, not to ask me about whom I have discussions with. Don't forget yourself."

"Yes, sir. My apologies." Bostwick felt as if he'd just been kicked, and he didn't like it. He'd done a good job sorting through Sinclair's finances, had been discreet with his inquiries, and had even made the information comprehensible enough for a man like Updegraff to follow. He didn't deserve to be spoken to as Updegraff had just done. "There is one more piece of information that might be of interest to you." He hadn't intended to mention it, but decided to do so since it might cause Updegraff some anxiety— and right now Bostwick wanted to see him squirm.

"What's that?"

"I recently spoke with Lyman Sinclair's sister—to inquire about his personal finances. When I did, I learned that someone had already been to see her: a gentleman from *Harper's Weekly* named Marshall Webb. Apparently, he's a writer and he's—"

Updegraff spun around and Bostwick almost rejoiced at seeing the sheer panic in his boss's countenance. "*Webb*, you say?"

"Yes, sir. He—"

"I know who he is," Updgraff growled. "That no account son of a bitch has been sparking my sister-in-law for the last year. He's after the family fortune, if you ask me. You say he's writing about Mr. Sinclair for *Harper's?*"

Bostwick hadn't said that, but it seemed a reasonable conclusion. "That would be my assumption, sir, yes."

Updegraff violently ground his cigar into an ashtray. "It would be a disaster if this Western Continental business gets into print."

That was another reasonable conclusion, Bostwick thought.

Marshall Webb had had a productive morning at the courthouse. His notebook now contained the names of the judges who'd been involved in the competency hearings and naturalization proceedings orchestrated by Tammany Hall at the time of the last election. He also had the names of those who'd been released from the Lunatic Asylum, along with the dates of their releases and recommitments.

Eager to write about what he had learned for his next *Harper's* installment, Webb decided to forgo lunch at any of the restaurants he passed by in Union Square, and walked directly home. He was already working out the outline of the article in his head.

As Webb came to the steps of his brownstone, he couldn't help but notice the elegant carriage stopped on Fourteenth Street directly in front of the place. The carriage's black enamel panels were polished to a mirror finish, and its gold trim and brass driving lanterns sparkled. Both the horses hitched to the carriage looked like champion thoroughbreds. Although the carriage was pulled next to the curb, it was blocking traffic and causing a variety of bells, horns, and whistles to be sounded by other drivers angry at being obstructed. Webb muttered to himself a few unkind words about how the rich always thought they owned the streets.

Inside his apartment, Webb eagerly laid out his papers on his desk. The abuses of the electoral process that he'd uncovered might be exactly the sort of thing to trigger public outrage, he thought, increasingly optimistic that his *Harper's Weekly* series might really help bring about changes in the corrupt system. Voting was the only recourse citizens had to change the government, and if that privilege was given to those who didn't deserve it, what did it really mean anymore to be a citizen?

Before he could sit down, there was a polite knock at his door. Webb wasn't expecting company and didn't particularly want any, but he went to answer the knock.

A tall, thin gray-haired man, garbed in servant's livery that might have once been worn by a French courtier, said, "Please pardon my intrusion, Mr. Webb." His posture was rigid and he sported a mustache and whiskers that could rival Webb's own for impeccable grooming.

"Quite all right," Webb answered with some uncertainty. He didn't know what a man dressed like this could possibly want with him.

"I didn't wish to accost you on the street." The servant held out a small linen envelope. "This is from Mr. Jacob Updegraff." He said the banker's name as if invoking the name of a deity.

Webb ripped open the envelope and read the brief note it contained:

I would appreciate your company for lunch today.
J. Updegraff

There wasn't even a greeting, Webb noted, and it sounded more like a summons than an invitation.

Updegraff's messenger cleared his throat. "The carriage is waiting, sir," he prodded.

"That's convenient," said Webb. "Because you can use it to bring him my reply." He went to his desk and scribbled a note of his own on a piece of torn foolscap:

I regret that my schedule precludes me from accepting your exceptionally gracious invitation.
M. Webb

He handed it to the servant, who appeared slightly taken aback. "Be so kind as to give this to Mr. Updegraff, please."

"Yes, sir. As you wish." He made a slight bow and moved toward the stairs.

As soon as the man began walking down the steps, Webb reconsidered. For Rebecca's sake, perhaps he should accept Updegraff's invitation, he thought. Offending him might cause family friction. Besides which, the banker was the one person who would know the most about what had become of Rebecca's money. Webb had failed to learn anything at the Schulmerich home, and so far he had heard nothing from Lawrence Pritchard. He called out to the servant, "One moment, uh . . ."

The man stopped in his tracks and turned to look back at him. "Ramsey, sir."

"One moment, Ramsey. Let me get my coat."

"*Very* good, sir."

A few minutes later, Webb was seated inside the richly upholstered carriage, with the note he'd given to Ramsey now crumpled in his pocket. The servant rode on the back of the vehicle.

Despite the heavy midday traffic, Updegraff's driver made good time. He was frequently aided by police officers who held up other vehicles to give the obviously more important coach priority. Webb didn't grouse about the rich thinking they owned the streets; he realized that, as much as he disliked it, for all practical purposes men like Jacob Updegraff did indeed own every part of the city. Also, he noticed that it was rather nice to be inside a carriage that was being accorded such a favored treatment.

In no time at all, they reached the corner of Fifth Avenue and 21st Street. Although this elegant area was home to some of the most splendid houses in the city, the one at the corner, an imposing Florentine mansion, was truly spectacular. It was within its walls that the members of the exclusive Union Club met to drink and dine.

The carriage pulled in front of the club's massive oak door, and Webb was let out of the vehicle by Updegraff's servant, who wished him a pleasant meal. He was then allowed inside by a uniformed doorman, but barely got two steps into the broad entrance hall before he was stopped by a butler, who courteously asked his name and checked to see that he was indeed on Jacob Updegraff's guest list.

This was the first time Webb had been inside the establishment, but he certainly knew its reputation. Very few men ever got through its doors, and fewer still got onto the membership rolls. It wasn't the exorbitant costs that kept them out; there were more than enough millionaires in the city who could afford the three-hundred-dollar entrance fee and seventy-five-dollar-a-year dues. Membership was strictly limited to those who had pedigrees as well as money. Department store magnate A. T. Stewart had been blackballed because of his Irish heritage, and this year J. P. Morgan had been rejected because his wealth had been acquired too recently. Only men from established, reputable families were eligible for membership—and then only after spending at least a decade on the Union Club's waiting list. Those who tired of the wait sometimes joined the rival Knickerbocker Club, which had been formed after the war by Alexander Hamilton, John J. Astor, and Philip Schuyler, who themselves ran out of patience with the Union Club's membership committee.

Another butler escorted Webb upstairs to the library, a spacious room heavy with dark wood, thick carpeting, and a haze of cigar smoke. Jacob Updegraff was seated in a red leather wing chair, with a long, black cigar in one hand and a snifter of brandy in the other. He motioned with his cigar for Webb to take the chair next to him. "Good of you to come, Webb," he said, with what sounded like forced enthusiasm. To the butler, Updegraff said, "Bring Mr. Webb a brandy."

Webb contradicted him. "Port, please."

The butler bowed and left to get the drink.

Updegraff said, "Lunch will be ready shortly. I took the liberty of ordering for both of us—roast venison and sweetbreads. I thought we might talk for a few minutes first."

"That's fine with me."

Updegraff took a sip from his snifter, then rested the glass against his belly. "Do you have a club, Webb?"

"No, I don't." The banker had asked him that almost every time they'd met, and the answer was always the same.

"Well, maybe someday you can join this one. I might even sponsor you—after all, there might be a family connection in our future." He winked broadly. "You and Miss Davies make a fine couple."

Webb ignored the mention of Rebecca. He looked around the room, at all the stiff, grim old men who appeared to be atrophying in their expensive armchairs; except for their neckties, the men were almost indistinguishable from the furniture. Webb was certain he wouldn't fit in with this membership until after he'd been embalmed. "That's very kind of you," he replied with no enthusiasm.

"Always glad to do a favor when I can." Updegraff took another sip of brandy. Webb noticed that his hand trembled slightly and it steadied only when pressed again against his silk vest. "In fact, I'm going to do you one right now." He didn't look directly at Webb.

"What's that?"

"I understand you've been asking some questions about one of my bankers, Lyman Sinclair. Planning to write an article, I suppose?" He gave Webb a sidelong glance.

Webb shrugged noncommittally. He was content to let Updegraff assume whatever he chose.

"Well," the banker said, "I realize that's your job, but Mr. Sinclair is dead—there's no way for him to defend himself against any allegations you might make. Doesn't seem quite fair for you to put his name in print."

Thus far, Webb wasn't aware of any allegations, nor did he have any plans to write a story on the banker. All he wanted was to help Rebecca get her money back. But if Updegraff was concerned, Webb figured it was worth pretending that he did have a story in mind. "I realize that," he said. "I would never make allegations that I couldn't support with proof."

"What kind of proof do you think you have?"

"I haven't finished my research yet."

Updegraff did look at him directly now. "There is no reason for you to continue to investigate. The banking business is in some turmoil at present—due to the economy, not due to any fault of ours. And what may appear to be irregularities at our institution could merely be the inevitable result of the present financial panic."

Webb interrupted, "What is the favor you're doing for me?"

"The favor is that I'm telling you to find another story to write about. I happen to be a personal friend of several editors at *Harper's*, and I would prefer to put a stop to this through you instead of by talking to them." He smiled. "I'd like to spare you whatever trouble you might get into with your superiors if you were to pursue this."

"I don't expect any trouble," Webb said calmly. "What I *do* expect—and you should too—is that I will pursue any story that I find to be of interest, no matter whom it might involve."

"I thought you were smarter than this!" Updegraff's voice rose so much that several men nearby shot looks of reprimand at him. "You'll leave me no choice but to go to your superiors."

Webb wasn't worried about that a bit. Knowing what he did of the banker's nature, if Updegraff did have some influence with his editors he would have gone to them first to try to have the story killed. "My editor thinks the story is a fine idea," he replied. "You won't be able to get it stopped." Webb almost smiled to himself—there was, after all, no story at all. "But I am willing to do *you* a favor."

Updegraff slumped back in his chair and raised his eyebrows as if to ask what the favor was.

Webb went on, "Your best chance for a favorable article is if I choose to be selective about the material I include—and exclude. And I prefer to make informed choices, so tell me this: What happened to the money Miss Davies gave to Lyman Sinclair?"

The banker hesitated. "I honestly don't know. We've been in-

vestigating the matter but haven't been able to track it down yet."
From his tone, Webb thought he was being truthful, if reluctant.

"How does an established bank like the New Amsterdam Trust
Company manage to misplace money?"

"It depends on who's handling that money," Updegraff said
weakly.

"Lyman Sinclair—he stole it?"

Updegraff sat upright. Bursting with indignation, he said, "You
don't have any evidence of that! The fact is—" He got himself
under control and settled back again. "The fact is, I simply don't
know yet what he did with the money." He finished his brandy in
a gulp.

"But you suspect him. Has he stolen money from other accounts?"

"I don't know. Mr. Sinclair's records were incomplete, and it's
been taking some time to make sense of them. I've had one of my
best accountants working on his books, but we're still missing
some information."

"Such as what became of the money."

Updegraff nodded sadly. Then he looked at Webb. "You said
you want to make informed decisions about what to include in
your story."

"That's right."

"Since not all the information is in yet, what I can tell you is
rather limited right now. But I *have* told you what I know. Will you
do me the courtesy of waiting until more facts are available before
submitting your story for publication?"

That seemed fair—especially since there was no story—so
Webb agreed that he would.

The butler came and announced that lunch was served.
Although Webb had little appetite for more of Updegraff's company, and the banker appeared to have no appetite for anything
other than more brandy, the two adjourned to the dining room.

CHAPTER 21

Burns, Fish & Company, located in Sixth Avenue's posh shopping district known as "The Ladies' Mile" because of all the shops catering to women customers, had been established so long ago that not Burns, Fish, or any of their original company was still involved in the management of the famous jewelry store. Nicholas Bostwick soon found that the tradition they had established, however—that of making customers feel as if human beings were far inferior to crystallized minerals—remained in full effect.

When Bostwick entered the store, a richly appointed shop with thick carpets and dark wood display cases, the only attention he received from the sales clerks were looks of suspicion. Although he was wearing one of his better blue serge suits, he clearly wasn't attired in a manner that projected sufficient wealth or status for him to receive service.

Bostwick ventured a cautious "Excuse me?" to one of the clerks, who tilted his nose in the air, pretended not to hear, and glided past him to help a well-dressed matron instead. He finally waited until one of the clerks was alone behind a display case of pearl necklaces and went over to him. "Excuse me, could you help me, please?"

The clerk, a dapper young man with a pointed goatee and waxed mustache, looked up at him, then glanced about to see if there were any more promising prospects in the vicinity. Seeing none, and with the display case blocking a quick exit, he said, "Yes, sir. How may I be of service?" There was a tone of contempt in the "sir," Bostwick thought.

"I'm looking for a Mr. Daniel Kroencke. He's one of your sales staff, I believe."

The clerk appeared taken aback. "I'm Mr. Kroencke." He eyed Bostwick up and down. "Has someone recommended me to you?" Kroencke didn't appear to believe that any of his fine customers would know a man as obviously low on the social scale as Nicholas Bostwick.

"You sold quite a bit of jewelry to Mr. Lyman Sinclair."

Kroencke hesitated. "We have quite a few customers. What makes you think Mr. Sinclair bought his jewelry here?"

"Your name is on the sales receipts." Among the papers in the late banker's apartment had been receipts for expensive necklaces, rings, and bracelets, many of them adorned with rubies or emeralds. The papers each had *Burns, Fish & Company* on their letterhead, Sinclair's name as the purchaser, and the signature of the sales clerk. Bostwick took the receipts from his coat pocket and showed them to the clerk.

"Yes, well . . ." Kroencke coughed. "I trust there is nothing wrong with the merchandise."

"I wouldn't know; I've never seen them." The jewelry hadn't been in Sinclair's apartment, and although it was possible that the gems had been looted by the police in what they believed to be a perquisite of their job, Bostwick didn't think Lyman Sinclair had bought jewelry like that for himself. Necklaces and bracelets were gifts for ladies. "What I'd like to know is for whom the jewels were purchased."

Kroencke laughed. "I can't tell you that. Even if a customer reveals such information, we are expected to be discreet. We must maintain our customers' confidence, you know." He shook his head emphatically. "The only person who can answer your questions is Mr. Sinclair, and unfortunately he is . . . in no position to do so."

Bostwick persisted. "Nor is he in a position to object."

"Good day, sir." Kroencke nodded toward the door. "I'm sorry I can't be of assistance."

"So am I." Bostwick wasn't sure what to do; he couldn't even afford to bribe the clerk for the information. Then he said, "Mr. Updegraff will be sorry to hear this, too."

"Mr. *Jacob* Updegraff?"

"Yes. Do you know him?"

Kroencke stammered. "I know of his family, of course. A fine family, the Updegraffs, and quite ... respected." Bostwick was certain that "wealthy" was the word in Kroencke's mind when he said "respected."

"I am here on Mr. Updegraff's behalf." Bostwick smiled. "I'm sorry I didn't introduce myself earlier. My name is Nicholas Bostwick and I am an associate of Mr. Updegraff at the New Amsterdam Trust Company. You may telephone the bank if you'd care to verify that."

"There's no need," Kroencke quickly said. "I take a gentleman at his word." He added apologetically, "I hope you realize that I was simply trying to protect the privacy of our customers."

Bostwick nodded. "I'm sure Mr. Updegraff will appreciate that. He will also be most grateful for any assistance you can give us."

The clerk thought for a moment—no doubt, about the prospect of future sales to Updegraff, rather than whether to reveal a confidence. "I shall be happy to be of service," he decided.

"Thank you. Now, about the jewelry: Did Mr. Sinclair say who it was intended for?"

"Not at first." Now that Kroencke had decided to be helpful, his words came pouring out like those of an old gossip. "Of course, some of our male customers do not wish to reveal the beneficiaries of their largesse for obvious reasons—and I never pry. Mr. Sinclair made several purchases from us over time, however, and I believe he was actually eager to say who the gems were for. Eventually, he revealed her name to me—then promptly pretended it was an accidental slip and swore me to secrecy."

"The name was?"

Kroencke looked left and right before answering in a tone of awe, "Miss Dolores Tenison."

Bostwick was awed himself—more like thunderstruck. What was a junior banker like Lyman Sinclair doing with one of the stage's most famous actresses, besides showering her with expensive jewelry? "You're certain of this? He bought the jewelry for *Dolores Tenison?*"

Kroencke appeared a bit miffed that Bostwick doubted him. "I'm certain that that's the name Mr. Sinclair gave me, yes. As to whether she was indeed the recipient of his gifts ..." The clerk spread his hands.

The only way to confirm that, Bostwick thought, was to speak with Miss Tenison—but that prospect scared him down to his union suit. It made the new assignment Jacob Updegraff had given him, one that he had previously been dreading, seem far more appealing in comparison. "Thank you for your help, Mr. Kroencke," he said.

"You *will* inform Mr. Updegraff of my cooperation, I trust?" The clerk was almost salivating at the thought of winning favor with the wealthy banker and chalking up lucrative sales.

"I certainly shall," Bostwick promised.

"Perhaps you could also mention that we presently have some exceptionally fine pearls in stock—of a quality that only a man like Mr. Updegraff could appreciate."

Or afford, thought Bostwick.

This was one of those rare times when the words just flowed from his gold-nibbed fountain pen onto the paper. They seemed to organize themselves into sentences and paragraphs, all structured and coherent. Marshall Webb had such a clear idea in his mind of how he wanted to present the information on Tammany Hall's activities that the only effort was in moving his writing hand fast enough to get it all down.

The first two installments of his series were already at the *Harper's* offices, ready to be typeset. The initial piece gave a detailed history of the Tammany Society and some of the characters, like Boss Tweed, who ran it. Although Webb would have preferred to start with a stronger story, at least the article provided context for the current political activities of the organization—and it was fairly innocuous, unlikely to get the rest of the series quashed. The second installment described the organization's current structure and included an office-by-office listing of all the Tammany hacks who currently held political office in the city. At the top of the list was Thomas F. Gilroy, who was both Tammany grand sachem and New York City mayor, and below him was the Board of Aldermen, where all thirty seats were held by men who had openly run on a Tammany slate. There were also numerous commissioners and superintendents of dozens of public works departments who were awarded their titles and salaries by Tammany

Hall—and collected those salaries despite rarely carrying out the duties that their positions entailed.

It wasn't until the series' third article, which Webb was now writing, that there was anything the majority of New Yorkers didn't already know. Webb was detailing exactly how those politicians and appointees got their positions and retained their power: through fraudulent votes.

Webb described the voters first, especially the criminals and asylum patients who had been released to provide Tammany Hall with an army of illicit, obedient voters who would carry out their orders. He then detailed the manner in which they'd been given their freedom, naming those in the courts, prisons, and hospitals who had facilitated the releases. Webb knew that people expected Tammany to be corrupt; it was his hope that they expected more of their public institutions and would demand reforms.

He was writing at a furious pace when there was a tentative knock at his apartment door. Webb kept writing until the visitor knocked again; then he reluctantly laid down his pen, intending to send whomever it was promptly on his way.

Webb opened the door to see a clean-shaven little fellow with sharp features standing there. He was about five years younger than himself, Webb estimated.

"Mr. Webb?" the man asked in a high voice.

"I'm Marshall Webb."

"Allow me to introduce myself." He took off his hat and offered his hand, then paused as if trying to remember his own name. "My name is Nicholas Bostwick. I work for Mr. Jacob Updegraff at the New Amsterdam Trust Company. He asked that I come to see you." Bostwick spoke as if he'd been reading from notes.

Webb's interest was piqued, and he decided that it might be worth putting off his writing for a while. He shook hands with the man and stepped to the side. "Please come in, Mr. Bostwick."

"That's very kind of you." Bostwick twitched his lips into something that was nearly a smile.

After closing the door behind him, Webb took the man's derby and overcoat, and deduced from the cut of his plain suit that Updegraff didn't pay much of a salary. He offered his visitor a seat, which was accepted, and a drink, which wasn't. "What can I do for you, Mr. Bostwick?" he asked after they sat down.

"Well . . . you see . . ." He must have lost his place in the mental notes he'd prepared, Webb thought. "That is, Mr. Updegraff believes that we can be of help to each other."

"In what way?"

"Mr. Updegraff says you are writing a story for *Harper's Weekly* which involves one of my late colleagues, Mr. Lyman Sinclair." His voice rose on the last words, making it more of a question than a statement.

Neither confirming nor denying Bostwick's words, Webb waited silently for him to continue.

The young man coughed and went on. "Upon Mr. Sinclair's untimely death, I was charged by Mr. Updegraff with reviewing his accounts and putting them in order. So you might say that you and I are working along similar lines." Bostwick attempted another small smile. "Therefore, Mr. Updegraff suggested that it might be beneficial to both of us to work together and share whatever information we each acquire."

Webb almost burst out laughing and managed to maintain his composure only with a valiant effort. He had no doubt that Updegraff had sent his employee to get information or to keep tabs on Webb's efforts, not to make a joint investigation. "That sounds like a fine idea," he said. "What information do you have to share with me?"

Bostwick wasn't prepared for a question that direct. "Not much," he hedged. "I've only begun my own investigations."

Webb pressed him. "Lyman Sinclair has been dead for a month. You just told me that Mr. Updegraff assigned you to examine Sinclair's accounts 'upon his death.' Surely, you must have been able to learn *something* about him in the last month."

Bostwick looked frozen, unable to respond. "What have *you* learned?" he finally asked weakly.

"About the same," Webb answered. This was proving thoroughly unproductive for both of them.

Webb then turned to a safer topic, asking Bostwick how long he had worked at the bank and what his position was.

Bostwick countered with the same questions about Webb's work for *Harper's Weekly*.

After a brief conversation that was polite but not illuminating, Webb said that he needed to go back to his writing. Bostwick took the hint and left, obviously relieved to be done with the mission Updegraff had given him.

Webb planned that he would speak with the man again, but another time, when he didn't have his defenses up.

CHAPTER 22

This was one of those special nights when their voices seemed to blend perfectly, Nicholas Bostwick thought. Chris Flynn's bass notes were a rock-solid foundation, Bob Stump was putting his heart and soul into the melody, Kenyon MacLeod filled out the chords on baritone, and Bostwick's tenor harmony added the sparkle to their sound.

They had sung half a dozen tunes and were just beginning "Aura Lee," when Bostwick was startled to see Marshall Webb walk into the barbershop. Taken by surprise at the writer's unexpected arrival, Bostwick's voice caught in his throat, causing him to emit a thoroughly nonmusical squeak. He stopped singing, and the other three singers quickly fell silent, too.

"Mr. Bostwick," Webb said cheerfully. "I'm so glad I found you." He had an easy smile on his chiseled face.

Instead of a greeting, Bostwick blurted out the question that was in his mind: "How *did* you find me?"

"I went to your apartment," the writer answered. "A neighbor of yours—Mrs. Johnson, a rather talkative lady across the hall from you—kindly came out and told me you were usually here on Thursday nights." Webb nodded in greeting to the other men. "I hope I'm not intruding."

That dratted Mrs. Johnson never could mind her own business, Bostwick thought. "No intrusion at all," he said with forced courtesy. In fact, he did resent Webb's invasion of his sanctuary. Every Thursday night for the past few years, Bostwick got together in Al Napoli's two-chair barbershop to harmonize with his friends amid the scents of bay rum, brilliantine, and pomade. The four of them never talked about business or family matters, concentrating only on their singing and producing a ringing sound that could carry them away from their daily cares. Bostwick was sure that Marshall Webb was here for a reason that had nothing to do with music—and it probably involved the sort of concern that Bostwick came here to forget.

"You sound good," Webb said to the group in general, receiving several thank-yous in response. To Bostwick he said, "I hate to ask this, but could we go someplace and talk for a few minutes?"

Before he could answer, Flynn asked in his basso profundo, "Who's your friend, Nicholas?"

Bostwick politely made the introductions, presenting Webb to the members of his Village Four quartet.

"Bully!" said Flynn. "Now that were all acquainted, you'll sing a song with us, Mr. Webb."

For the first time, Bostwick saw Webb's composure slip. "I can't sing," the writer said.

"Nonsense," answered Flynn. "Nobody comes in here without singing a song."

From one of the chairs, where he was reading an old issue of the *Police Gazette*, Al Napoli called to them, "They sure don't come in here for shaves and haircuts. Not when you're singing, anyway."

Bostwick chuckled to himself; he knew that the aging barber actually enjoyed having them sing in his shop—and they were four of his most regular customers.

Not letting Webb off the hook, Flynn told him, "Just pick a song you know—as simple a tune as you like. You take the melody and we'll harmonize around you."

After a moment's consideration, Webb said, "I've always liked 'I'll Take You Home Again, Kathleen.'"

Bostwick was curious to hear this, and rather looking forward to hearing Webb stumble. He knew that liking a song and being able to sing it were two entirely different things. "Then give it a go," he said. "We'll come in on our parts as soon as you start."

After Webb removed his hat and coat, Stump stepped aside to let him take his place. The writer began, tentatively at first, to sing. Within a few notes, Bostwick began harmonizing the tenor line just above Webb's voice, and Flynn and MacLeod filled in their parts. Bostwick was pleasantly surprised at the results;

Webb had a naturally rich baritone voice, so the key was rather low, but his notes were accurate.

The final chord was still ringing when Flynn slapped Webb on the back. "Fine job! You can sing with us anytime."

"Thank you." Webb looked as though he'd genuinely enjoyed the experience. He then said to Bostwick, "I hate to take you away from this, but I was hoping that we could speak for a few minutes."

Bostwick hesitated. "Yes, certainly." He then called to Napoli to sing tenor until he returned.

The barber, who had once been an operatic tenor in Italy, pulled himself out of his chair. "Might as well," he grumbled in mock reluctance. "It's not like there's any chance of a customer coming in here."

Out on Bleeker Street, Webb suggested they stop in at a nearby café to talk. Bostwick readily accepted the offer; he could use something to wet his lips after all the singing.

Once they'd found an empty table and been served their drinks—port for Webb and pilsner for Bostwick—the writer said, "We didn't seem to make much progress the last time we spoke."

They couldn't, Bostwick thought. Not under the circumstances. Jacob Updegraff had instructed him to glean whatever information he could get from Webb without revealing anything himself. And of course, the cautious writer was probably used to obtaining intelligence, not providing it. "I suppose that's true," he allowed.

"I was hoping we might be able to do a bit better," Webb said. "It occurred to me that there might be something which will give us a hint as to what Lyman Sinclair did with the money, something which neither of us has considered." He flashed a self-deprecating smile. "I know I hadn't."

"What's that?"

"How did Lyman Sinclair die?"

That was easy to answer. "He fell from his balcony."

"Fell?"

"Or jumped." Bostwick remembered his assumption that officials might have ruled the suicide an "accident" to spare the family some anguish and allow him a Catholic burial.

"Are those the only possibilities?" Webb toyed with his wineglass, giving no indication of what he was driving at.

"I don't know. I really haven't thought about it." Bostwick had only been assigned to make sense of Sinclair's accounts, not investigate his death. And he tended to focus strictly on whatever the task was at hand without allowing himself to get sidetracked—single-mindedness was part of the reason he was such a good accountant.

Webb looked up at him. "Here's what I'm suggesting: Lyman Sinclair's death might have resulted from something he'd been involved with while he was alive. So if we know *why* he died, we may know *what* he did that brought that about."

Bostwick thought over the suggestion and agreed there was some sense to Webb's reasoning.

"There are only a few possibilities," Webb said. "Let's consider the simplest first: Accident. Of course, by definition that would mean there was no motive for his death and we can learn nothing from it. Let me ask you: do you believe his fall was accidental?"

Bostwick recalled being out on Sinclair's balcony. "No. I was in his apartment. There's a high railing around the balcony; he could have walked right into it and not fallen over." He briefly wondered if that was something he was permitted to reveal to the writer. Jacob Updegraff had stressed that he was to tell Webb nothing.

"Very well, so we'll eliminate accident as a cause of death. Next possibility: suicide. Did Sinclair take his own life?"

Bostwick had assumed so but hadn't really thought about it. "I don't know."

"What drives a man to commit suicide?" Webb asked. Obviously not expecting Bostwick to answer that question, he began answering it himself. "Life seems hopeless to him. He's unhappy about something, or looking to escape from something." The next question was directed at Bostwick, as were Webb's probing eyes. "Was there anything in his personal life that he was upset about—a failed romance, maybe?"

"I didn't know him well," answered Bostwick. "We never discussed personal matters."

"From what you did know of him, you must have gained some impression of the man. Do you think Lyman Sinclair was the sort of man who would take his own life?"

Despite being peppered with questions, Bostwick found himself warming up to the writer. Webb appeared to value his opinion, unlike Mr. Updegraff, who wanted only the facts and numbers he could provide. He gave some thought to his answer. "No," he decided. "Although it's impossible to know what's in another man's mind, of course, I would have to say that Mr. Sinclair was not the type to concede defeat in any situation. And he was, if I may speak ill of the dead, a rather conceited and headstrong young man. Suicide, I believe, would not have been in his character."

Webb nodded thoughtfully and slowly sipped his wine. "What if he was engaged in some illegalities with the bank's money and feared that he was about to get caught? You still don't think he would take his own life?"

Bostwick passed up the opportunity to comment on possible illegalities. "My impression is that Mr. Sinclair was sufficiently arrogant to believe that he could overcome any situation."

Webb nodded again and put down his glass. "That leaves one final possibility then: murder."

"*Murder?*" That possibility had never entered Bostwick's mind, and it wasn't one that he wanted to contemplate.

"Yes. Again, assuming there was some financial impropriety—let's say, just for the sake of argument, that Mr. Sinclair was taking money from investors and using it for his own purposes. Perhaps one of those investors took exception to losing his money and decided to kill him."

What *did* Webb really know about Sinclair's financial activities? Bostwick wondered. The man seemed to be awfully close to the truth. Then Bostwick began considering the scenario Webb had just suggested. Bostwick happily had had no experience with violence in his life, and didn't know what would drive someone to commit murder. But the accountant in him did forge a ready opinion. "Murder wouldn't make fiscal sense. Killing Mr. Sinclair would mean never getting the money back. If it was a substantial enough amount to want to kill over, it must have also been a large enough sum to want it back."

"I hadn't considered that." Webb smiled. "That's a good point, Mr. Bostwick. You do have an acute financial sense."

Nodding his thanks at the compliment, Bostwick decided to share some information with the writer. If Mr. Updegraff should happen to find out, Bostwick could always claim that he had to give some information in order to get some in return. "Your supposition is correct, by the way," he said.

"What do you mean?"

"I am not at liberty to give you any details, but according to the records I've found, Mr. Sinclair was indeed taking money without making the investments he promised."

"Do you know what he did with the money?"

Bostwick thought that he had better not reveal any more at this point. "I'm still trying to determine that," he said.

Webb raised his glass and finished the contents. "Well, I've kept you from your friends long enough. It has been good talking with you, Mr. Bostwick. I appreciate your candor and I hope we'll be able to speak again soon." As he stood, he added, "Oh, and please thank your friends for letting me sing with them—I quite enjoyed it."

Bostwick repeated Chris Flynn's invitation to come and sing with them again, and was pleased when Webb promised that he would do that.

CHAPTER 23

There was a sizzle, and a small cloud that was more steam than smoke; then the feeble flame sputtered and died. The wood was still too green and simply refused to light.

Rebecca Davies crouched low and stuck her hands into the ancient iron range, feeling around for some dry pieces that she could use for kindling. As she did, she muttered mild oaths—at the wood burning stove, which had probably been installed when the house was built in the 1700s, at the fact that Colden House couldn't afford a new coal-burning stove, at the fact that even if they could get a coal stove they couldn't afford the fuel for it, and at having to conserve even the cheaper wood fuel. In the past, the stove would be kept burning from morning to night, as breakfast preparations went into lunch and then into dinner. A week ago, Rebecca had decided to save wood by letting the stove grow cold after each meal, and now the lighting of each new fire had become a cumbersome ritual.

"Pardon me, Miss Davies."

Rebecca pulled her head out of the stove to see Miss Hummel standing in the kitchen doorway. A folded newspaper was in her hand. "Thank you," she said. "But I've already put paper in the stove; it's the wood that's giving me trouble."

"No, ma'am," the older woman said. "This isn't for the fire. I brought this for you to read."

Rebecca sighed and stood. She was making no progress in getting the wood to ignite anyway. She grabbed an old towel and wiped soot and ash from her hands and forearms. "Good news or bad news?"

"Is it ever good news, ma'am?"

Not in recent memory, Rebecca thought sadly.

Miss Hummel handed her the afternoon edition of the *New York Herald,* folded back to page six. "There," she said, pointing a wrinkled finger at a single-column article.

The story was a short one—only three paragraphs. But Rebecca continued to stare at it for some time after reading its words. According to the article, the Western Continental Railroad, which had recently come under the controlling interest of New York financier Benjamin Freese, had just gone bankrupt. The company's stockholders were now left with nothing more than worthless paper. Rebecca didn't even have that much—she never had received her stock certificates.

Miss Hummel tried to prod Rebecca out of her daze. "I'm sorry to have to show you this, Miss Davies, but I thought you would want to know what's happened."

"I appreciate that. And you were quite correct—I do want to know." Then Rebecca looked at her assistant, somewhat puzzled. "How did you happen to notice the story?" As far as she knew, Miss Hummel's preferred reading material was limited to the illustrated weeklies and the theatrical news in the *New York Mirror.*

The older woman explained, "After you gave all that money to Mr. Sinclair, I took to reading the financial pages—I wanted to keep track of any news on our railroad. I thought our future depended on the railroad making money, and I wanted to see if it did. I've been awful worried about keeping the home going." She coughed softly. "You're not the only one who worries about Colden House, Miss Davies. It's my whole life, too, and—if you'll forgive me, ma'am—it has been for longer than it's been yours."

Rebecca was somewhat taken aback by the statement, but certainly not angry. Miss Hummel always did her work so quietly and efficiently, rarely showing emotion of any kind, that Rebecca never really considered what she might have on her mind. "There's nothing to forgive. You're quite right, Miss Hummel."

Her assistant went on, "I want you to know, Miss Davies, that there's no need to put everything on your own shoulders. You can always talk to me about anything—it's an awful burden for anyone to do so much worrying alone. Let me bear some of it. And I can do more here in other ways, and I'm glad to be of service."

"You've *always* been of great service. And I will certainly take you up on your kind offer. Thank you."

Miss Hummel nodded a "you're welcome," then suggested, "For example, you don't need to be the only one getting up at four in the morning to get the heat on. I have an alarm clock, too. Why don't we take turns?"

Rebecca was speechless for a moment. She didn't even know anyone was aware that she'd been doing that. A week earlier, the house had run completely out of coal in the middle of the night. It wasn't until morning that she had been able to coax a small delivery on credit. Every night since then, in order to stretch out their meager supply, Rebecca had been letting the house go cold from midnight to four, when everyone was asleep under bedcovers. And she'd been getting up early to make sure the place was warm again when they rose. "Thank you," she said again.

"Any time, ma'am," said Miss Hummel. A look of concern came over the woman's steely face. "About this railroad folding, though, ma'am—does that mean we're going to have to be closing our doors? We're already short on coal and wood, and we're serving more and more soup at mealtimes to stretch out the food. Are we going to be able to go on?"

"I intend to," answered Rebecca, although she had no idea how. "The money I gave to Mr. Sinclair was an investment, to provide us with an income for the future. We weren't counting on returns from it anytime soon." Now that she'd learned Miss Hummel had been worrying over the future of the home, too, Rebecca was eager to reassure her. "We do have a little money coming in from the letters I've been writing. That should help cover our everyday expenses; I've been using it mostly for groceries."

"But there's not enough to keep a fire going?"

No, not enough for that, Rebecca thought with some frustration. And although she wanted to reassure Miss Hummel, she didn't want to mislead the woman. "We do have to cut costs where we can, but we will keep food on the table and a roof over these girls' heads. We'll at least get them through the rest of this winter."

"Yes, ma'am." Miss Hummel had a determined set to her jaw. "If you'll forgive me again, ma'am, there's one other thing."

Not more news like what she'd just read in the paper, Rebecca hoped. "What's that?"

"Let me start the fire. I have more of a knack for it than you do."

Rebecca laughed. "I shall be happy to have you take over that duty—if you'll give one of your chores to me."

Miss Hummel took a long match from a shelf and bent down to the stove. "There's nothing I can think of that I want to give up, ma'am." Then she looked back. "But there is something you could do for me. Mr. Sehlinger asked me to go to the theater with him Saturday night—there's a new play opening at the Knickerbocker. If you could cover for me then . . ."

Rebecca promptly agreed. Then, while Miss Hummel rearranged the wood in the stove, she took another look at the *Herald* article.

According to the report, Benjamin Freese had been majority stockholder of the Western Continental Railroad for little more than a week. What Rebecca couldn't understand was how a man known to be such a savvy financier could buy a railroad unless he was convinced that it was a good deal. And if it *was* such a good deal, why did he have to declare bankruptcy so soon after making the purchase?

"I don't know," said Marshall Webb. Freese's purchase of the railroad, and its immediate demise, didn't make sense to him, either.

"Oh! Look at that one! Isn't he adorable?"

Webb followed the direction of Rebecca's finger. A small rhesus monkey was making a mess of peeling and eating a banana while chattering at several other monkeys in the same cage. "He has better table manners than some men I've seen at free-lunch counters," Webb said.

The two of them were walking through the menagerie in Central Park, one of Rebecca's favorite spots in the city. Next to the New York State Arsenal, on the east side of the park near Sixty-fourth Street, the zoological garden boasted eight hundred species of animals. It was always refreshing to see wildlife in New York that wasn't of the human variety.

Webb had been somewhat surprised by Rebecca's suggestion that they go to the park. She had been spending almost all her time at Colden House lately and had had to decline his past couple of invitations to dinner. Webb had been happy to take her up on the idea, though, and to take a break from his own work for the afternoon.

And it was certainly a glorious day for an outing. There were finally signs of the coming spring; the temperature was mild and the sky clear blue. Trees, though still bare, no longer appeared to be shivering, and the earth appeared to be softening, ready for flowers to push their way through and blossom. Young men played baseball in the open areas of the park, children flew kites, and bicyclists of both sexes rode the pathways.

To his mild disappointment, it soon became clear to Webb that not all of Rebecca's attention was on him or the caged animals. She'd reported to him the news about Benjamin Freese and the failure of the Western Continental Railroad; the two of them discussed it as they walked, but neither of them knew quite what to make of the development.

After watching the monkeys for a few minutes, Webb said, "I don't know much about Freese, except what I read in the papers from time to time. From what I understand, he's a maverick, and unpredictable, but a smart man when it comes to making money."

"Smart and *ruthless,* according to my brother-in-law," Rebecca said. "Mr. Freese would sell his own mother if he could make a profit on her." She added wryly, "Although that's not quite as bad as it sounds—the expression Mr. Updegraff usually uses when he refers to the man would mean that his mother is just a female dog, anyway."

"He's talked to you about him?" Webb was surprised that Jacob Updegraff would discuss business practices with Rebecca; the banker made no secret of his belief that women were incapable of comprehending matters of finance.

"No, I can't say that we've 'talked' about him; mostly, I've heard my brother-in-law *complain* about Mr. Freese." Still looking into the cage, Rebecca scratched her head in an exaggerated way, trying to get the monkey to mimic her. "Actually, I've heard quite a few complaints about Mr. Freese from quite a few people." She then bared her teeth at the monkey when it continued to pay more attention to its lunch than to her.

"About the way he does business?"

"More about the way he lives—he does as he pleases with no regard for social decorum." Rebecca smiled. "So I suppose he and I have something in common—oh!" She reached for her watch and flipped open the engraved case. "A quarter to five. I promised Miss Hummel that I'd be back before six—she's going to the theater tonight with her Mr. Sehlinger. I'd like to see the cats before I leave."

"Certainly." Webb knew that the big cats were Rebecca's favorite creatures. He personally didn't find them to be any more appealing than the household variety, which he detested. As they strolled to the section of the zoo that housed the lions and tigers, he asked her, "What were the complaints you've heard about Benjamin Freese?"

"Primarily about his social aspirations—and pretensions. Friends of my parents always seemed to enjoy ridiculing anyone who lacked a pedigree like their own, and Mr. Freese was a frequent target of their criticism. It's no secret that Freese came from the slums of Five Points, and he's managed to make a fortune for himself since then. Now he has a mansion on Fifth Avenue filled with fine art, rare books, and expensive furnishings, but he's a social outcast—blackballed from all the clubs and never invited to social functions. I personally think part of the reason is envy—he's better at making money than many of the city's established families."

They came to a cage where an ancient male lion was stretched out, almost covering the entire floor of his small prison. He didn't appear any more lifelike than he would have if he'd been killed and turned into a rug. Webb didn't care to look at the miserable animal. He said, "I've heard that some of Freese's business deals were on the shady side."

"Hmph." Rebecca waved her beaded purse at the lion, trying to elicit some response. "You don't want to know how many of New York's most 'respectable' families made their fortunes in the slave trade." She turned to Webb. "But what I still can't understand is, if Mr. Freese is such a smart investor, how can he buy a railroad and go bankrupt in so short a time. It's as if he just burned the money that he'd put into it." She paused and added in a softer voice, "And burned mine along with it. We'll never get that money back now."

Webb could tell that the news about her lost investment was causing her quite a bit of anguish. He got the sense that Colden House's financial problems must be particularly acute, although Rebecca would say nothing about them directly. He decided to share some of what Nicholas Bostwick had revealed to him, hoping it would lessen the pain of the news. "You might not have gotten the money back even if the railroad had stayed in business. Lyman Sinclair was apparently stealing from investors."

"Why, that—" Rebecca suddenly looked about to pounce, appearing far more like a big cat than the real one in the cage. "He should be . . ." She left the sentence unfinished. There was nothing that could be done to Sinclair now—at least, nothing more than what somebody may have already done to him.

CHAPTER 24

Mozart or Verdi? Nicholas Bostwick couldn't decide. He knew that he should probably play neither and instead conserve his precious cylinders. One of the unfortunate qualities of the wax phonograph cylinders was that they were soft and easily worn away by metal styluses. It would be at least another paycheck before he would be able to buy a new cylinder, and he should really try to make them last. Nevertheless, he felt a need for music, a desire to be transported to a place where only music could take him. It would be Mozart, he finally decided, who would take him on that journey.

He'd carefully removed the cylinder from its protective carton and pulled away the cotton packing when there was a knock at the door. Bostwick rarely had company; except for deliveries and unwanted salesmen, there were few callers at his apartment. He wasn't expecting a delivery and didn't want anything that a salesman might be hawking, but he nevertheless went to see who was there.

Marshall Webb stood in the hallway, wearing a spring-weight worsted suit with a blue-and-black pin-check pattern. It was finer than anything in Bostwick's wardrobe. "I'm sorry to disturb you, Mr. Bostwick." He removed his brown derby. "I would have telephoned, but . . ."

But Bostwick didn't have one of those instruments. "That's quite all right, Mr. Webb." He held the door wide. "Please come in." After their last conversation, and especially after having sung with the man, he was actually pleased to see the writer again.

As soon as Webb's tall frame entered the cramped one-room flat, it seemed overcrowded. Bostwick was somewhat embarrassed both by the lack of space and by the poverty of his furnishings. At least the apartment didn't smell too bad now; with the warmer weather, he was able to keep the window open to allow fresh air to circulate.

Bostwick immediately directed Webb's attention to the one high-quality object in the place. "Have you seen Edison's new Perfected Phonograph?" he asked his visitor.

"No, I haven't."

"I was just about to play a song on it, if you'd care to listen." Bostwick hoped that Webb would realize what an extraordinary opportunity he was offering him. Most of Edison's devices were in commercial phonograph parlors, where customers had to pay to listen to recordings through tubes and earpieces. It was only recently that the instruments had become available for home use, and Bostwick had used most of his meager savings to purchase one.

"Certainly, I would."

Webb didn't sound enthusiastic, but that didn't discourage Bostwick. "It just came out," he said as he picked up the brown wax cylinder he'd selected earlier. "The Perfected replaces his Improved Phonograph. And I must say, this new model does seem just about perfect." He carefully positioned the cylinder on the mandrel that would make it spin, and explained to Webb that the newly invented automatic reproducer ensured that the stylus would line up perfectly in the grooves of the recording. The stylus itself was also lighter in weight, so that it wouldn't erode the wax cylinders as quickly. When the spoken introduction to the music was made, Bostwick explained how the vibrations of the stylus were transferred to a thin glass diaphragm in the reproducer and then out through the conical brass horn.

Webb didn't appear particularly enthralled with the explanation of the machine's mechanics, but Bostwick was certain that his expression would change as soon as the music began. When the beautiful voice of soprano Amelia Carroquino began to sing "Ah, chi mi dice mai," an aria from *Don Giovanni*, Bostwick glanced at the writer again. He saw that Webb appeared to be in pain; the man obviously was not an opera lover, and Bostwick instantly regretted having wasted a play of the valuable cylinder on him.

Bostwick's own enjoyment of the music was dampened by

Webb's attitude, and the two-minute recording seemed inter-minable. "I apologize," he said as soon as the horn was silent. "Here I went making you listen to this without asking the pur-pose of your visit."

"Not at all," Webb said politely. "It was quite . . . enjoyable. And there's no urgency to my call."

Since he had no parlor, Bostwick offered a seat at the dining table and a glass of sherry, both of which were readily accepted.

Once they were seated and the wine poured, Webb said, "The last time we spoke, you were kind enough to share some of the in-formation you'd learned from Lyman Sinclair's accounts."

Bostwick smiled to himself, recalling what he had reported to Mr. Updegraff the next day. All he had told his boss was that there was no reason to be concerned about Marshall Webb. He'd reas-sured Updegraff that Webb had uncovered no information of his own, that the writer had no understanding of finance, and that the only information he'd revealed to the writer was intended to mis-lead him.

Webb went on, "Now something has come up which I simply do not understand. You have a greater understanding of financial matters than I do, so I was hoping you might be able to shed some light on it for me."

Bostwick was flattered but wary. "What is it you're interested in?"

"Benjamin Freese," Webb answered. "He recently bought con-trolling interest in the Western Continental Railroad—the same railroad Sinclair had been promoting to investors. And immedi-ately after buying the railroad, he declared bankruptcy. My ques-tion is, why would a shrewd businessman like Freese do something like that?"

Bostwick didn't have a ready answer to that. He'd wondered about it himself when he first heard the news. Only one possibil-ity had occurred to him, but he wasn't sure he should share it with the writer.

In response to his silence, Webb reached into a small portfolio. "I realize you are in a sensitive position, Mr. Bostwick. Jacob Upde-graff has given you the task of discerning what I might know about Sinclair's business dealings without revealing to me any confidential bank matters."

"Well . . ." Bostwick again found himself with nothing to say. He hadn't realized it had been so obvious, but Webb had summed up the situation quite accurately. All Bostwick could do was shrug uncomfortably and venture a smile of apology.

"I can't very well ask you to reveal confidences to me unless I am willing to share some of my own." Webb removed some papers and a couple of thin paperbound volumes from the portfolio. "The fact is, however, I know almost nothing about Mr. Sinclair that you don't know yourself. The truth is also that I have no intention of writing about the matter for *Harper's*. Mr. Updegraff mistakenly jumped to that conclusion, and I simply saw no reason to correct that assumption."

Bostwick held back a laugh. He enjoyed the fact that Webb had let his boss worry for no reason.

"The only subject I am presently writing about is Tammany Hall." Webb slid a copy of the latest issue of *Harper's Weekly* across the table; it was opened to an article that promised to be the first in a series on the corrupt political organization. "My only interest in your bank and in Mr. Sinclair's activities are as a favor to a very dear friend of mine who invested with him. She is experiencing some financial difficulties and badly needs to recover the money she gave him. I am trying to help her do so."

Bostwick sympathized but felt powerless to help. Besides, he didn't want to give false hope—he knew there was no chance that any of Sinclair's investors would get their money back. "I hope you realize," he said, "that whether you intend to make the information public or not, I do have to comply with the wishes of Mr. Updegraff—he *is* my employer."

"Of course," Webb said. "But what if you could be assured that I will maintain any confidences you may share with me? If I can assure you that Mr. Updegraff will never find out . . ."

"How can you guarantee that?"

"By sharing a secret with you—one of which *my* employers at *Harper's* are unaware, and which would certainly cost me my position if they learned of it." He pushed the rest of the papers to the middle of the table; from the middle of the stack, he plucked a dime novel and put it on top. The full-color cover illustration was of a Union cavalryman about to slash a Confederate soldier with his saber, and the bold lettering read:

Pritchard's Dime Library Presents
THE COURAGEOUS CAVALRYMAN
or
How Sergeant Frazier Saved the Day
by David A. Byrd

Bostwick was familiar with the book. "I've read it," he said. "It was quite a good story."

Webb appeared taken aback to hear that. Finally, he said, "Thank you." In answer to Bostwick's quizzical frown, he explained, "I wrote it. I'm David A. Byrd."

"You—?" Bostwick was at first impressed, then skepticism took over—anyone could make that claim, he realized.

Webb took a few sheets of correspondence that had *Pritchard's Dime Library* printed on their letterhead and handed the papers to him. "These will confirm it."

They did. Bostwick read them over carefully; they were in regard to payments, publishing schedules, and sales figures. Evidently, Marshall Webb was indeed the writer behind the David A. Byrd pseudonym. "I enjoy your books, Mr. Byrd," he said. Just as music took him somewhere ethereal, Byrd's dime novels, especially the Westerns, took him outside of crowded Manhattan and into the open spaces of the Wild West.

"Thank you. And, please, it's Webb—not even my family knows that I write dime novels."

"I'll keep your secret," Bostwick promised. He thought for a few moments. "Just as I'll trust you to keep whatever I may tell you confidential." When Webb nodded in agreement, Bostwick went on, "I may have an answer to your question about Benjamin Freese."

Webb cocked his head, obviously eager to hear what Bostwick had to tell him.

"Mr. Freese was one of the first investors in Western Continental—his is one of the first names to appear in Lyman Sinclair's ledger, at least. And he's one of the few who made a profit—quite a handsome profit, I must say—on his investment."

Webb nodded. "So that may be what led him to believe that buying controlling interest in the railroad would be a good deal. Still . . . to fold only a week or two after he bought it seems awfully coincidental." The writer pursed his lips, causing his mustache to drape over his entire mouth. "It also might make Freese feel like he'd been duped by Lyman. That could be a motive for murder, except that . . ."

"Except that Mr. Sinclair was already dead by the time the railroad went bankrupt."

"Exactly." Webb appeared to be disappointed that the timing didn't work out.

"There's something else I haven't mentioned," Bostwick said. "And it might shed some light on the circumstances of Mr. Sinclair's death."

"What's that?"

"Perhaps Mr. Sinclair had had an unhappy love affair." Bostwick wasn't quite comfortable with such a matter, but he thought it might be relevant. "There was nothing in his papers to indicate a romance—no love letters or photographs of a woman. I noticed a silver picture frame in his parlor, though; it was empty, but it was the elaborate kind of frame that would be used to hold a picture of a lady. It occurred to me that a romance might have gone badly for him and he'd discarded the photograph."

"Could be," Webb agreed. "But an empty picture frame isn't really evidence of anything."

"Not by itself, no. But Mr. Sinclair also purchased quite a bit of jewelry—over forty-five thousand dollars' worth, as a matter of fact. I went to the store where he made those purchases and learned that they were intended for Miss Dolores Tenison."

"The actress?" Webb appeared as startled as Bostwick had felt when he'd first learned the name.

"Yes." Bostwick stood and went to the sideboard. From the wall next to it, he unpinned a tinted postcard put out by Old Judge cigarettes as part of their "Stars of the Stage" series. "She's quite a lovely woman." He handed the pasteboard to Webb.

Webb briefly studied the photograph of the actress. "She is, indeed." With a pronounced tone of skepticism, he added, "And you really believe she could have been romantically involved with *Sinclair?*"

"If not with *him,* then perhaps with almost fifty thousand dollars' worth of gold, rubies, and emeralds." Bostwick cleared his throat. "I was planning to call on Miss Tenison to see if she might confirm this, but I haven't yet had the opportunity." He didn't add that what he'd really lacked was the nerve. "Perhaps you . . ."

"Would join you? Certainly."

What Bostwick wanted to suggest was that Webb be the one to try to speak to her, not the two of them together. But at least that would be preferable to trying to see her alone. "Very good," he said. "Perhaps"—he wanted to delay it a bit and give himself a chance to get used to the idea of meeting the famous actress—"perhaps Tuesday evening, if that's convenient for you?"

"Tuesday it is," said Webb. He stood to go. "It's been good talking with you, Mr. Bostwick. And the discussion *will* remain between the two of us?"

Bostwick agreed that it would. As he handed Webb his derby, he added, "I do hope you'll write some more Westerns. I tried your last book, the one about the Homestead Strike, but I didn't care for it, I'm sorry to say."

"Don't be sorry." Webb smiled wryly. "You're in good company—my publisher didn't care for it, either." He put his hat on. "He prefers the Westerns, too, so I will have another one of those written soon."

"What's the title? I'll look for it."

"I don't have one yet. But no need for you to look; I'll be happy to give you a copy as soon as it comes out."

Bostwick thanked him for the offer, and they agreed on a time to meet Tuesday night.

"Ambush at Grizzly Mountain," Webb read aloud. "How can you give the book a title when I don't even have it written yet?" Not only was the title already decided upon, but it was emblazoned over a lurid front cover illustration of a frontiersman being shot by Indians. This one was gruesome even by dime novel standards; all the arrows sticking in the victim's bloody chest made him look like a human pincushion.

"My usual illustrator is moving to San Francisco next month," Lawrence Pritchard replied. "He's gotten a job as a newspaper artist out there—although why anyone would want to go to California is unfathomable to me. In any event, I had him do some covers in advance before he left. He needed the extra money for his travel expenses, and I was able to obtain his services rather cheaply." He smiled smugly at having got a bargain.

Cheap was the way Pritchard operated when it came to business, Webb knew. One glance around Pritchard's cluttered one-room office made that obvious: warped shelves of various woods and finishes overflowed with books and papers, a battered file cabinet in the corner was missing a drawer, the small throw rug in front of his chipped pine desk was moth-eaten, and the two chairs that were squeezed close to the desk belonged to a kitchen set. "That works out well for you," Webb said, "But what about the story? What if this cover isn't suitable for it?"

"That's easy enough to solve." The publisher smiled, which, with his balding head and bony features, tended to make him look like a grinning skull. "You simply include a scene of an ambush at a place called Grizzly Mountain." He shook his head. "Honestly, sometimes I don't know what you writers would do without editors."

"Yes, well, thank you. That clears it up for me." Webb hadn't come to Pritchard's office to talk about books, anyway. He stretched out his legs as much as he could in the close quarters. "The last time we spoke, you were going to learn what you could about Lyman Sinclair and Jacob Updegraff," he reminded the publisher.

"Ah, yes. I did make some inquiries about those gentlemen." Pritchard pushed at the bridge of his pince-nez. "I didn't learn much more than I'd already told you. Nothing at all about Updegraff, in fact—he's really quite a boring man, only interested in making money and not terribly clever about doing so. The only thing more that I learned about Lyman Sinclair was that he'd been pitching a railroad investment to some people. Those who did invest appeared to profit quite nicely."

"All of them?"

"I don't know. Perhaps those who profited were the only ones who would admit investing with him." He smiled. "Have you ever heard a man say that he did any worse than 'break even' after a card game? The losers generally keep their losses to themselves."

That could be, thought Webb. "There's someone else I want to ask you about."

"More interesting than Lyman Sinclair and Jacob Updegraff, I hope." Pritchard didn't believe it was worth knowing about someone unless there was something scandalous to learn.

"Certainly more attractive, at least," Webb said. "Her name is Dolores Tenison."

"*The* Dolores Tenison?" Merely at the mention of her name, Pritchard took on the expression of a gawking schoolboy.

"Yes, the actress."

Pritchard let out a long breath that turned into a whistle. "Now, *she* is the topic of a great deal of discussion. She always has been, and she always seems willing to provide fresh material— Dolores Tenison revels in attention, and doesn't seem to care if it's positive or negative."

Webb knew that by "discussion" the publisher actually meant "gossip." "Specifics, please," he said.

"To be polite, I will simply say that her true talents cannot be exhibited on the public stage." He raised his eyebrows to be sure that Webb got his meaning. "Her acting style is so broad that it's almost pantomime, and her singing voice is like that of a mewling cat."

"But she *is* popular."

"Primarily based on her past reputation. Miss Tenison was certainly a beautiful young woman in her day, and a rather charming actress. But now she must be the oldest perennial ingenue on stage. She still has a great deal of sex appeal, however, and doesn't lack for male admirers—some of whom probably first admired her when they were still in knee pants." Pritchard nodded his head with admiration. "I have to hand it to the lady: however she's accomplished it, she has managed to remain popular for more years than most women who take the stage."

"Are there any particular admirers that you know of?" Webb was hoping to hear Lyman Sinclair's name.

"There should only be *one*," Pritchard said. "And that's her 'benefactor,' Benjamin Freese."

"Freese?"

"Yes." Pritchard appeared surprised that this came as news to Webb. "It's common knowledge that Miss Tenison is Freese's mistress. He pays the rent on her apartment, buys her clothes and jewels, and provides her with all the comforts a woman like Miss Tenison could want." He hesitated. "Well, *almost* all the comforts."

Webb prodded him to explain what he meant.

"Mr. Freese is not a young man anymore," Pritchard elaborated. "And he has a family of his own. That leaves Miss Tenison free to accept the attentions of other admirers."

"And he knows about this?" From what Webb had heard about Benjamin Freese, he doubted that the man would take any attentions paid to his mistress in stride.

"That's a good question." Pritchard took a few moments to think about it before continuing. "Dolores Tension is a social creature; she loves parties and dinners and dancing until the wee hours. Benjamin Freese, however, is not a sociable man at all; he tends to be quite independent-minded and something of a loner." Pritchard paused and scowled slightly. "Of course, that might not be by his choice. Freese came from the streets—rumor is that he was even a member of the Dead Rabbit gang when he was a young man—and so he's shunned by proper society. Since he's a bit isolated from everyone, it could very well be that he hasn't heard about Miss Tenison's—what shall we call them?—*extracurricular* activities."

Webb pondered the information. "From what you've heard of Freese, what do you expect he would do if he learned that another man was providing Miss Tenison with his, uh, company?"

It didn't take long for Pritchard to answer. "I certainly wouldn't want to be that man." The publisher squirmed uncomfortably in his swivel chair. "I have no desire to be a soprano."

Webb wasn't sure if that was a fate worse than death, but Lyman Sinclair probably hadn't been given the choice.

CHAPTER 25

Tuesday evening, after a light supper together at a small German restaurant in Union Square, Marshall Webb and Nicholas Bostwick took a streetcar up Broadway to West Fortieth Street. There, they walked to the stage door on the side of the Empire Theatre.

It was an hour before the early show, but Webb was surprised to find there was already a small army of young men gathered there. They looked almost identical in age, dress, and facial hair, with most of them sporting straggly mustaches that accentuated their youth rather than making them appear more mature. Their style of dress was similar to Bostwick's: cheap, nondescript dark suits, stiff high collars, and black derbies tilted in an attempt to look jaunty. Many of them clutched bouquets of flowers or boxes of candy.

Webb tried to politely work his way through the crowd to the door, with Bostwick silently following behind him. He encountered more than a few murmurs of protest as well as several elbows. Ignoring the comments, and making use of his own elbows as needed, Webb reached the heavy stage door and knocked on it. When there was no response, the angry murmurs behind him turned to chuckles.

After two more series of insistent knocks, Webb heard a lock slide open, and a heavyset man with a walrus mustache and a bulbous nose cracked the door open enough to look out. Immediately, there was a press against Webb's back, as the crowd surged forward and the young men shouted messages that they wanted conveyed to Dolores Tenison.

With a couple of sharp backward jabs of his elbow—one of

which unfortunately struck Bostwick in the ribs—Webb gave himself some breathing room. "Are you the stage manager?" he asked the droopy-faced fellow in the doorway.

"That I am." He wiped the back of his thick neck with a wadded red handkerchief. "George Evans is the name. Showtime's not for an hour yet, though, and this ain't the entrance, anyways."

"I'm not here for the show," said Webb. "I've come to see Miss Tenison. Is she available?"

Evans laughed so hard that the chortle turned into a cough. "If that's what you're here for, you might as well just get in line with the rest of the stage-door Johnnys behind you." He began to pull the door closed. "But you won't have any more luck than the rest of them."

Webb grabbed the edge of the door. "It's important that I see her. And I can assure you I am *not* a stage-door Johnny."

The manager hesitated and looked Webb up and down. "Well, you're at least dressed like a gentleman, I'll give you that," he said. In a low voice, he added, "Listen, mister, the truth is Miss Tenison *never* sees anyone before a show. But . . ." He turned to see that there was no one listening behind him. "She will occasionally see a gentleman after a show. Why don't you go watch the show and come back here afterward?"

"Thank you," said Webb. "I'll do that."

"And be sure you have something nice for her. She likes for her admirers to bring her gifts." With another glance behind him, Evans added, "And I expect you'll have a little something for me, too, considering the trouble I'm putting myself through."

"I understand," Webb said, although he wasn't sure that he truly did understand. It sounded as if the stage manager was functioning as Dolores Tenison's pimp.

When the door closed and the bolt had been drawn to lock it, Webb nudged Bostwick and nodded toward the corner of the street. The two of them worked their way back through the crowd of Miss Tenison's young admirers and went to the ticket booth next to the main entrance on Broadway. Webb insisted on buying the tickets and sprang for second-row orchestra seats at a dollar twenty-five apiece.

After a brief wait, the main doors opened and they were among the first inside the plush auditorium. The Empire Theatre wasn't the best in New York, but it was a reputable place with modern fixtures, and well maintained. Electric bulbs in the chandeliers and in the sconces on the walls provided adequate light to see throughout the interior, which was decorated almost entirely in shades of red and gold. The carpeting was clean, the heavy drapes across the stage showed no signs of needing repair, and the upholstered seats with padded armrests looked as comfortable as easy chairs.

When they took their numbered seats behind the orchestra pit, Webb found that the chairs were just as comfortable as they appeared. He and Bostwick killed some time by chatting about nothing in particular—with the accountant doing most of the talking—until the orchestra began to play.

"The strings are out of tune," Bostwick said with a grimace. "And one of the clarinets is behind the tempo."

Webb hadn't noticed; to his untrained ear, the orchestra sounded rather good. "I don't think people are here for the music," he said, turning his head to look at the rows of filled seats behind them. The theater was packed with an audience that was almost entirely male. Younger men for the most part were in general seating, and older men, some of them wearing full dress suits, dominated the orchestra section and the private boxes in the balcony.

The music came to a crescendo, the lights were dimmed, and the curtains opened to reveal a set decorated to look like a medieval banquet hall. A castle was painted on a backdrop—which led Webb to wonder how the exterior of the castle could be visible from within its banquet hall—and a number of men costumed as knights and pages stood in position like mannequins. One dwarf, dressed in brightly colored jester's garb, cavorted about the stage, doing handstands and cartwheels.

Then, with a blare of trumpets, a single spotlight was aimed stage left, and Miss Dolores Tenison stepped into its glow. Her appearance was greeted with wild applause from the audience. She hadn't spoken a line or sung a note; it was simply enough for her fans to see her appear onstage in a flowing gown with a low-cut bodice, made up in the role of a royal princess.

Webb couldn't help but notice that Miss Tenison did make a pleasant sight. She had large, round, marvelously expressive eyes; golden hair in long curls; full, red bee-stung lips; and a petite hourglass figure that seemed to be in perpetual motion.

As the show unfolded, Webb kept his attention on Dolores

Tenison. That wasn't hard to do, since everything in the program was intended to highlight Miss Tenison's charms. And it had to focus on her charms, since she didn't have much acting or singing ability, Webb could tell. The show was a revue, simply called *Scenes of Spring*, and consisted of a series of costume vignettes unrelated to each other—or to spring, for that matter. Dolores Tenison was the only woman in the cast; perhaps she didn't want any competition for the attention of the predominantly male audience, Webb thought.

She certainly did all she could to maintain that attention, performing more as a seductress than an actress. Although she was far more subtle than the chorines who danced in the sin palaces of the Tenderloin, her every move and and gesture exuded sex appeal. There was a lascivious swing to her hips, a come-hither glint in her eyes, and her speech was full of suggestive inflections. The knowing smile on her lips made it clear that she knew exactly what effect her performance was having on the audience.

As Dolores Tenison broke into a song, Bostwick leaned toward Webb and said, "She does have a marvelous voice, doesn't she?"

Webb looked at him incredulously. Although her smoky voice had an enticing quality to it, even Webb could tell that she wasn't carrying the tune entirely on pitch. Bostwick looked enraptured, however, and Webb thought the woman certainly had a remarkable power to affect men's senses if she could make the accountant enjoy her music.

After the show, which earned Miss Tenison a standing ovation and a deluge of flowers that were thrown onto the stage, Webb elbowed Bostwick. "Let's go see her."

Bostwick stammered nervously, "Are you sure about this? I don't think we can simply go back there."

"We can try." Webb stood and found an usher who, for a quarter, was willing to take them to the stage manager.

Led by the usher, Webb and Bostwick proceeded backstage, trying to stay out of the way of the stagehands who were moving sets around to get ready for the next performance. When they came to the hallway that led to the dressing rooms, Webb spotted George Evans lounging against the wall, a smoldering cigar stub clamped between his teeth.

"Not yet," he grunted at Webb. "She don't see nobody till after the last show of the night."

"I'd prefer not to wait," Webb said. He took out a dollar bill and one of his *Harper's* business cards. "And you may assure Miss Tenison that my intentions are entirely honorable."

The manager looked at the bill with disappointment; he had probably been looking forward to the greater sum that *dis*honorable intentions might have brought him. "A writer, huh?" he said. "Well, we could use a favorable notice. Let me check if Miss Tenison will see you."

Evans knocked on a dressing room that had a large gold star on the door, gave his name, and went inside. He soon came back out. "Miss Tenison has agreed to see you for a few minutes."

Webb started toward the door. When Bostwick followed, the manager grabbed him by his shoulder. "I only asked if Mr. Webb could talk to her," he said. "Not nobody else."

"Mr. Bostwick is my associate," Webb said firmly. "We *both* need to speak with Miss Tenison."

Evans bit down on his cigar butt. "Well, it don't make no never-mind to me," he grudgingly decided. "But don't be surprised if she throws you out on your ass."

She didn't. When Webb and Bostwick entered the dressing room, Dolores Tenison greeted them with a fetching smile. "Mr. Webb?" she said, looking from one to the other. She extended her hand, palm down and with her dainty fingers curled.

"I'm Marshall Webb." Webb touched her fingers and made a slight bow. "And this," he said, gesturing to the accountant, "is Nicholas Bostwick."

When she offered Bostwick her hand, the accountant took hold of her fingers as if he would never release them and kissed the back of her hand. "A pleasure to meet you, Miss Tenison," he said. "I have your picture on my wall, but I must say you are much lovelier in person."

Somewhat embarrassed for the gushing Bostwick, Webb averted his eyes and looked around the room. He thought it had the appearance of another stage set, one designed to look like the dressing room of a prima donna. There were Japanese silk screens, a mirror that covered half a wall, a damask bed lounge, a cherry sideboard that held a silver champagne bucket, and racks and racks of clothes and costumes. A thick-waisted maid in a drab green uniform was hanging a gown on one of the racks.

After Dolores Tenison had retrieved her hand from Bostwick,

Webb said to her, "We are most grateful to you for seeing us on such short notice, Miss Tenison."

"The pleasure is mine," she said, tugging at the floral kimono that was pulled tight around her well-shaped figure. "According to your card, you write for *Harper's Weekly,* Mr. Webb. I don't believe *Harper's* has ever given me a notice before."

"An inexcusable omission," said Webb with an apologetic bow. He didn't mention that he had no intention of rectifying that omission, but Miss Tenison was welcome to believe so, if she chose.

The actress smiled coyly. "You know," she said, "most of my callers arrive with flowers or chocolates." She added with a lift of her eyebrows, "Or perhaps a bracelet or necklace. I do believe you're the first man to get in here with only a card." She paused, as if expecting that they did have a gift for her. Her smile faltered when none was forthcoming. She called to the maid, "Bring me a glass of champagne, Myra!" Her tone was imperious and impatient.

Webb took the opportunity to study Dolores Tenison. She wasn't quite as attractive close up as she was on the stage. Her large, bright eyes were certainly appealing, but the wrinkles around them were caked with face powder. The golden color of her hair was clearly not a natural one, and the fullness of her lips was primarily an illusion produced by a liberal use of rouge. Through the thin fabric of the kimono, Webb could see the outline of a corset, which was probably what gave her figure much of its shape.

Myra handed Miss Tenison a filled champagne flute. Webb thought the maid had probably been chosen for her job as if she were joining the cast of a play starring Dolores Tenison. Although not unattractive, the woman's dark hair was pulled back in a severe style and she wore no rouge or powder. Overall, her appearance was as drab as her starched uniform—there was nothing about her that would divert attention from the star whom she served.

Miss Tenison held the glass up to the light before drinking. "Myra," she said with an exasperated sigh, "how many times have I told you to check for water spots before you serve me?" Not waiting for an answer, she went on, "This glass is filthy. Bring me a new one—and make sure it's sparkling!"

"Yes, ma'am. I am so sorry." The maid obediently took the

glass, but Webb was amused to see that she rolled her eyes the moment she was out of her mistress's line of sight.

The actress called after her, "And make sure you pour *fresh* champagne—the champagne in that glass has been ruined." To Webb and Bostwick, she said, "It's always so difficult to get good help."

When the new drink arrived, Miss Tenison examined the glass carefully and nodded a rather reluctant approval. She took a long sip and sashayed over to the bed lounge, where she gracefully sat down. She then tossed her long curls and assumed a half-sitting, half-reclining position that caused her kimono to gape open slightly. It was a pose as carefully choreographed as any that she had adopted on the stage.

Although Webb was by no means oblivious to the seductive power she wielded, he forced himself to remain focused on the reason for their visit. "You mentioned gentlemen who come to see you," he said. "I was hoping you could tell us about one of those men: Lyman Sinclair."

She took another sip of champagne and betrayed no recognition of the name. "I have many admirers, Mr. Webb. There are probably dozens standing outside the stage door at this very moment, and they'll be happy to stand there for hours and hours just hoping that I might step outside and acknowledge their existence." She shrugged. "I don't know their names and I don't know Mr. Lyman Sinclair."

"I don't believe Mr. Sinclair would have stood outside," Webb said. "He was a rather well-to-do banker, and I've been given to understand that you've met him personally."

"I go to many parties and meet many people, but again, I don't know the names of everyone I meet." She laughed brightly, then asked, "What does that have to do with my performance, anyway? Aren't you here to write about the show?"

Nicholas Bostwick broke free from the trance that had kept him silent. "Lyman Sinclair was very generous to you," the accountant said. "He gave you jewelry worth almost fifty thousand dollars."

Miss Tenison laughed again, but little humor remained in her tone. "My dear young man, I have more jewels than you have neckties." She gave him an exaggerated once-over. "*Many* more, from the looks of you. And some of them are individually worth more than fifty thousand dollars. Of course, I don't really care about monetary value; I appreciate the beauty of fine jewels. Some of my gentlemen friends say they are the only things that come close to matching my own beauty."

"I'm afraid that my bank will have to consider their monetary value, not their aesthetic value," said Bostwick.

She snapped at him, "What on earth are you talking about?"

The accountant answered, "I am employed by the New Amsterdam Trust Company, the same bank where Mr. Sinclair worked. We have discovered that the money he used to purchase your jewelry was not his own; in fact, he may have used bank assets."

"I knew nothing of that!" Miss Tenison called to the maid for another glass of champagne. "I don't ask where my gifts come from; that would be rude. I simply accept them."

Bostwick quickly reassured her, "No one is accusing you of anything improper, Miss Tenison. Whatever wrongdoing may have taken place was entirely Mr. Sinclair's." He paused to let her sip from the fresh glass. Then he said, "But it is only fair to tell you that the bank may have to go after those jewels to retrieve its assets."

She threw the half-filled glass on the floor, smashing the glass. "You think *you're* going to go into my jewelry box, little man? You just try and take them from me."

The theatrics had Bostwick visibly upset. He stammered, "No, I . . . I didn't mean me . . . I wouldn't . . ."

"I thought not." There was nothing pretty in the actress's smile of victory. "Nor will anyone else."

Webb took over for the shaken accountant. "They very well might," he said. "Mr. Sinclair is dead. I'm sure the police are curious to know how and why."

Dolores Tenison immediately retorted, "The newspapers said it was a suicide."

"Oh, so you *have* heard of him," said Webb. "Earlier, you claimed that you hadn't."

"I said I didn't *know* him. There's a difference between *knowing* someone and *hearing* of him." She was now positively pouting and didn't look at all pretty.

The actress had a point, but Webb wasn't about to concede it. "It appears that you don't intend to be straightforward with us,

Miss Tenison. Perhaps the authorities will have more success." He nudged Bostwick and nodded toward the door.

Tenison whined, "I must say, this conversation has been a thorough bore. Myra! Show these men out."

Since they were already at the door, there was no need for the maid to do as she'd been bidden. Before going outside, though, Webb decided to ask one more question. "Tell me, Miss Tenison: did Benjamin Freese *know* about you and Mr. Sinclair, or had he only *heard* of the affair?"

While Dolores Tenison looked around for something more to throw, Webb and Bostwick stepped safely out the door.

CHAPTER 26

Rebecca Davies was suspicious of most of the remedies prescribed by doctors—she believed that far too many of them relied on quackery more than medicine. But there were always a few girls at Colden House who were in need of them, and Rebecca didn't want to withhold anything that might help. So every morning she went through the same routine in which she was now engaged, that of gathering the daily medicines. Today's medications included Dr. Rowland's System Builder and Lung Restorer for a girl with bronchitis, Bromo Vichy for one who'd been suffering from chronic headaches, and a bottle of Electricating Liniment for a young woman who'd sprained her ankle after being pushed down a flight of stairs.

Rebecca had gathered a few more bottles of pills and tonics together on a tray when the telephone rang. "Miss Hummel!" she called. "Could you get that, please?"

The telephone continued to ring until Rebecca remembered that Miss Hummel had gone to Lamy's Fish Market to buy some sardines for lunch. Leaving the medicines in the infirmary, Rebecca hurried to the hall telephone and picked up the receiver. "Hello?" she said with some annoyance at the interruption.

"Rebecca?"

She didn't recognize the strained voice on the line. "Yes, this is Rebecca Davies."

"This is Alice." There was the unmistakable sound of sobbing. "Could you come see me?"

"Of course. What's the matter, Alice?" Rebecca was startled to hear her sister sound so upset. She was usually so composed and proper.

"It's Jacob," Alice answered with another sob. "I think there's something awful that's happening."

"Is he there now?"

"No, he just left for the bank." Alice's breath caught. "I know you're busy, Rebecca, but can you *please* come?"

"Yes, I'll be right there."

Rebecca didn't like leaving Colden House unattended, but she knew that Miss Hummel would be back soon. After leaving her a note, she rushed outside to hail a hansom cab.

On the ride to Fifth Avenue, Rebecca wondered what it could be that had her sister so upset. Rebecca was usually so preoccupied with poor girls who lacked the basic necessities of life that she rarely considered whether those in her own family had any troubles other than choosing what gown to wear to a particular ball.

Rebecca thought back to when she and Alice had spoken in Himmer & Corey's dress shop. That was the only other time in recent memory that she had heard her sister sound so upset. She recalled Alice's saying that Jacob Updegraff had been angry and that Alice had found herself frightened for the first time. Rebecca had spoken with her a couple of times since then, and although Alice reported no improvement in her husband's behavior, it hadn't worsened, either—until today, apparently.

When Rebecca arrived at the Updegraff mansion, the front door swung open within seconds of her knock. Instead of requesting that she wait in the reception hall, the maid who answered the door said simply, "Mrs. Updegraff is in the drawing room." Three other servants stood along the hallway, all of them with concern etched on their usually implacable faces.

Rebecca immediately headed off for the drawing room, her shoes clacking like castanets on the tile floor. She strode so quickly that the maid who was trying to lead her there couldn't keep up and eventually came to a stop. Indifferent to social decorum, Rebecca opened the carved door herself and stepped alone into the tropically adorned room.

"Rebecca!" Alice squealed. Her tremulous voice contained the first note of pleasure that Rebecca had heard in it this morning. "I am so grateful to you for coming."

Alice, reclining on a bed lounge, was in a brocade dressing gown that was tied slightly askew, her blond hair wasn't quite in place, and if she had put on face powder this morning, much of it had been dissolved by the tears that filled her red, puffy eyes. Rebecca didn't remember the last time she'd seen her sister in such a condition.

Rebecca sat next to her sister on the bed lounge and took one of her hands. "Tell me what's the matter."

Alice's other hand held a crumpled lace handkerchief, with which she dabbed her eyes before answering. "It's Jacob. He's turned into a completely different man." She turned her damp eyes to Rebecca. "I know you've never cared for him, but he has always treated me with kindness—until recently, when he started worrying about money all the time."

"You told me about that at the dress shop," Rebecca said. "Has he been worse?"

Alice bit her lip and nodded.

Rebecca tensed. "Did he—"

"He didn't strike me, no. But he certainly acted like he was about to." Alice began to weep. "It's a terrible thing to be afraid of your own husband," she said, shaking her head.

Rebecca put her arm around her sister and let her cry it out for a while. When Alice had recovered somewhat, Rebecca said gently, "Tell me what happened. How did it start?"

Alice took a deep, ragged breath and collected herself. "It began at breakfast. Jacob was absorbed in the morning newspaper and didn't talk to me at all. That's not unusual—he's usually preoccupied with reading the news and the financial page. But this morning, he was obviously upset by something he read—he looked angry and scared at the same time, and he didn't touch his food. When I asked him what the matter was, all he would say was that it was 'business' and none of my concern."

Rebecca wasn't sure she understood. Was this all that had her sister so upset? "What then?"

"Papa telephoned for Jacob during breakfast. And when Jacob went to speak with him, I looked at the newspaper he'd been reading. There was a story on the front page about the State of New York buying Fire Island. The curious thing was that Jacob's name was in the story—he owns the island!" She looked at Rebecca. "I never knew that. And the state is buying it for almost a quarter million dollars—that sounds like a lot of money."

"It is," said Rebecca with a sigh. While she fretted over nickels and dimes at Colden House, her sister had never had to consider the cost of anything that she wanted. To her, there wasn't much of a difference between a thousand dollars and a million.

Alice went on, "When Jacob came back to the table, I told him I'd seen the news. I congratulated him—I thought it was good news and that he'd be happy about it." She shook her head. "He's been so worried about the bank lately. Anyway, I told him this was something to celebrate and that we should consider throwing a spring ball." She choked up, then continued, "Jacob just lashed out at me. He called me a silly, stupid thing who had no idea what it took to survive in the real world. He said all I worry about is balls and gowns, while he's involved in matters of life and death."

"Life and death?" Rebecca repeated.

Alice nodded. "That's what he said, and I asked him what he meant. He went into a rage, not making any sense. He started to blame all sorts of people, including me, for chipping away at the family fortune, and saying we had no idea of all that he had to do to build it up again." She looked at Rebecca with pleading eyes. "I tried to understand what he was talking about. I asked him what he did do, and then he stopped talking completely. He called for the carriage and went off to the bank."

Rebecca was at as much of a loss as her sister. "Maybe he'll be calm by tonight again."

"I don't understand," Alice said with genuine bewilderment. "I thought maybe Papa might know, so I telephoned him after Jacob left for the bank. Papa said he'd only called to congratulate Jacob on the Fire Island business." She looked up at Rebecca again. "That *was* good news, wasn't it?"

"I would think so," she answered. How could a quarter-million-dollar sale not be good news?

"What did Jacob mean, 'life and death'?" Alice asked. "Are we going to starve?"

Rebecca assured her that Jacob Updegraff hadn't meant that. But she was unable to explain what he did mean.

He had turned in the third installment of his Tammany Hall series to his *Harper's* editor a day early, so Marshall Webb decided to do some work for his other publisher. He was already past the date that he'd promised, and wanted to give Lawrence Pritchard something to go inside that garish cover of *Ambush at Grizzly Mountain.*

He'd barely got five pages into the manuscript when he was interrupted by a knock at his door. He was surprised to find Rebecca standing there, but as always he was happy to see her face. Except this time, he noticed, it bore a most anxious expression.

"What's the matter?" Webb asked before she'd even stepped foot inside the apartment.

"Jacob Updegraff." Rebecca shrugged out of her coat and handed it to Webb. She had a folded newspaper in her hand. "And Alice—she's the one I'm really worried about. She's always been so sheltered, and now . . ." She bit her lower lip and shook her head.

Webb led her to the couch. He offered tea, which she declined. "Tell me about it," he said.

"Take a look at this." Rebecca handed him a copy of the *New York Sun* and pointed to a headline that read, State Buys Fire Island for Quarantine."

Webb gave the brief article a quick read. According to the story, Governor Roswell P. Flower had just signed a bill to purchase Fire Island. The state intended to use the sandy strip of land as a permanent quarantine station for incoming immigrants. The purchase price was $210,000, which was to be paid to the island's current owner, Jacob Updegraff of the New Amsterdam Trust Company. "But Updegraff doesn't own the island," Webb said, mystified by the newspaper's error.

"He doesn't?"

"No. The inhabited part is owned by a fellow named Eric Christensen, who built the hotel there." Webb had met Christensen when he was working on his dime novel *Welcome to America,* about the immigrants who'd been quarantined in the hotel during the cholera scare. Although there were a couple of small parcels owned by other residents, Eric Christensen, not Jacob Updegraff, held the title to most of the island.

Rebecca looked puzzled. "Alice didn't know that her husband owned the island, either. Anyway, she assumed that the sale was good news, but Mr. Updegraff was inexplicably angry." She went on to tell him about her visit to her sister this morning. "Alice is very worried," Rebecca concluded. "She's never seen her husband like this, and she thinks he might have gotten mixed up in something dangerous. He said something to her about being involved in 'a matter of life and death.' " She shook her head. "I never did understand that man."

"What do you think he meant by that?" Webb asked.

"I don't know." Rebecca sighed sadly. "Men like Jacob Updegraff will do foolish, destructive things sometimes, though. It's happened to more than one of my family's friends. Some people posses so much wealth, they become virtual prisoners to it—all they can think about is protecting their fortunes. With Mr. Updegraff, it's even worse; he believes protecting his money isn't enough—he has to *grow* the family fortune. And I suspect he may go to extreme lengths to do so. I only hope Alice won't have to suffer for whatever her husband might be involved in."

"Let me make some inquiries," Webb offered. "I may be able to find out about this Fire Island business, at least, and I'll let you know as soon as I learn anything."

He hoped that Rebecca would stay for a while, but she thanked him and insisted that she had to get back to Colden House.

Something was clearly amiss, Nicholas Bostwick could tell. Harold Nantz actually smiled at him when he entered the boss's office, and it appeared to be a smile of gratitude. Nantz then almost darted past him to the door, obviously happy for the chance to leave.

One look at Jacob Updegraff was enough to explain his secretary's eagerness to depart the smoke-filled room. Bostwick had never seen the bank president so angry. It wasn't a raging anger, though. Instead, it seemed to be a suppressed sort of anger that had been bottled up, as if the rage was entirely within. Or had he simply been storing that anger until Bostwick came in to bear the brunt of its explosion? Bostwick wondered.

"You asked to see me, sir," Bostwick gently reminded the fuming bank president.

Jacob rapidly chewed the end of his fat cigar and looked up at Bostwick with fire in his eyes. "You're finished," he said.

Bostwick felt his knees tremble and nearly give way. He *needed* this job. "You mean—"

"I mean exactly what I said. Your work on the Lyman Sinclair accounts has concluded."

"Oh!" Bostwick consciously had to force his breathing to return to normal. Now his knees wanted to give way with relief.

Updegraff exhaled a cloud of smoke. "You did fine work, Bostwick."

"Thank you, sir."

"Don't interrupt."

Bostwick hadn't realized that he *had* interrupted his boss. He nodded and meekly added, "Yes, sir," hoping that the words wouldn't be taken as another interruption.

"As I was saying . . ." Updegraff paused to glare at Bostwick, as if challenging him to interrupt again. ". . . you did a good job, and you were discreet in your efforts. Now that your assignment is over, I hope you realize that you must continue to keep whatever you've learned about Mr. Sinclair's activities completely confidential."

Bostwick waited until he was sure that he was expected to respond. "Yes, sir. I understand."

"Very well." Updegraff leaned back. "I mentioned before that your efforts merit an increase in salary."

Yes, Bostwick recalled, but he hadn't been given one.

"As of next week," Updegraff went on, "you will be at fifteen dollars a week. A rather generous increase, if you ask me."

"It is indeed, sir!" From eleven to fifteen dollars a week was more than Bostwick could have imagined. "Thank you!"

Updegraff jerked his head at the door, indicating that Bostwick's presence was no longer wanted. He left, both happy and perplexed. The boss had looked as if he were about to fire him, yet the result was the complete opposite.

By the time Bostwick reached his desk, he still couldn't understand the contrast between Updegraff's angry demeanor and generous act, but his thoughts were starting to drift to the consequences of the raise. He would be able to do a lot with the extra four dollars a week.

"Bostwick! Telephone!"

He looked back at Jeffrey Kutner, who was in charge of the accountants on the main floor. "Me?" No one ever telephoned for Bostwick.

"Yes! Hurry up," Kutner barked. "We need to keep the line open for *important* calls."

Bostwick hurried to Kutner's desk and took the receiver. "This is Nicholas Bostwick."

The voice on the other end said, "It's Marshall Webb. Sorry to bother you at work, but I was hoping you could tell me about this Fire Island business."

"What?" Bostwick didn't know what the writer was talking about.

"The newspapers are reporting that the State of New York is buying Fire Island—and that it's buying it *from* Jacob Updegraff. Do you know anything about that?"

"No, I'm sorry, I don't."

"Do you think you could check? I'd like to know when Updegraff purchased the island."

That was a request Bostwick couldn't agree to. He hadn't minded sharing what he knew about Lyman Sinclair with the writer, but to inquire about his own boss seemed disloyal. "I'm afraid that wouldn't be possible," he answered emphatically.

CHAPTER 27

Marshall Webb would have preferred to be making the long, slow journey in the company of Rebecca Davies. But Rebecca couldn't get away from her duties at Colden House, and this wasn't a pleasure outing anyway, so Webb traveled alone.

Rebecca was in his thoughts, however. Webb hadn't realized until she'd left his apartment how tired and worried she had looked. Whenever he was with her, he thought only how much he enjoyed seeing her and how much he was coming to care for her; he tended not to notice when her eyes were red or her expression careworn. He knew that Rebecca already had enough on her mind with the problems at Colden House, and the added worry about her sister, Alice, seemed to be wearing her down even further. Webb hoped that he might learn something today that would alleviate some of Rebecca's concerns and put her mind at ease.

From time to time, Webb looked out the train window and considered how pleasant it would be a few months from now, at the beginning of summer, when a trip to the beach would be a welcome reprieve from the city's streets, and Rebecca and he could take it together.

Most of Webb's forty-mile journey was spent on the Long Island Railroad, which carried him through Brooklyn and all the way southeast to Babylon, Long Island. From there, he caught a small steam ferry that took him across Great South Bay to Fire Island.

The sandy barrier island, which was thirty miles long but not more than half a mile across at its widest point, ran west to east below the southern shore of Long Island, separated from it by the waters of Great South Bay. Most of Fire Island, which was covered by small groves of pitch pine and high thickets in its sheltered areas, and stretches of beach grass and low shrubs along the Atlantic shoreline, was completely uninhabited except by white-tailed deer, rabbits, foxes, and shore birds.

The only signs of civilization were at the western end of the island, where the ferry dropped him off. Rising high above the sandy beach at the westernmost point was the landmark red-and-white-striped lighthouse, which had provided a warning beacon to sailors for most of the century. Just inland from the lighthouse was the island's largest building, the Surf Hotel, which in August of last year had become the temporary home of five hundred immigrants being quarantined by the State of New York.

Webb made his way on foot along a narrow dirt path to the hotel, a sprawling, three-story frame dwelling with covered pathways that led to nearby cottages. The hotel and the cottages all showed the ravages of time. Much of the wood was weather-beaten and bare of paint, some of the shutters were crooked and barely hanging on their window frames, and quite a few shingles were missing from the sloping roofs.

The grounds of the Surf Hotel looked deserted, and Webb feared that his journey might have been in vain. It was a risk he'd had to take, however; the island had no electricity or telephone service—isolation was an attractive feature for New Yorkers who wanted to get away from the bustle of the city—so he couldn't have called ahead.

Webb first walked up the creaking front steps of the hotel to find the door locked. Looking through the windows, he saw no sign of life inside; there were no curtains on the windows, he noticed, and the furniture had been removed from the lobby. He then went out back to find the rear door also secured. It wasn't until he checked the outer buildings that he found Eric Christensen carrying a wicker chair from one of the cottages.

"Mr. Christensen!" he called.

The hotel's former proprietor put down the chair with a grunt. "I know you?"

"My name's Marshall Webb. I spoke with you last fall, back when your hotel was being used for the quarantine."

Christensen, a trim, tanned man with iron gray hair and close-cropped side-whiskers, clapped his hands together to brush off the dirt. "What a hell of a time that was," he said. "But at least it still *was* my hotel." He squinted at Webb. "You're that writer fellow."

"Yes. I'm with *Harper's.*" When he'd spoken with the hotel owner last year, he had never told him that his inquiries were actually for use in a dime novel. "I saw that you're in the news again. I read that the state is buying the entire island."

Christensen sat down in the chair and sighed. "Not from me. I'm not getting a cent of that state money."

Webb already knew that. Yesterday he had gone to Brooklyn, where the King's County records were kept, and learned from a tax clerk that Jacob Updegraff had bought the property from Christensen less than two weeks ago. "It doesn't seem fair," Webb said. "After all that you were put through last year—losing all your paying guests so that the state could bring in those immigrants—you should have gotten some compensation."

"Not a penny," Christensen said wistfully. He looked around the grounds. "I know the place isn't what it used to be, but what can you expect of buildings that were put up before the war? And my old guests were probably never coming back anyway—everyone's terrified that the immigrants left the hotel infected with cholera somehow. I hardly had a dozen guests all winter—and they only stayed in the cottages, because they hadn't been used during the quarantine." He sighed again. "Like I said, the hotel isn't much, but I used to own a hundred twenty acres of this damn island. Between the land and the buildings, I should have gotten something."

"You got something from Jacob Updegraff, didn't you?" Webb said. "He bought it from you."

Christensen spat on the ground. "Fifteen thousand dollars. And a week later, he gets two hundred, ten thousand from the state. Made himself a handsome profit, didn't he?" He shook his head. "Should have been me getting that money."

"Why wasn't it? How did Jacob Updegraff come to buy the hotel from you?"

Christensen didn't answer for a while. Then he pointed to a nearby cottage, which had a window shade flapping in a broken window. "There's another chair in there. Why don't you go get it for yourself?"

Webb did that. He placed it next to Christensen's and sat down. "When did you decide to sell the place?" he asked.

"When I decided I wanted to keep breathing."

"You mean Updegraff threatened you?" Webb couldn't imagine the banker getting violent.

"Hell, I never even met Jacob Updegraff. A few men who called themselves 'associates' of his came by to see me." He snorted. " 'Associates,' hell—they were nothing but New York street thugs. They *told* me I was going to sell my property to Updegraff. And they said I should be grateful that he was paying me anything for it."

"So you agreed to sell."

"Hell, no! I told them exactly where they could go, and what they could do to themselves when they got there."

"And?"

"They left. They went to see the Lamonettins, an older couple who own a cottage and about ten acres just east of my property."

"Did the Lamonettins agree to sell their land?"

"Not at first. But a couple of days later, Mrs. Lamonettin did. Her husband was no longer in a position to object—he was found on the shore, beaten to death." He shook his head. "Tom Lamonettin was one of the kindest men I've ever known—never hurt a soul. In fact, he and his wife were always taking in injured birds and rabbits and trying to nurse them back to health." Christensen's jaw clenched. "Lousy bastards didn't even wait for Mrs. Lamonettin to give her husband a funeral before they came back with papers for her to sign."

Webb was shocked. He never imagined that Jacob Updegraff would be involved in cold-blooded murder. When he recovered from the news enough to speak, he asked, "The police didn't go after the men who killed him?"

"Sheriff came over from West Islip. But there were no witnesses and no real evidence. The sheriff said it could have been coincidence that Mr. Lamonettin was killed just after refusing to sell his property."

"But you don't believe that."

"No. I've been able to add two plus two since I was in knee pants. I knew what the deal was. So when they came back to see me, I signed the papers, too. Hell, at least I'm alive and I got some money for the old place." He looked around again. "I figure I'll try to buy a small place in Jersey—Atlantic City, maybe—and start up again. They didn't even care about keeping the furnishings; that's why I've been clearing them out a little at a time and having them ferried to the mainland. Them bastards must have had some advance word about the state buying the island. All they wanted it for was to turn a quick profit."

"You said you never met Jacob Updegraff, so he wasn't one of the men who came here."

"No, just his damn 'associates.' "

"Did they give their names?"

Christensen shook his head. "They didn't say much at all. Just told me to sell."

"Could you identify them?"

"I *could*, sure. But I don't *want* to. I don't ever want to see those plug-uglies again." He looked at Webb with a touch of fear in his eyes. "Hey, I really shouldn't be saying anything about this at all. I've just been steamed at the way they made their deal."

Webb assured Christensen that he would try to keep what he'd revealed confidential. Then he asked, "How many were there?"

"Three. An older one, about my age, and a couple more in their twenties, I'd guess. All three of them were big bruisers." He looked at Webb. "What kind of men kill over a little plot of land?"

Webb shook his head. "It wasn't the land they were after. They wanted the money." Webb wondered what percentage they earned for getting the land signed over to Updegraff.

"Oh, one of them did mention a name," Christensen remembered. "One of the younger men, a fellow with red hair and a broken nose, called the older one 'Rabbit.' "

That name was a familiar one to Marshall Webb. But could it have been Rabbit Doyle? He didn't believe that Jacob Updegraff would have any association with a man like Doyle. But then, this entire business about Updegraff and Fire Island had come as a most disturbing surprise.

CHAPTER 28

Nicholas Bostwick felt that he had been a bit more abrupt than he'd intended when he had last spoken with Marshall Webb on the telephone. Of course, it had been difficult for him to speak openly at the bank, with Jeffrey Kutner hovering next to him, but Bostwick still regretted having been so terse and wanted to apologize. Besides, he had come to a decision and wanted to tell Webb about it in person.

The writer answered his knock and greeted him with a smile. "Come in, Mr. Bostwick."

"Thank you." Bostwick took off his derby and stepped inside Webb's apartment. "I'll only take a moment."

"Drink?"

"No, thank you." Webb motioned to the sofa, but Bostwick declined that as well. "I shan't be staying long." He began to turn the brim of his hat slowly around in his hands. "I'm sorry I wasn't able to be of any help when you telephoned the other day."

"No need for apology," Webb said. "I shouldn't have bothered you at work. I know Mr. Updegraff must keep you busy."

"Well, the thing is . . ." Bostwick tried to find a way to say what he had come to tell him. "The fact is, Mr. Updegraff has terminated my assignment regarding Mr. Sinclair's finances."

"You've been fired?" Webb frowned. "I *am* sorry to hear that. I hope it wasn't because—"

"No, no. *I* wasn't terminated," Bostwick quickly corrected. "Only the assignment." He couldn't help but add with pride, "As a matter of fact, Mr. Updegraff was quite pleased with my work. He's given me a rather substantial increase in pay."

"Congratulations! I'm sure it was well deserved." Webb looked as though he was genuinely happy for him.

"Thank you." Bostwick shifted his weight from one leg to the other. "However, that means I will no longer be able to be of any assistance to you. Mr. Updegraff made it emphatically clear that all of my work on the Sinclair matter is concluded."

"I see." Webb appeared thoughtful. "Do you think that may be because Mr. Updegraff fears you might be close to uncovering something that he doesn't want revealed?"

Bostwick was momentarily speechless. "I don't know." He honestly hadn't considered that possibility; he'd been too busy thinking about all he could do with the increase in salary. "But it doesn't matter *why* he wants me to stop looking into Mr. Sinclair's affairs. I work for Mr. Updegraff, and whether he gives me an assignment or takes one away, I am compelled to follow his instruction." He decided to reveal to Webb something of a personal nature, and again, it was in large part out of pride. "The fact is, I cannot afford to lose my position at the bank. I've recently been calling on Miss Liesl Schulmerich, Lyman Sinclair's sister. And of course, I cannot court a young lady if I am without gainful employment."

"I understand."

Bostwick had thought he would. A man could explain any act, no matter how irrational, by saying that it was to woo a woman, and any other man would accept the explanation. He offered his hand. "I have enjoyed our conversations, Mr. Webb. And if you should ever like to stop by the barbershop to do some singing, you would be most welcome."

Webb shook his hand firmly and promised that he would take him up on that offer sometime. The last thing he said was, "Best of luck with Miss Shulmerich."

Bostwick then left to catch a streetcar for Flatbush.

Before letting Bostwick leave, Webb had considered asking him whether Jacob Updegraff had mentioned anything about the Fire Island purchase. It was clear the question would have gone unanswered, though; Bostwick was obviously loyal to his employer and unlikely to betray a confidence.

Webb had also considered inviting Bostwick to join him in visiting Benjamin Freese. He thought that both of them might be able to learn something useful from Freese. But the accountant had made it plain that he intended to comply with Updegraff's orders and end his inquiries into Lyman Sinclair's finances. Webb still thought he might be able to learn something from Freese, however. There were a couple of coincidences that led him to believe there might be some connection between Freese and Updegraff. Webb wanted to know if it was some business deal with Freese that had made Jacob Updegraff so angry lately and had caused Rebecca Davies to become so worried about her sister's well-being.

After a light lunch Thursday afternoon, Webb struck off by himself to pay a call on the reclusive financier. Since it was a glorious spring day, with soft sunshine and mild winds that seemed to blow clean the city's air, he elected to walk.

As he strolled through Union Square and along Broadway, Webb reviewed what he knew of Benjamin Freese. He had made some inquires about the man, speaking with a couple of *Harper's* writers, among others. What he'd learned was that Freese was a maverick, not active in any clubs, charities, or fraternal organizations, and was apparently disinterested in politics. The solitude was not entirely self-imposed—the "better" elements of New York society excluded him because of his humble beginnings and lack of social graces. Now, working from an office in his home, Freese seemed to relish his notoriety as a hard-nosed individualist who managed to do much better for himself working outside the system than the insiders were able to do from within.

By the time he turned onto the broad sidewalk of Fifth Avenue, Webb's thoughts had turned to the strange coincidences that had lately occurred, and he sought a link to make sense of them. It seemed odd to him that Benjamin Freese, who initially made a great deal of money by investing in a railroad with Lyman Sinclair, subsequently suffered a failure after buying control of that same railroad. Meanwhile, Jacob Updegraff, whose bank suffered losses due to Sinclair's theft, managed to make a profit of almost two hundred thousand dollars by selling an island that he hadn't even owned until a week before the state decided to purchase the land. Were Freese and Updegraff somehow connected together through the deceased Lyman Sinclair? Webb wondered.

Webb reached the stately Freese mansion, on Fifth Avenue just north of Madison Square Park, still unclear on how recent events had transpired. He was especially perplexed by the Fire Island deal that had brought about the death of one of the landowners—it didn't seem like anything Jacob Updegraff would be involved with, but the banker had been the one to profit from its sale. Webb wasn't sure if Benjamin Freese could provide him with any answers, but he intended to ask the questions.

Freese's home was a splendid three-story structure of white marble and yellow brick, with a colonnade that gave the impression of a bank or government building. At the double-doored entrance, Webb pulled the cord of what he assumed was a doorbell, but he heard no sound from inside.

The bell must have worked, because a stiff old butler in a stiff old suit promptly opened the door. "Can I help you, sir?"

"Yes, my name is Marshall Webb. I'm here to see Mr. Freese." He presented his *Harper's Weekly* card. "I telephoned this morning to make an appointment."

The butler didn't touch the card. Instead, he reached for a silver salver from a table near the door and held it out for Webb to place his card on it. "One moment, sir." He left Webb waiting outside and closed the door in his face. Apparently, Benjamin Freese's disregard for social courtesies had been adopted by his servants as well, Webb thought.

It was some time before the butler returned. He opened the door and held out the salver, offering Webb his card back. "Mr. Freese's secretary confirms that you did indeed call to make an appointment, but he says your request was denied. I'm sorry, sir." He pushed the salver out as if trying to push Webb away.

"That's true—Mr. Freese did decline to see me when I phoned." Webb left the card on the tray. "But I hoped that if I came in person, he might change his mind. It is a matter of some importance."

The butler hesitated. "Very well, sir." He opened the door wider. "You may wait in the foyer while I convey your request."

"Thank you." Webb stepped inside the wide hall and remained there while the butler headed for a curving staircase. He looked around the place, astonished at how much furniture and artwork had been crammed into the house. There were Greek statues, Persian rugs, Chippendale chairs, and Louis the Fourteenth tables. Individually, each piece was magnificent, but collectively, there was no stylistic theme or order. Altogether, it appeared as if the items had been accumulated rather than collected or designed, and the place looked not like a museum but more like a museum's storage room. It occurred to Webb that his editor at *Harper's*, Harry M. Hargis, would have been quite envious of the Freese home.

When the butler returned, his face had the first emotion on it that Webb had seen; it was a look of bewilderment. "Mr. Freese will see you," he said. "This way, sir."

Webb was led to a second-floor den that was as rich in furnishings as the rooms downstairs, but more consistent in its decor. It had the appearance of an English hunting lodge, with a beamed ceiling, bearskins on the parquet floor, and the mounted heads of a dozen animals hanging among the guns and swords that adorned the paneled walls.

At one end of the room, behind a broad walnut desk that was almost barren of papers, sat a barrel-chested man in a chocolate brown business suit with a gold silk vest. He shifted a massive bulge in his left cheek with his tongue. "Mr. Webb," he said in a raspy voice. "I admire your persistence. You have five minutes." He nodded at the butler, who silently exited, leaving the two of them alone.

"Thank you, Mr. Freese." Webb glanced at a carved Dante chair facing the desk; receiving a nod from Freese, he sat down and briefly studied his host.

Benjamin Freese looked like a human battering ram who'd used his head for that purpose a few times too often. The man had no visible neck, which was partly because Freese's square head seemed to emerge directly from his shoulders, and partly because his bushy spade beard obscured everything below his chin. Unlike his reddish hair, which was well on its way to turning gray, Freese's deep-set eyes showed no sign of fading; they were glossy black and probing.

"Let me save you some time, Mr. Webb." Freese spat into a brass cuspidor next to the desk. "I won't speak with you on the record. The press has treated me rather shabbily over the years; therefore, I do not give interviews. Whatever I say is *not* to appear in print. Do you understand?"

"Yes," Webb answered. "But one thing I don't understand: *why* has the press been so unkind to you?"

Freese chuckled. "That's a question that would be better answered by the newspaper editors, not by me." He propped his elbows on his desk and tented his fingers. "But I believe they simply do not approve of my rather humble origins. I'm no foreigner, I'll have you know." He shot a look at Webb as if he had just accused the financier of being such. "I was born right here in New York. But not on Fifth Avenue; I grew up in Five Points, and that's too humble for the society swells in this city."

"You have my word," Webb said. "I won't publish anything you tell me. Actually, I'm here because you are considered one of the best financial minds in the city." He noted that Freese appeared pleased at the compliment. "My editor is thinking of publishing some articles on the growing financial panic. I must confess"—Webb smiled—"although I did *not* confess it to my editor, that I'm largely ignorant of affairs of business. I was hoping you could enlighten me on a couple of matters."

"If I can," Freese agreed, nodding. "But remember, I don't operate out of a fancy bank with a staff of bookkeepers and accountants to tell me how to do business. I rely on my wits."

"I've heard that your wits are quite sharp," Webb said.

"You've heard correctly." Freese spat again. "Tell me: What is it you want to know?"

"There have been a number of important commercial concerns that have recently failed: banks, manufacturers, railroads, along with dozens of small businesses. What I'd like to understand is how they can go from prosperity from bankruptcy so quickly."

Freese leaned back in his thronelike chair. "For many of them it *hasn't* been quick. Some have been floundering for some time, and the current shortage of capital is merely the final blow."

"What about the Western Continental Railroad?" Webb asked. "About a year ago, you invested in that concern with a Mr. Lyman Sinclair of the New Amsterdam Trust Company, and you earned quite a handsome return on your investment. How—"

"Where did you hear that?" Freese rasped.

Webb didn't want to betray Nicholas Bostwick's confidence. "From one of my editors," he lied. "Apparently, Mr. Sinclair wasn't very discreet when it came to discussing his clients' investments. He often mentioned the names of his successful investors, such as yourself, in order to attract additional clients."

Freese's only response was a grunt.

"But recently," Webb went on, "you bought controlling interest in the railroad only to go bankrupt two weeks later. It must have cost you a great deal of money to purchase Western Continental, and it is now worth nothing. My question again is, how can there be such a change of fortune in such a short amount of time?"

It was several moments before Freese responded in words, but his skin began to take on the same shade of red as his whiskers. "I must say that I find it rather impudent of you to ask about my personal business." Webb could tell that by the tone of his voice. "In a general sense, however, I will say that an investor can only make judgments based on the best information he has available to him at the time. Sometimes, that information is not complete."

"So you're saying Lyman Sinclair misled you?"

The rasp in Freese's voice became a low growl. "I said nothing of the kind. Mr. Webb, you're reminding me why I do not speak to the press. Your five minutes is up."

Webb decided to risk one more question. "Did Mr. Sinclair also mislead you about his interest in Miss Dolores Tenison?"

Freese's beard quivered, and his eyes narrowed to the point where they were barely visible. *"What,* exactly, do you mean by that, Mr. Webb?"

"Oh, I assumed you knew. Lyman Sinclair was calling on Miss Tenison and giving her quite a few presents—jewels, mostly. Isn't Miss Tenison *your,* uh, friend?"

"I knew of no such thing. And yes, Miss Tenison is a very dear friend of mine—and I expect she shall remain so." He continued to drill Webb with his eyes. "You see, when something becomes mine, it remains mine until I decide to part with it."

He hadn't denied his relationship with the actress, but then Webb didn't think that he would. Judging by all the objets d'art cluttering his home, Benjamin Freese liked to flaunt his possessions. And from the words he'd just spoken, that was exactly what he considered Miss Tenison to be: a possession, something to keep and flaunt as a trophy.

"Our conversation is concluded," Freese reminded him.

Webb stood. "Thank you for your time." Before he reached the door, he turned back and added, "By the way, I come from Five Points, too. I was born in a tenement called the Gates of Hell, on Little Water Street." None of those existed anymore, the tenements having been razed and Little Water Street paved over.

CHAPTER 29

It was a sound that Rebecca Davies had come to dread: a late-night knock at the door. It usually signaled either a girl needing a place to stay—and by this time of night Colden House was almost always at capacity—or a husband or father looking to take back a girl who'd fled an abusive home. Sometimes the knocking was produced by a police officer looking for a "suspect" in a local crime—no such suspects were ever found, but crude patrolmen seemed to think it great fun to roust the sleeping residents of Colden House. By now, Rebecca had learned to distinguish between the sharp rap of a nightstick, the pounding of an angry husband, and the tentative knock of a girl needing shelter; the sound of this one was the last, she thought.

It was with some pleasant surprise that Rebecca opened the door to see Sarah Zietlow, the young woman who had come to her just a couple of months ago suffering the symptoms of poisoning. She looked better than Rebecca had ever seen her. Unfortunately, the petite dark-haired woman next to her looked close to death.

"Do you remember me, Miss Davies?"

"Of course, Sarah. Please come in. Who's your friend?"

"This is Melissa Ostertag. I'm so sorry to bother you, but Melissa has the same thing I did. And there was no place else I could take her."

Miss Ostertag, keeping her eyes directed downward, mumbled, "Good evening, ma'am." She wasn't much older than Sarah, Rebecca thought, but her young life had clearly been a hard one, evidenced by scars on her lips and chin and an odd bend to her elbow where it may have once been broken and not healed properly.

"Come in. Come in." She saw that Miss Ostertag certainly had the same symptoms that Sarah had had: jaundiced skin, loss of hair, emaciated body. "Let's get you upstairs."

Rebecca took one of Miss Ostertag's arms and led the two young women up to the infirmary. The "infirmary" differed from a small bedroom primarily in that almost everything in the room was painted white, and it had a cabinet in which Rebecca kept some basic medical supplies.

At Rebecca's urging, Miss Ostertag lay down on the iron-rail bed. She immediately curled up, clutching her stomach. "I got a real bad belly pain," she said through clenched teeth that had had little dental care.

"See ma'am? Same as what I had," said Sarah.

Rebecca was concerned about Miss Ostertag's condition, but since Sarah Zietlow had gone through it and was now healthy, she believed that Miss Ostertag would soon recover too. Remembering Doc Abraham's advice, Rebecca told the dark-haired girl, "We'll get you some milk. See if you can keep it down." To Sarah, she said, "Come with me."

"I hate to leave Melissa alone, ma'am."

"We're only going to the kitchen. We'll be right back."

Downstairs, Rebecca was happy to find that there was still enough milk in the icebox to fill half a glass for Miss Ostertag. As she poured, she said to Sarah, "You told me when you were sick that it was your 'own doing.'" There was no tactful way to say it, so Rebecca simply asked, "Is that what Miss Ostertag did, too—did she try to poison herself?"

Sarah Zietlow's jaw dropped. "Oh, no, ma'am! Is that what you thought I meant? No! I only meant . . ." She drew a deep breath. "I meant that I brought it on myself—as punishment. I was living on stolen food for a while—I just couldn't afford to buy any and I would never sell myself to get the money. So I figured the sickness was to punish me for stealing."

"And Miss Ostertag has been doing the same thing?"

"No, ma'am. She used to work where they make it: Fluitt and Schlichting Confectioners. They make candy—lots of different kinds—and Melissa's worked for them for almost five years. I worked there, too, for a while, and that's how Melissa and me got to be friends. But I got fired." Miss Zietlow looked up at Rebecca.

"I didn't do nothing wrong, ma'am; it's just business was slow, they said. Anyway, after I had to start living on the streets, Melissa would bring me candy almost every night. I'd have starved if she hadn't. Please, ma'am, can Melissa stay the night? She got fired last month—they said she wasn't working fast enough anymore, but it's only because she was feeling so sickly. And then she got evicted from her boardinghouse when she couldn't pay the rent. She don't got no one else to care for her."

"Yes, of course she can stay. And tomorrow, we'll take her to Dr. Abraham." She headed back to the stairs.

"I can pay for the doctor, ma'am. I been working in the lunchroom regular and tomorrow is payday."

Rebecca was impressed with the offer; Sarah Zietlow had just started to get back on her own feet, and here she was willing to help someone else in need. "We'll worry about that tomorrow."

Miss Zietlow also insisted on sitting with her friend through the night, so Rebecca left the two of them together with instructions to call her immediately if Miss Ostertag got any worse.

"It never seems to end, does it?" Webb said after Rebecca told him the story over lunch. It was a late lunch, so late that there were few other customers in the Greenwich Street café, and the two of them were free to speak without being overheard.

"No, it doesn't," said Rebecca. "All I can do is hope that Miss Ostertag will soon be as healthy as Sarah Zietlow is again." She put down her fork. "Miss Zietlow did insist on going to pick up her pay from the luncheonette, and then she came back to Doc Abraham to take care of her friend's bill."

"He's certain that Miss Ostertag will recover?"

"Not certain. All he would say is that he's 'hopeful.' I'm going to take her to Columbus Hospital; they can do some tests to see if it really is arsenic poisoning, as Dr. Abraham suspects."

"I hope she'll be all right." Webb had hardly touched his food, or even his utensils. He continued to make interlocking condensation rings on the tabletop with his water glass.

Rebecca must have noticed. "What is it?" she asked. "You've been distracted ever since you picked me up."

Webb thought for a moment. He hadn't figured out a good way to tell her about Jacob Updegraff's business on Fire Island. "It's about your brother-in-law," he said, deciding just to spit it out and get it over with. "I may have found out what he meant about being involved in a matter of 'life-and-death.' "

"What's that?" Rebecca visibly braced herself for the news.

"When he wanted to buy Fire Island, the owners didn't want to sell. In fact, they refused to sell—until one of them, who owned only a small piece of property, was murdered."

Rebecca gasped. "And you think—"

Webb held up his hand and went on. "That convinced the man's widow to sell. It also convinced Eric Christensen, who owned the Surf Hotel and most of the island's west end. He signed his property over to your brother-in-law for fifteen thousand dollars."

"I can't believe that."

"It's true. I checked with the tax clerk, and I saw the papers." Webb added, "But there is some question about exactly how much Updegraff was involved—Christensen says he never talked to him personally, never even met him."

"Then whom *did* he speak with?"

"Three thugs. I think I know who they are, and I can't imagine how your brother-in-law would know them." Webb was sure they were the three men he'd met in the Lucky Star Saloon, and the same three that Craig Rettew had encountered at the polling booth. Eric Christensen had mentioned that the red-haired young man who'd been to see him had a broken nose, and Rettew had given Brick Fessler a broken nose while trying to defend himself on election night. Between that similarity and Rabbit's being the older man of the three in each case, Webb thought there couldn't be another trio in New York to match those descriptions.

"So maybe Mr. Updegraff had nothing to do with that man's death." Rebecca shuddered. "Alice would be devastated if he did."

"That's possible. But he must have known about it, at least— why else his 'life and death' comment?"

Rebecca shook her head. "I don't know."

"I'd like to talk to your brother-in-law and ask him directly what he's been doing."

"Well, perhaps that's the best thing to do. He won't tell Alice anything, and he certainly wouldn't tell me."

Webb said, "There's only one problem: If I come to him with questions like this, he'll just throw me out of his bank."

Rebecca considered that. "He'd throw you out of his house, too." She brightened. "But not my parents' house. Why don't you come to dinner this Sunday? We haven't been for a while, anyway. You can talk to him after dinner, and there's nothing he can do to stop you."

Dinner with Rebecca's family wasn't something Webb particularly wanted to endure, but it could be his only chance to talk with Jacob Updegraff. He agreed and tried to appear as if he would be looking forward to it.

CHAPTER 30

As always, the food prepared by the Davieses' cook was excellent. From the first course, of terrapin soup, to the roast pheasant, to the dessert of almond cheesecake, the dishes were as tasty as anything prepared in Delmonico's Restaurant. The table conversation, however, was as enjoyable as listening to the drip of a leaking faucet.

Dinner at the Davies home was always a trying affair for Marshall Webb. Striving to endure the company of Rebecca's pompous family, he adopted his most polite smile and used it in response to almost anything that was said to him. It came into service once when Rebecca's aunt hinted that she hoped there would soon be a marriage in the family; he used it several times, augmented by occasional nods, when Rebecca's father repeated interminable "humorous" stories that he'd heard at the Union Club; and he used the smile to save himself whenever his attention strayed and he found himself having to answer a question that he couldn't remember hearing. The only time his smile was genuine was when he caught Rebecca's eye and the two of them were able to share a look of commiseration.

At the conclusion of the dinner, the ladies adjourned to the music room and Webb followed Mr. Davies and Jacob Updegraff into the library for the customary brandy and cigars.

Updegraff, who hadn't spoken a word to Webb throughout the meal, continued his silence as he poured three snifters of cognac and held out a cedar cigar box. Webb and Mr. Davies each took one of the fragrant dark cigars.

Rebecca's cotton-haired father asked, "Have you learned to play chess yet, Mr. Webb?"

"I'm sorry, I haven't," Webb lied. The meal was dreary enough; he didn't want to test the limit of his tolerance for boredom by following that ordeal with a chess game.

Mr. Davies cast a wistful glance at the chessboard. "Oh, I'm sorry to hear that. There's nothing like chess to exercise the mind."

Or to numb it, thought Webb. "Actually, I was hoping I might have a word with Mr. Updegraff," he said.

Mr. Davies waved his cigar. "By all means." He then ambled over to a corner chair, where he sat down and amused himself by blowing smoke rings. He smiled like a child every time he succeeded in shooting a small ring through a larger one.

Updegraff did not look pleased that Rebecca's father had given them leave to talk between themselves, but he sat down in one of a pair of wing chairs and Webb took the one next to him.

Webb drew on his cigar, then paused to remove a piece of tobacco from his tongue. He rarely smoked, but did so on occasion primarily to see if he could figure out the appeal of the habit. "I wanted to congratulate you," he said to Updegraff. "I read about Governor Flower buying Fire Island. The state is going to be paying you quite a nice sum."

"Thank you," the banker said grudgingly. "But I would have preferred that the newspapers kept my name out of their reports." He shot Webb a sidelong glance. "I believe that one's personal finances are a private matter. I do not discuss them."

Webb chose to ignore the pointed hint. "So it was your own money, not the bank's, that you used to buy the island?"

"That's really not your concern, is it?"

"Well, it could be." Webb puffed away at the cigar. "You remember when we spoke at your club? I told you that what I choose to write depends on what information I have."

Updegraff smiled smugly. "I don't believe you have *any* information that could be of concern to me."

"I didn't get any from your Mr. Bostwick, that's for sure," Webb said, trying to sound disappointed. "He even told me that he was no longer looking into Lyman Sinclair's accounts, and that there was to be no more communication between us."

"That's true. The matter is closed." Updegraff was almost beaming. Webb was certain that the accountant's position at the bank was now secure, and he was happy to give Updegraff the impression that Bostwick had revealed nothing to him.

Webb went on, "I suppose with all the money you'll be getting from the state, there's no need to look for whatever Sinclair might have, uh, misplaced." He sipped his cognac, which helped kill the smoky taste in his mouth. "By the way, will Rebecca be getting her investment back?"

Updegraff, keeping his own eyes directed at the end of his cigar, answered coldly, "Miss Davies purchased stock in the Western Continental Railroad. That venture went bankrupt. Its stockholders are entitled to nothing."

"That's awfully convenient, isn't it?"

"What do you mean?"

"Well, let's say somebody gives Mr. Sinclair money to buy stock in the railroad. But instead of investing the money, he uses it for other purposes—his own, perhaps. Once the railroad goes bankrupt, there's no reason to look into what Sinclair really did with the money, is there? The investor is simply told his stock is worthless." Webb nodded. "Very convenient."

"You're talking nonsense." Updegraff drained half his snifter in a gulp. "Bankruptcies occur all the time—especially in hard times like these. That's a risk every investor has to accept."

"But you don't take risks yourself."

"*Every* investment has some risk associated with it."

"Not your Fire Island purchase," Webb said. "There was no risk in it for *you*, at least. You made *certain* that you'd come out ahead on that deal." He looked at the banker. "You sent some thugs to the island to convince the owners to sell their land cheap, and they even killed an old man named Tom Lamonettin in order to clinch the deal for you."

Updegraff began to breathe heavily. "You don't know what you're talking about. I would never be involved in any such thing."

"On the contrary," replied Webb. "I know exactly what I'm talking about—I've been to the island. When I'm working on a story, I do my research. Tell me, how do you happen to know a man like Rabbit Doyle? I don't expect he's a member of the Union Club."

"I don't know anyone by that name." Updegraff was clearly so shaken that by now Webb couldn't determine whether he was telling the truth or not. The banker turned to Webb and fixed his angry eyes upon him. "And the last thing I'm going to say to you is: damn you and your goddamn story. You put my name in print and I'll sue you for libel."

Webb said calmly, "Then I have only two things to say to you. One: the truth is a perfectly adequate defense in a libel suit, and I will only write what I know to be true. Two: before you try bringing me into civil court, you'd better make sure you can clear yourself in criminal court first."

"Bah! I've committed no crimes."

"The police might feel differently. A man was murdered so that *you* could make a killing in a real estate deal. And whether or not you ever go to jail for it, you're never going to be able to escape that truth."

Updegraff chomped into the end of his cigar and carried through on his vow to say nothing more to Marshall Webb.

CHAPTER 31

Old Doc Abraham came out of his examination room rubbing his hands on his frayed black frock coat. "I'm sorry to keep you waiting, Miss Davies. I have a patient who wasn't quite as proficient with a skinning knife as he thought he was. The darned fool went to work drunk, and a slaughterhouse is no place for drunks." He smiled, causing the wrinkles on his upper lip to fan out. "But I've got him all stitched up again."

Rebecca tried not to look at the fresh blood splattered on the doctor's coat. "The wait was no trouble at all. I just came by to find out if you've gotten the test results from the hospital yet." She noticed that there was also a bloody smudge on the doctor's fringe of white chin whiskers, and vowed never to bring one of her girls to Abraham for surgery—at least not until he began working in cleaner conditions.

"Yes. I heard from Columbus this morning. The tests on Miss Ostertag's hair were positive for arsenic, as I suspected." A small smile of satisfaction twitched the corners of his mouth; he was apparently pleased that his diagnosis had been proved correct. He then asked in his soft voice, "Does she know who might have poisoned her?"

"She believes it was in some candy that she made," Rebecca answered. "Sarah Zietlow ate quite a bit of the same candy, which must be how she was poisoned, too."

Abraham frowned. "Candy? What kind?"

"I don't know." Nor could Rebecca fathom what difference the type of candy could possibly make. "It was made at Fluitt and Schlichting Confectioners. Miss Ostertag worked there, and she'd been giving candy to Miss Zietlow for some time."

"Gum drops?" the doctor asked. "Sour balls? Lollipops? Chocolate? What was it?"

"I really don't know."

"It would help to find out." The doctor tugged at his beard, leaving a few more bloody smudges. "Some of the candy makers use colorings that contain arsenic."

"Arsenic? In *candy?*" That made no sense to Rebecca. "But children eat candy."

"Exactly," Abraham said, as if the logic was obvious. "And the candy manufacturers want to make sure their wares are attractive to children, so they put chemicals in the mix that give them pretty, bright colors. There probably isn't enough arsenic in the candy to do much harm unless someone eats a lot of it at a time, though."

Just as Sarah Zietlow had done, thought Rebecca. The unfortunate young woman had practically been living on the candies that Melissa Ostertag had been giving her. Miss Ostertag had been working with the chemicals and eating the candy every day, too. "I'll see if I can find out what kind it was," Rebecca said. She reached for her purse. "I know Miss Zietlow paid you for Miss Ostertag's visit. But I believe I still owe you for a couple of girls who came to see you last month."

"No, you don't," the doctor replied. "Miss Zietlow came back and paid off your entire bill."

"She did?" Rebecca didn't want the young woman to be spending all of her hard-earned money helping girls that Colden House should be taking care of. "Well, I'm going to pay her back, then."

Doc Abraham coughed. "I know it's none of my business, Miss Davies, but I suggest you don't do that." A warm smile came over his wizened face. "You should have seen Miss Zietlow—she was so proud at being able to pay the bill. She's grateful to you for helping her, and she's determined to do the same for others. You know, there aren't many folks willing to give of themselves, and I don't think you should discourage her. It made her feel good about herself, Miss Davies."

Rebecca thanked him for his help and his advice. She left, thinking that he was probably right.

The New York City Health Department, housed in a nondescript brick office building on the northwest corner of Mott Street and Houston, had more rooms and corridors than Rebecca Davies had imagined. And she'd already spent a good part of the afternoon going from one office to another without finding anyone who could—or would—help her.

So Rebecca wandered from office to office, patiently being kept waiting at each one until some petty bureaucrat told her to try elsewhere. The Health Department had numerous inspectors listed on its directory; some were in charge of investigating contagious diseases, others were responsible for ventilation and plumbing systems, and some were supposed to resolve sanitation problems. But there was no one willing to take a report on poisoned candy being manufactured in the city.

Rebecca knew that part of the reason for the disinterest was no doubt due to the fact that the Health Department had more inspectors collecting salaries than it had doing actual inspections. Like all city departments, many of the jobs it provided were no-show positions awarded by Tammany Hall as patronage. Not giving up, however, she finally checked the directory once again and decided to try the department's chemist. Arsenic was, after all, a chemical, so perhaps he would be interested—if he was at his job.

She went downstairs to a basement room which had *Jeffrey Cokeroft, Chemist* stenciled on a frosted-glass door. In answer to her knock, a voice called, "Come in, if you must!"

Rebecca cautiously stepped inside. Amid rows of glass flasks, test tubes, and beakers, one thin, clean-shaven young man in a white lab coat was lighting a flame under a beaker of white liquid. He had large gray eyes and mussed brown hair that was almost standing on end, giving him a look of perpetual surprise. "Mr. Cokeroft?" she ventured.

He looked up from his flame. "Yes, ma'am."

She introduced herself. "I'm hoping you can help me. There's a candy manufacturer in the city that's putting arsenic in its gumballs and stick candy." Melissa Ostertag and Sarah Zietlow had told her those were the most brightly colored of the candies they'd eaten.

"Which manufacturer?" Cokeroft asked.

"Fluitt and Schlichting Confectionary."

The chemist nodded. "Yes, they're one of the largest. The arsenic is actually in the colors they use." He adjusted the height of the flame and looked back up at her. "So: how can I help you?"

Rebecca thought she had just explained that. "By arresting them, or closing them down, or whatever it is you do to stop them."

He frowned, obviously puzzled. "I'm afraid I don't understand. Why would we want to close them down?"

"Because they're poisoning people!" *Can this man really be so dense?* she wondered.

"Who's been poisoned?"

"Two young women in the last couple of months alone. One worked in the factory; another ate a lot of their candy."

"They died?"

"No, but they were both quite ill. One of them still is."

"Oh." Cokeroft appeared disappointed. "Well, then there really isn't anything we can do."

Rebecca was growing increasingly frustrated, and it was all she could do to speak civilly. "What do you mean, there isn't anything you can do? If this isn't a matter for your office, then where should I go?"

"I don't believe you can go anywhere—not in the Health Department." He ran his fingers through his unruly hair. "You see, we're only authorized to deal with *adulterated* food."

"Doesn't *arsenic* count as adulteration?"

"No, I'm afraid it doesn't." Cokeroft pointed to bottles of white liquid. "Those are milk samples. I test hundreds of those every week, and I find all sorts of fillers and whiteners being used— chalk, bleach, plaster of Paris. And if I told you what they put in butter, it would make you sick. Now, those samples are 'adulterated' because the milk and butter are advertised as being pure when they're not. But candy is different; it's not sold as a pure food product, so a manufacturer can use any additives they like— including arsenic."

Rebecca was aghast. "So there's nothing I can do?"

"Well, you can avoid eating the candy," Cokeroft suggested. "Or change the law."

CHAPTER 32

Nicholas Bostwick had heard soprano Amy Goodpaster sing several times before and had always considered her voice to be tinny and her pitch perception to be tenuous at best. But this evening, as she sang a duet with Spanish tenor Roberto Moreno in the music room of the Eden Musee, her voice sounded bright, clear, and in tune. Bostwick looked to his right, where Liesl Schulmerich was seated next to him. Yes, he thought, since the two of them had begun keeping company, music sounded better, the taste of food improved, and his life in general was much happier.

When the performance was over, the two of them went into the variety house's main gallery, where the waxwork figures for which the Eden Musee was famous were on display. They passed full-scale wax sculptures of famous people ranging from heavyweight champion John L. Sullivan to General George Armstrong Custer. Bostwick barely looked at the remarkably lifelike figures, however; his eyes were largely focused on Liesl. In the bright light of the gallery, her hair seemed almost translucent and her fair skin was so white that it positively appeared to glow like an incandescent bulb.

"My brother and I used to sing together when we were young," Liesl said wistfully. Apparently, she wasn't paying attention to the sculptures, either.

Bostwick wasn't sure how to reply. Too often for his comfort, there would be something that reminded Liesl of Lyman Sinclair, as the duet they'd just heard must have done. "Opera?" he asked.

"German folk songs, mostly. He had quite a nice voice." She sighed. "I would give anything to be able to sing one more song with him."

Lyman Sinclair might be a closed matter as far as Jacob Updegraff was concerned, Bostwick thought, but that didn't erase the memory of the banker. Liesl Schulmerich had lost her brother, and that loss would affect her for some time. Bostwick wished there was something he could do or say to make her feel better, but he knew of no words or actions that might help.

The two of them decided to pass up the Eden Musee's other attractions, which included Ajeeb the Chess Automaton and a magician who billed himself as "The Peerless Panulla," and left the variety house. Outside on West Twenty-third Street, the rain that had been falling most of the day had tapered off to nothing more than a light mist. Although it wasn't necessary for protection, Bostwick opened his umbrella and held it for Liesl, who walked close by his side.

As they strolled toward Broadway, Liesl continued to talk longingly of her late brother. Bostwick's responses were limited for the most part to sympathetic murmurs. But when she mentioned that her family still hadn't been allowed access to Sinclair's apartment, Bostwick spoke up, eager to do something for her. "I believe I can get you in, if you'd like to see it."

Liesl turned to him, her eyes big and hopeful. "You can? Of course I want to see where he lived!"

Bostwick was pleased to give her such hope, but suddenly fearful that he might not be able to justify it. He would have to check with Mr. Updegraff, of course. . . .

"How soon can we go?" Liesl asked.

Bostwick studied her eager face for only a moment before answering with more confidence than he felt, "I'll take you there now." He then hailed a hansom cab, helped Liesl into her seat, and gave the driver instructions to take them to the Langford Arms on West Fourth Street.

At the apartment house, the two of them went to the door of the building superintendent. The man remembered Bostwick from his earlier visit with Sergeant O'Melia and promptly agreed to let them into the Sinclair apartment. Bostwick enjoyed the sense of power, especially in being able to use it on behalf of Liesl Schulmerich.

When the superintendent unlocked the door to 4-D, he said, "I've kept the place sealed just like I was told. But it's been some time now, Mr. Bostwick. Do you know when I'll be able to rent it again?"

It was no surprise to Bostwick that when Jacob Updegraff closed the Sinclair investigation he had neglected to tell the police that the apartment could be opened again; Mr. Updegraff seldom did give much consideration to others. "I will see to it that you can make the apartment available again as soon as possible," Bostwick promised. With a glance at Liesl, he added, "After his family can take possession of his effects, of course."

The superintendent expressed his thanks, then left the two of them alone in the former home of Lyman Sinclair.

Liesl began to explore the spacious parlor with curiosity. She slowly moved around the room, stopping now and then to touch a Chippendale chair or peer at an oil painting on the wall. She looked over the figurines in the china cabinet, and the leather-bound books on the shelves. Bostwick could tell that her examination wasn't in the manner of an appraisal, but rather as if she was trying to absorb some sense of what her brother's life had been like.

She then looked at the French door that led out to the balcony. "That's where he . . ."

"Yes," said Bostwick.

"I'll never believe that he took his own life," Liesl said in a small voice. "But I don't see how he could have *fallen.*"

Bostwick chose not to mention the possibility that he and Marshall Webb had discussed—that her brother might have been murdered.

"My parents are totally devastated," Liesl went on. "And my mother hardly has the energy to do anything any more." She took a few steps toward the balcony. "You'd think the fact that they'd had so little contact with Lyman in the last few years would make it easier for them. But it doesn't. They'd always hoped that he would come back and be Ludwig again. Now that he's dead, it's like they've lost him twice, and the pain is something awful for them." She added softly, "And for me." She looked out the glass door. "I'll never get him back, but I do want to know how he lived—and why he died."

Bostwick stared at Liesl for some time. He wished that he could do something to relieve her mind. There was nothing he

224 / *Troy Soos*

could really do to help now, he realized, but he vowed to himself that he would find the answers she was seeking.

Rebecca would have almost preferred that the late-night rap at the door was the insistent pounding of a policeman or an angry husband. At least they wouldn't have wanted a bed for the night. But she could tell from the sound that the knock was probably that of a girl needing shelter.

As she wrapped her dressing gown around her and hurried from her small bedroom down the stairs of Colden House, Rebecca took a quick mental inventory of what space was available. Every bed was already taken, as well as a couple of folding cots. The infirmary was still occupied, too, by Melissa Ostertag, who was struggling to fight off the continuing effects of arsenic poisoning.

By the time Rebecca reached the front door, she almost wished that Colden House was a hotel so that she could simply announce, "No vacancy." As long as there was space on the floor, though, no girl was going to have to sleep in the street.

When Rebecca opened the door, she was astonished to see Alice standing there in a plain straw bonnet and simple traveling suit. A Gladstone bag was in her hand. Her sister's lips were trembling, and there was an ugly bruise below her left eye.

Alice simply stared at Rebecca for a few moments like a frightened child. Then she erupted into tears.

"Come in, come in," said Rebecca, quickly putting an arm around her sister's shoulders.

"Pardon me, ma'am," came a gruff male voice behind her. "There's the cab to be paid for."

For the first time, Rebecca looked past her sister to see a top-hatted cabdriver standing behind her. His vehicle was parked at the curb. "How much?" Rebecca asked. She knew her sister wouldn't have been practical enough to bring money of her own; everything Alice purchased was simply charged to Updegraff accounts.

"It was three miles, ma'am—all the way from Thirty-third and Fifth." The driver touched the brim of his hat and flashed an ingratiating smile. "That makes the fare a dollar-fifty."

"I'll get it." Rebecca hurried Alice into the sitting room and onto the sofa, then left her bawling sister to dig up the money. She found less than a dollar in her purse and a few more coins in her desk drawer and went to the front door, where she put the change in the hand of the driver.

He looked down at his palm with disappointment. "This is a dollar-fifty, ma'am."

"Yes, it's what you—" Rebecca caught on that he wanted a tip. "Oh, I'm sorry. It really is all I have." She then closed the door on the grumbling driver and hurried back to her sister.

Alice was trying valiantly to stem the flow of tears. She had a crumpled lace handkerchief pressed to her dainty nose. "I'm so sorry to come to you like this," she said.

"Nonsense." Rebecca sat down next to her. "I told you to come anytime and I meant it. Now tell me: what happened? Did Jacob strike you?" She didn't remember ever seeing her sister with an injury of any kind; even as children, Alice had been pampered and protected, never allowed to play any games that could result in the slightest harm.

"He didn't mean to," Alice replied in a small voice.

Rebecca hated to hear that. She'd heard the same thing from so many abused girls over the years, excusing the men who'd beaten them.

Alice went on, "He was drunk."

That, too, was something Rebecca had heard far too often. "That's no excuse," she said. "He should never have hit you." She gently touched her sister's cheek below the swollen, purple bruise. "I have a good mind to go give him a thrashing myself."

"No, really," Alice said. "He didn't mean to hurt me. It was an accident." She took a deep breath. "I told you before that I've been scared of him lately—because he's been acting so strangely, and so angry all the time."

"Yes, I remember." And, Rebecca thought, her fear had been justifiable, as it turned out.

"So I've been trying to avoid him. Most nights I stay in the drawing room until I think he's asleep. But tonight he came in to get me." She started crying again and took a moment to wipe her tears. "He'd been at the club and must have been drinking the whole evening—I've never seen him in such a state. He burst into the drawing room and insisted I go up to bed with him." Alice blushed; her sleeping arrangements with her husband weren't a topic for decent conversation, not even with her sister. "I refused, especially seeing his condition. Jacob went into a rage. He picked up a vase and threw it down on the table. I think he wanted to smash it, but the vase didn't break—it bounced off the table and hit me in the face."

"How did you get away from him?"

"As soon as he saw what happened, his mood changed. He began apologizing and telling me he loved me. I told him that I just wanted to be left alone, and eventually he went to bed by himself." Alice blew her nose into the handkerchief. "I didn't know what to do; I was almost in shock. All I knew for sure was that I didn't want to stay in the same house as Jacob tonight. So I waited until the servants had gone to bed, and left." She looked at Rebecca with pleading in her eyes. "Please, can I stay here?"

"Of course." Rebecca quickly decided that she would give Alice her own bed and spend the night on the sitting room sofa. "Let's put something on your eye first, though." She took Alice's bag and led the way upstairs.

After showing Alice the modest bedroom where she would be sleeping, the two of them went to the infirmary. Rebecca went in quietly, trying not to disturb Melissa Ostertag, sleeping fitfully on the iron-rail bed. The young woman was moaning pitifully in her sleep.

Alice whispered, "Who's that?"

Rebecca took some salve from the medicine cabinet. As she did, she quietly explained to her sister who Melissa Ostertag was and that she was suffering from arsenic poisoning.

They stepped into the hallway, where Rebecca began applying the balm to Alice's bruise. "This might sting a little," she said.

Alice flinched at the initial contact. Then she asked, "Will the poor girl be all right? She sounds close to death. And her skin— it's just hanging on her bones."

"The doctor thinks she'll recover," Rebecca answered. She knew that Miss Ostertag would probably recover more quickly in the care of a hospital, but there was no money to pay for that, and the hospital refused to keep her without payment. Sarah Zietlow had recovered while staying at Colden House, though, so Rebecca was hoping Miss Ostertag would pull through as well as Miss Zietlow had.

"And she was poisoned where she worked?" Alice sounded amazed that such a thing could happen.

Rebecca was glad to see that it was at least providing a distraction from her sister's own troubles. "A lot of girls who come here were hurt at work. There are several here right now who were maimed in factory accidents. And one who has lung problems from tobacco dust—she used to work stripping tobacco leaves in a tenement sweatshop." Rebecca stopped herself from continuing. There were a hundred similar tales, many of them far more disturbing, that she could have told her sister, but this was a time to comfort her, not cause her added distress. "There," she said. "That should keep it from hurting too much, and it should heal quickly." The skin wasn't broken, and she didn't think there would be any scar.

"Thank you," Alice said. She was still looking at the infirmary door, obviously thinking about Miss Ostertag inside. Perhaps, Rebecca thought, Alice was considering that she had something in common with the unfortunate woman from the other end of the social scale: Both of them, at least temporarily, needed the shelter of Colden House.

CHAPTER 33

Rebecca didn't get much sleep on the sofa. It was just as well; she'd forgotten to take the alarm clock from her room before Alice settled in for the night, and the only reason she was able to rouse herself early enough to get the heat going in the house was because she hadn't been sleeping anyway.

By five o'clock, long before the sun would begin to light the sky, Rebecca had got the coal furnace burning again and had kindled a fire in the kitchen stove. She'd also scraped together what little food was on hand for breakfast. There was no coffee left and very little tea, and the money that Rebecca had intended to use for milk this morning had instead gone for Alice's cab fare.

Leaving the bleak situation of the kitchen, Rebecca then quietly went upstairs to check on her sister. She almost panicked when she peeked inside her room and saw the bed empty. Her first thought was that Alice had decided to return home in the middle of the night. Then she realized that her sister wouldn't have been able to leave without Rebecca's hearing her go out the front door—especially since Rebecca hadn't done more than doze on the sofa.

On her way to the bathroom to see if Alice was there, Rebecca poked her head into the infirmary; ever since Melissa Ostertag had been released from the hospital, Rebecca had made it a point to check on her every few hours. To her surprise, Alice was seated in the room's one straight-backed chair, with a blanket draped around her petite figure. Miss Ostertag was asleep, regularly emitting an awful sound that was a combination of a snore and a moan.

"Alice?" Rebecca whispered.

"I'm awake." Alice's voice was soft and distant.

"What are you doing in here?"

"I couldn't sleep. So I thought I'd come in here and keep Miss Ostertag company. She sounded so bad last night that I was worried about her."

Considering how Alice's own comfortable world had become one of turmoil lately, Rebecca was impressed that her sister felt such compassion for someone she'd met only a few hours ago. "That was kind of you."

"Her moaning was awful—I think she must be in pain," Alice reported, "But she slept through the night." She shivered within her blanket. "I don't know how, though. It's freezing in here."

"We can't afford to heat the place," Rebecca said. "So I let the furnace die out at night." She'd calculated that by leaving the heat off for four hours a night, she saved a day's fuel every week. "It's back on now, though; the house should be warm again soon."

Alice gave her a puzzled look. "No heat?"

Rebecca knew it was an alien concept to her sister to have to be cold or go hungry. Wait until Alice found out that there was going to be nothing for breakfast but weak tea and day-old bread. "Let's go into my room," she suggested.

Once they were in the privacy of her own bedroom, and in a brighter light, Rebecca noticed that the ugly bruise under Alice's eye had grown more swollen and colorful; a mix of green and purple mottled her fair skin. "What about you, Alice?" she asked. "How are you feeling?"

"I'm not sure how I feel," her sister answered. "Afraid, angry, hurt. I've never felt anything like this before."

"What do you plan to do?"

Alice sat on the edge of the bed and lowered her head. "I don't know. I *won't* go back to Jacob—certainly not while he's behaving so strangely." She looked up. "Can I stay with you a little while?"

"Of course." Rebecca sat down next to her sister. "But don't you want to call home and say that you're all right? When he finds that you've left, Mr. Updegraff is going to be worried about you."

"Good! Let him worry about something besides money for a change."

It wasn't that Alice's absence might distress her husband that had Rebecca concerned. "No, I mean call *our* home—Mama and

Papa's. Mr. Updegraff will think you went there. And when he contacts them to ask about you, they'll be terribly worried. Please telephone them and tell Mama and Papa that you're safe."

Alice shook her head. "And what do I tell them about *why* I'm here?" She brought a fingertip up and gingerly touched her bruised cheek.

"The truth." It wouldn't hurt for them to learn what Jacob Updegraff was really like, Rebecca thought.

"No!" Alice looked appalled at the suggestion. "It would be far too humiliating. What if our friends found out? And what about the servants? What would *they* think?"

Rebecca thought she had encountered every possible situation at Colden House over the years, but this was a first. No girl who had ever before come to the place had expressed concern about what her servants would think.

"Marshall? Are you awake?"

At the sound of Rebecca's voice on the telephone, Webb tried to shake the sleep out of his head. "A little," he answered.

"Alice is here."

"At *Colden House?*" Rebecca had once told him that her sister had never been to the home. At this early hour, Webb realized, she certainly wouldn't be making her first social call. "Is something wrong?"

"She came last night. Jacob Updegraff was drunk and crazy. He threw a vase that hit her in the face."

"Is she hurt?"

"A bruise, nothing more serious—at least not physically. She *is* shaken up by what's happened, and she wants to stay with me for a while." Rebecca then told him how frightened her sister had looked and acted last night.

"How is she now?"

"Sleeping. She didn't sleep at all last night, so I'm glad she's getting some rest now."

"What is she going to do?"

"I honestly don't know. Maybe when she wakes up she can think about it more clearly." Rebecca sighed; it came out as a burst of static through the telephone wire. "Alice seems to think that her biggest problem is that someone might find out. She's as much embarrassed as she is frightened."

Webb didn't understand that kind of thinking. Jacob Updegraff was the one to be ashamed, he believed. "Is there anything I can do to help?" he asked, thinking to himself that giving Updegraff a good pummeling might be the most appropriate action.

"For now, just don't tell anyone that she's here."

Webb promised to keep the secret, and the two of them hung up.

He knew he wouldn't be going back to sleep, so he went to put on a pot of coffee. As it brewed, he wondered what it had been that set off Jacob Updegraff.

Was it his conversation with the banker at the Davies home? Webb worried that he might have been the trigger that sent Updegraff into the rage that resulted in his injuring Alice. Had he accused the banker unjustly? he wondered.

Or was everything Webb had said true, and fear of exposure and scandal what had Updegraff so upset?

Whichever the case, Webb was sure that nothing would be resolved until it was determined exactly how much Jacob Updegraff had been involved in the financial improprieties at his bank, and in the murder on Fire Island.

CHAPTER 34

Marshall Webb turned the corner from Delancey Street into cobblestoned Marion Alley and stepped inside the Lucky Star Saloon. As he did, the whistles and horns of the boat traffic on the East River were nearly drowned out by the low rumble of male conversation and the frequent clinking of glasses, bottles, and poker chips.

Webb took a moment to let his eyes get accustomed to the gloom that resulted from dim light and thick smoke, then looked around at the late-night crowd. The men he was seeking were huddled at a table, hunched together in earnest discussion.

Rabbit Doyle, the oldest of the three, looked as much like a bullmastiff as the first time Webb had seen him in the saloon; the beefy ward heeler even appeared to be frothing at the mouth because of the foam left clinging to his lips by his glass of beer. Of the two young bruisers with him, Webb picked out the rust red hair of Brick Fessler, and noticed with some satisfaction the bend in his nose that Craig Rettew had given him on election night. The third man at the table was the same one who'd been with Doyle before; although his name had never been given, Webb assumed that he was the Danny Alcock whom Rettew had mentioned.

Without invitation, Webb grabbed an empty chair from a nearby table. He swung it over to Doyle's table and sat down. Fessler and Alcock immediately began to rise. They had faces that belonged in the detective bureau's Rogues' Gallery, and their threatening expressions were enough to warn Webb that if he didn't leave they would throw him out.

Ignoring them, he said to Doyle, "My name is Marshall Webb. We've met before."

Doyle studied him for a long moment. "You were in here a couple months ago, claiming you worked at the Tombs." He scowled. "If you were an honest man, you would have told me you write for *Harper's* and that you were trying to dig up dirt on Tammany Hall."

Fessler asked, "You want we should take him outside, boss?"

The ward heeler considered that. "Not yet," he decided, waving the two young men back into their seats. Looking at Webb, he said, "You've been writing a lot of hogwash about us. And there's some people in the Society who wouldn't mind tackin' your hide to the wall."

"I checked my information quite thoroughly," replied Webb. "Anything in particular you'd like to correct?"

Doyle scowled again but could name nothing that Webb had got wrong in his articles. "Don't matter a damn, anyhow. You can write what you want and print what you want. Nothing's going to stop us. Better men than you have tried, and every one of them failed."

There was that same arrogance Webb had remembered from before. He had come here hoping that Doyle's belief in his own invincibility might make him feel that no harm could come of talking to Webb. "I realize that," Webb said. "But you know how it is: every few years some newspaper or weekly starts another anti-corruption campaign." He shrugged. "This year it happens to be *Harper's* turn. I'm not looking to stop you; I'm just doing my job."

All Doyle could think to reply was a grunt.

Webb went on, "Just like I assume you were only doing your job when you and your friends here went to Fire Island to convince the owners to sell their properties."

Danny Alcock made a gasping sound. Rabbit Doyle steeled himself so much to avoid looking shaken that Webb knew he'd been correct in his assumption that these were the men Eric Christensen had met.

"What I'd like to know," Webb continued, "is whom were you working *for*: Tammany Hall or Jacob Updegraff?"

Doyle quickly downed a long draught of beer, splashing some of it onto his shirt. "You're just full of questions, ain't ya?"

"Oh, yes. Here's another: How do you happen to know a man like Jacob Updegraff, anyway? You're not exactly of his social class." At Doyle's stony silence, Webb pressed on. "He's not like

Benjamin Freese—you and Freese were in the Dead Rabbits together, weren't you? Are you still pals?" Webb had been convinced for some time that there was some kind of connection between Updegraff and Freese, but he didn't know if that connection was Lyman Sinclair or the Fire Island deal, or maybe Rabbit Doyle. He was spitting out questions and hoping for a response that might narrow the possibilities.

Fessler spoke up again. "No good is gonna come of talking to this guy, Rabbit. Let's take him outside and shut him up." He seemed to be the most nervous of the three. Webb wondered if the red-haired young thug wanted to make sure the conversation was over with before it got around to the murdered man on Fire Island—perhaps it had been Fessler who'd administered the fatal blows. Webb decided to forgo asking that question for now.

Rabbit Doyle downed the rest of his beer and put the glass on the table with a heavy *thunk*. "Not a bad idea, Brick. I'm tired of his questions."

Fessler and Alcock scraped back their chairs.

Trying not to sound afraid, Webb said, "That won't accomplish anything. You boys will get in some shots, but so will I." He looked to Alcock. "Maybe I'll give you a nose like Fessler's here."

"You just try—" Alcock began.

"I will. And I'll succeed." Webb shrugged. "There's three of you and one of me, so you'll end up getting in most of the punches, but I promise you'll know you've been in a fight. And no matter how many shots you get in, you won't stop what I'm doing."

"Oh, we can stop you," Doyle said quietly. "Permanently."

Forcing himself to remain calm, Webb replied, "You'd end up doing yourself more harm than good. For one thing, killing a *Harper's* writer would bring a storm of attention to you and to Tammany Hall."

"We've weathered storms before." Doyle nodded at his accomplices. They stood up and reached out to grab hold of Webb.

"Not like this one—and I don't think Tammany will be protecting you this time."

Doyle held up his hand; Fessler and Alcock lowered their arms. "What do you mean?"

"I've left the rest of my series on Tammany with my editor. I can only change them if I'm alive. If I'm dead, they get published as is—and believe me, you don't want that."

"You're gonna print them anyway."

"I've added some embellishments that I intend to take out as long as I'm able to do so. It's something of an insurance policy to make sure I remain healthy." Webb flashed a smile that he hoped would look confident. "Right now, there's enough about you in there that both the police and your bosses at Tammany will be after your scalp."

Rabbit Doyle mulled that over for a while. "Wait here," he said, rising from the table. "I'm gonna make a call."

While Doyle went to the back of the bar, the three men remaining at the table sat in silence, waiting for his return.

The ward heeler came back a few minutes later. "Webb, you're coming with us," he said.

"Where?"

"To the man who can answer your questions."

Webb had no doubt that he would indeed be going with them whether he wanted to or not. Only two thoughts comforted him. One was that he truly didn't believe they would harm a writer from *Harper's*—it would cause too much attention for them. The other consoling thought was that he might really learn the answers to his questions.

The four men squeezed into a hansom together and rode from the East Side to Fifth Avenue, where they traveled north past the mansions for which the avenue was famous. As instructed by Doyle, the driver pulled to the curb in front of a home that Webb had visited not long ago. It was the marble-and-yellow brick mansion of Benjamin Freese.

This time, Webb wasn't let in the front door. Instead, Doyle led the way to the rear of the house. Brick Fessler and Danny Alcock walked on either side of Webb, close enough to make sure that he couldn't get away. A butler who appeared to recognize Doyle let them in through the servants' entrance, and they marched up the back staircase to Benjamin Freese's den.

As they entered the room, Webb couldn't help but give a nervous glance at all the animal skins on the floor and the mounted heads on the walls. He had the sense that Doyle would have liked to add Webb's to the collection.

Freese was seated behind his imposing desk. At the sight of his visitors, his face flushed to nearly the same shade as his bushy beard. "I can't say that this is a pleasure," he wheezed in his raspy voice.

"Wait here," ordered Doyle.

Fessler and Alcock remained next to Webb, just inside the door, while Doyle went to speak with Freese. They talked for some minutes, and Webb kept a close eye on them to see what he could determine from their agitated appearance and gestures.

Why the ward healer had chosen to bring Webb to Benjamin Freese's home was something Webb found curious. Rabbit Doyle worked for Tammany Hall, and Webb knew that Freese wasn't part of that organization. So why didn't Doyle bring Webb to one of his Tammany bosses? Did Doyle and Freese have another business of their own? If so, it was clear from their demeanor that Freese was the dominant partner.

Most likely, Webb thought, Doyle had brought him here so that Freese could size him up and perhaps determine if Webb had been bluffing about having an incriminating story in the hands of his editor at *Harper's*. If so, Webb had to worry about two things. One was the possibility that Freese had some kind of influence at *Harper's* that could get the story squelched. The other was that the financier would correctly deduce that Webb's claim was a bluff and that he could be killed without fear of repercussion.

Benjamin Freese held up his hand, motioning for Doyle to step aside. "Mr. Webb," Freese said, beckoning with his finger.

Webb walked closer to the desk but didn't take a seat. He nodded at the financier. "Mr. Freese."

Freese didn't even extend the courtesy of a nod. He spat into the brass cuspidor next to the desk. "You ask a lot of questions."

"Occupational hazard."

"*And* you're impertinent." Freese's dark eyes were narrow.

Webb shrugged.

"Mr. Doyle tells me that you claim to have a story in at *Harper's* that could reflect badly on some people."

"That's true. And if I'm not around to stop it, the story appears in print for everyone to read."

"You're lying."

"Ask Doyle," Webb said. "He knows I write for *Harper's*, and he knows there's been an installment of my Tammany series coming out every week."

"I don't need to ask Mr. Doyle," Freese rasped. "I've read your articles, too."

"Then you know I have to have more ready to print." Webb asked in an incredulous tone, "You don't think *Harper's* would begin a series unless they had the next installments ready to go, do you?"

Freese fixed his stare on him for what seemed like a full minute. "No, I'm sure they wouldn't," he decided.

Webb tried not to let his relief show on his face.

Freese leaned back in his thronelike chair and worked the wad of tobacco in his cheek. After some moments, he said, "The last time you were here, you asked me about Lyman Sinclair. I've decided that I will tell you about my dealings with him, which I expect will put an end to your questions about that matter."

Webb said nothing in reply; he felt under no obligation to meet Freese's expectations.

The financier continued. "You seemed to imply that I had reason to want revenge against Mr. Sinclair, either because of my unfortunate Western Continental investment or because of a relation between him and Miss Dolores Tenison."

"That crossed my mind," said Webb. Only the second possibility that Freese mentioned struck him as a likely motive for revenge, though, since Sinclair had already been dead by the time Freese purchased his controlling interest in the railroad.

"Then you were mistaken. I had nothing to do with Mr. Sinclair's death—in fact, my dealings with the man were quite profitable."

"How so?"

Freese spat and paused to wipe tobacco juice from his lower lip. "About a year ago, Mr. Sinclair came to me with a proposal. He told me he needed investors for a growing railroad company out west, and he knew that I'm viewed as a rather astute businessman. Mr. Sinclair suggested that if I invested and made a profit, then he would soon have others lining up to give him their money."

"What if you lost money?" Webb asked.

"Ah, but that couldn't happen. Mr. Sinclair *guaranteed* me a return of twenty-five percent within two months."

"How could he guarantee something like that?"

"It doesn't matter how he did it. That fact is, he kept his word and in two months gave me a check for exactly the sum that he'd promised." Freese smiled. "Of course, he had no alternative. When a man makes me a promise, he had better keep it. Otherwise, I have some associates of mine pay a call and convince him to keep his word."

Webb glanced back at the young thugs standing by the door. "Did your 'associates' have to convince Lyman Sinclair?"

"No. Mr. Sinclair was not the sort of man who would want to let matters get to that point. He brought me the money on time and in full. Then he let it be known that I had profited hand-somely from my investment with him, and, as he'd predicted, there were society types eager to give him their money, too." He spread his hands. "So you see, my dealings with Mr. Sinclair were entirely satisfactory."

"But you ended up losing it all when you bought controlling interest in the railroad."

"True, but I have to take the blame for that error in judgment. Mr. Sinclair was already dead by then." Freese's expression dark-ened as he seemed to anticipate Webb's next questions. "As for Mr. Sinclair's relationship with Miss Tenison, you will simply have to take my word for it that I was unaware of that—until you brought it to my attention. And, in case you're interested, my con-nection with her is now severed."

What Webb was actually interested in was why Freese had chosen to tell him about his deal with Lyman Sinclair. Was it to di-vert Webb's attention from a different matter? Webb hadn't even mentioned Sinclair at the Lucky Star Saloon. It was the subject of Fire Island that had upset Rabbit Doyle and his comrades.

"What about Fire Island?" Webb jerked his thumb at the men behind him. "Why were *your* associates helping Jacob Updegraff buy the island?"

Freese shifted his wad of tobacco and didn't answer for some moments. "My understanding from the newspapers," he finally said, "was that Jacob Updegraff owned Fire Island. So your ques-tions on that matter would best be directed to him. I am in no po-sition to comment on Mr. Updegraff's affairs—we do not exactly socialize." Freese looked from Doyle to Alcock to Fessler. "As for these men, however, I can vouch for their characters. I'm sure they would never be involved in anything inappropriate."

Webb followed Freese's gaze. The fact that Alcock and Fessler both had grins on their tough faces did nothing to bolster Freese's ridiculous claim. "One of the landowners was beaten to death," Webb said. "That doesn't count as 'inappropriate'?"

Freese scowled. "I've said all I intend to say. Our conversation is over, and it is the last one you and I will ever have." He gave a curt nod at Rabbit Doyle, and Webb soon had Alcock and Fessler on either side of him again. To Doyle, he said, "Take him out and don't ever bring him back."

How final was this to be? Webb suddenly wondered.

His thoughts must have been apparent on his face, because Freese grinned with amusement. "Don't worry. They won't harm you. A reporter can't just disappear. It would raise too many questions—and, as you know, I value my privacy."

And he undoubtedly wanted to avoid publication of the articles Webb claimed to have written.

Freese spat. "Besides, we know more about you than you perhaps realize. For example, you have a lady friend named Rebecca Davies—a sister-in-law of Jacob Updegraff. If you were to publish anything damaging to Mr. Doyle or myself, it could seriously affect her well-being. I'm sure you wouldn't want any harm to come to her. Do we understand each other?"

Before the men next to him could grab his arms, Webb lunged forward and reached across Freese's desk. He grabbed hold of the financier's necktie and gave it a sharp twist. Freese made a choking sound, and tobacco juice bubbled from his lips. "You'd better come after *me*, not Miss Davies," Webb said through clenched teeth. "Because if anything ever happens to her, you better believe that I'll be going after *you*." Both of Webb's arms were grabbed from behind, and he struggled to keep hold of Freese's tie. Just before he was pulled off of the financier, Webb asked him, "Do we understand each other?"

It took Freese some time to regain his breath. His face was so red that his head looked like an inflamed boil that needed to be lanced, and there was fury in his eyes. Eventually, he rasped, "Very well, Mr. Webb. We'll do it your way. If you give us any more difficulty, you can count on us coming after *you*."

Webb had the sense that Freese would be hoping for an excuse to do just that.

CHAPTER 35

Merchants near Colden House had long ago stopped extending additional credit to Rebecca, so she was having to travel farther and farther to obtain goods for the shelter. This morning she'd had to go all the way up to Christopher Street to find a grocer who was willing to give her two dollars' worth of food on credit.

When she returned to Colden House with her meager groceries, Rebecca first went to the infirmary to check on Alice and Melissa Ostertag. The room was empty. So were Alice's room and the bathroom.

Growing frightened, Rebecca ran down the stairs, calling, "Miss Hummel!" She almost collided with her gray-haired assistant coming into the hallway from the kitchen. "Where's my sister?"

"At the hospital, ma'am."

"What happened to her?" Rebecca began buttoning her coat again, ready to go to whatever hospital Alice was in.

"Not to her, ma'am. It was the young lady—Miss Ostertag. Her pains got worse and your sister insisted on taking her to the hospital."

"Which one? Where did they go?"

"I don't know." Miss Hummel looked somewhat miffed. "Mrs. Updegraff didn't tell me much. She just took it on herself to get Miss Ostertag into a hospital." The older woman added, "I lent her the money for cab fare."

"That was kind of you. I'll see that you get it back." Rebecca was relieved that her sister was all right, but worried now about Miss Ostertag. Alice had been so reluctant to go outside, embarrassed by her bruised face, that the young woman must have really taken a turn for the worse for Alice to take her out for medical care.

Since there was nothing she could do now but wait, Rebecca worked with Miss Hummel in the kitchen. The older woman did her best to keep Rebecca distracted, chatting endlessly about her latest evening at the theater, but Rebecca couldn't do much of anything but worry.

It wasn't until shortly before dinnertime that Alice returned to Colden House. Rebecca ran into the hall to greet her. "Where's—" Alice was alone, and Rebecca feared the worst about Melissa Ostertag.

"Don't worry," said Alice, unpinning one of Rebecca's wide-brimmed bonnets from her blond hair. "Miss Ostertag is in the hospital. She's going to stay there, in a private room, until she recovers. And the doctors assure me that she *will* recover."

Rebecca was happy to hear the answer to that important question, but there were others that immediately came to mind. "What happened? Why did she have to go to the hospital?"

Alice looked at the silk-trimmed black hat in her hand. "This is very pretty. I hope you don't mind me borrowing it, but I wanted a broad brim to hide . . ." She pointed to her eye.

Not only had Alice worn the hat tilted down to help hide the bruise, but she had covered the skin below her eye with a thick coat of face powder. "I don't mind at all," Rebecca answered, once again amazed at how easily her sister's attention could be diverted. "But what about Miss Ostertag?"

Alice unbuttoned her coat. "She told me her stomach pain was much worse this morning. And when she tried to eat some breakfast, it wouldn't stay down. She also had a numbness in her legs— she could barely walk." Alice frowned. "I hated to see her suffering like that, and I thought she would recover better in a hospital than here."

Of course she would, thought Rebecca, but there was no money to pay for medical care. "Columbus Hospital?" she asked.

"Oh, no. Roosevelt Hospital—it's much better than Columbus. Don't worry; she will be very comfortable there."

Rebecca explained to her sister, "Alice, I can't even afford to pay for a ward bed at Columbus. The bill for a private bed at Roosevelt is going to be enormous."

"But you won't have to pay it." Alice smiled brightly. "I told them to send the bill to Mr. Updegraff. I'm his wife, so he'll have to pay it."

Rebecca wished that she could get goods and services on her name alone. The merchants she dealt with all wanted cash. "What about Mr. Updegraff? Have you spoken to him?" She led Alice to the sitting room.

"No. And I don't think I will—at least not for a while. I'm more concerned about Miss Ostertag right now; I'm going back to the hospital tonight to stay with her again." She turned to look at Rebecca. "I can understand why you do this now. It feels good to help someone."

Rebecca thought for a moment. She'd lately become so frustrated with trying to keep Colden House in operation that she didn't let herself enjoy the fact that so many girls were helped by the shelter. "Yes, it does," she said. "Oh—have you contacted Mama or Papa yet?"

Alice shook her head.

"You'd better. Otherwise, they're going to hear from Mr. Updegraff that he's gotten a bill for you from Roosevelt Hospital, and they're going to worry that you're hurt."

With a little coaxing, Alice agreed to write a note to their parents saying that she was fine but without revealing where she was staying.

CHAPTER 36

Marshall Webb had lately been focused on Jacob Updegraff's purchase of Fire Island, trying to determine if the banker had any role in the murder that helped him acquire that property. But now it was once again the death of Lyman Sinclair that was on his mind.

First, Benjamin Freese had told him about his business arrangement with Sinclair—probably to distract him from the Fire Island deal, Webb believed. And then Updegraff's accountant, Nicholas Bostwick, telephoned him to ask if he'd learned anything new about Sinclair.

Bostwick claimed that he was calling on behalf of Liesl Schulmerich, who simply wanted to know more about her brother's recent life. Webb could understand that desire; it sounded similar to the one Alice and Rebecca had to learn about Jacob Updegraff, and what was driving Webb to continue in his investigations. Webb told Bostwick about Sinclair's deal with the financier and promised to contact him again if he learned anything more. He also told the accountant that he'd leave it to his judgment how much to reveal to Sinclair's sister—she might not want to know of his fraudulent investment scheme.

Webb later wondered if Jacob Updegraff had actually been behind Bostwick's call in an effort to determine whether Webb had discovered anything new. But if that was the case, why had Bostwick only asked about Lyman Sinclair? Why hadn't he asked about Fire Island—wasn't that the deal that could be the most incriminating for Updegraff?

That led Webb to reconsider Sinclair's death. If Benjamin Freese had indeed broken off his relationship with Dolores Tenison *after* Webb had spoken with him, then perhaps it was true that he knew nothing of her involvement with Lyman Sinclair. And if that was true, then Freese had no apparent motive to want Sinclair killed.

For the first time, Webb thought of another possible suspect in Sinclair's murder: Jacob Updegraff. It would never have occurred to him before that Updegraff could be involved in a murder. But then, he had never thought that the banker could be mixed up with the likes of Rabbit Doyle and his cronies. They killed the landowner on Fire Island to secure a sale for Updegraff, so perhaps they carried out another errand for him: killing a banker who was using his position at the New Amsterdam Trust Company to commit fraud and perhaps bring ruin to the business that the Updegraff family had spent generations building.

Shortly after lunch on Friday, Webb went to the Hotel Normandie at Broadway and Thirty-eighth Street, a stone's throw from where Dolores Tenison's show *Scenes of Spring* was running at the Empire Theatre. Webb thought he might learn two things from the actress. One was whether Benjamin Freese had indeed ended their affair. The other question he had was whether Lyman Sinclair had ever said anything to indicate that Updegraff was suspicious of his financial dealings.

When Webb knocked at the door of Miss Tenison's suite, he found that she was in no mood to tell him anything.

Tenison's maid answered the door. "Yes, sir?" She sounded tired, and her uniform was rumpled.

Before he could say anything, Miss Tenison's voice called from inside, "Who's there, Myra?"

Webb gave his name, and the maid relayed it to her employer.

"Tell Mr. Webb he can go straight to hell!" was Miss Tenison's immediate response.

The maid said, "I'm sorry, sir, but Miss Tenison says—"

"Yes, I heard. Please tell her that I have something she might like to see. I believe she will be quite pleased."

"One moment, sir." Myra closed the door and retreated inside for a couple of minutes. When she reappeared, she said, "Miss Tenison says she will see you, sir."

Webb stepped into a perfume-scented parlor that was in complete disarray. There were partially packed crates, two large steamer trunks, and several racks of clothes. Other clothes were strewn on an elegant divan.

Dolores Tenison made a theatrical entry from the bedroom, whisking through the doorway, the hem of her purple velvet gown brushing across the carpet. "How nice to see you again, Mr. Webb." As she neared him, she held out her hand.

Webb took her fingertips, bowed slightly at the waist, and made no mention that he had heard her earlier direction to send him "straight to hell." Instead, he said, "You look lovely as always, Miss Tenison."

The statement wasn't quite a lie, but it was certainly an exaggeration. The actress's long golden curls needed the attention of a hairbrush, the rouge that gave her lips their bee-stung pout was smudged at one corner of her mouth, and she'd neglected to powder her pallid face. Miss Tenison's large eyes looked as if she'd been crying most of the night, and her forced smile deepened the laugh lines around them. "I'm told you have something for me," she said, trying hard to sound cheerful.

"Yes, I do." Webb reached into his jacket pocket.

"*Please* don't tell me it's another card."

He smiled. "No. It's more than that." He pulled out a folded sheet of foolscap and handed it to her.

Miss Tenison appeared disappointed. Whatever it said, it was still only paper, and she was probably hoping for something more valuable—jewelry, perhaps. She brightened somewhat at reading the story, as Webb thought she might. For the occasion, he had written a glowing review of her performance in *Scenes of Spring*. There was no chance of *Harper's* publishing it—especially since Webb had no intention of ever submitting it to them—so he'd been effusive in his praise of her talents and beauty, hoping only that it would make her willing to speak with him about more serious matters. "This is a very nice notice," was her verdict. "When is it going to run?"

"My editor hasn't given me a date yet."

"I hope it's soon. I could use some good news." She called to the maid, who was packing what must have been at least a dozen different pairs of ladies' boots into a trunk. "Myra! Make sure you wrap each shoe in a cloth before you pack them—I don't want them getting scuffed."

"Yes, ma'am." Myra sounded as if she'd have preferred to wrap a cloth around Miss Tenison's mouth.

"Going somewhere?" asked Webb.

"Unfortunately, yes." The actress gave him a sharp look. "My rent is only paid through the end of the week, and I need to be out by then."

"I'm sorry to hear that." Webb looked around the magnificently furnished parlor. "This is quite a beautiful place." Lawrence Pritchard had told Webb that Freese was the one paying her rent. Apparently, the financier *had* cut off his relationship with her—which included cutting off her financial support.

"Yes," she sighed. "I hate to leave it."

Webb suddenly had another idea about who might have wanted Lyman Sinclair killed. If it wasn't Benjamin Freese—and Webb was now convinced that it wasn't—then maybe it was Dolores Tenison.

Lyman Sinclair was not a discreet man in either his professional or personal life. He couldn't keep his mouth shut about his investors, for one thing. And according to Pritchard, he'd even paid newspaper writers to get his name in the society pages. Sinclair had also revealed to a jewelry store clerk that his purchases were gifts for Miss Tenison. Perhaps the actress worried that Sinclair wouldn't be able to keep their relationship a secret, and feared being cut off from Freese's money if the financier learned of their affair.

"I suppose it had to happen some time," he said. "Benjamin Freese was going to find out about you and Lyman Sinclair eventually."

"What are you talking about?" she asked coldly.

"What I'm talking about is that you can't very well expect Mr. Freese to continue paying the rent on this place if you're using it to keep company with another man."

Miss Tenison took a deep breath. Then she slapped Webb on the face—hard. "I've had quite enough of your company, Mr. Webb. I'll thank you to leave."

Webb ignored the sting on his cheek. "If I do," he answered calmly, "I'll be going directly to the detective bureau. I'm sure they would be interested to know that someone—namely *you*—had a motive to murder Mr. Sinclair. So it's your choice: you can talk to me or you can talk to the police."

Dolores Tenison stared at him with anger in her eyes. But she didn't strike him again, nor did she insist that he leave. She finally called, "Myra! Go down to the lobby and get me a cigarette."

"There are cigarettes in the bedroom, ma'am," the maid replied, standing up. "I'll fetch you one."

"No. Go down to the lobby and get something else, then. I want to speak to Mr. Webb alone."

"Very well, ma'am," Myra sighed.

When the maid left, Miss Tenison cleared a spot on the sofa and sat down. She put a lace handkerchief to her eyes, although there was no sign or sound of crying.

Webb remained standing, and he studied the actress closely, curious whether she would try to act her way out of this. "You were worried that Lyman Sinclair would reveal your affair, weren't you?" he said. "Because if Benjamin Freese got wind of it, your comfortable lifestyle would suddenly become a lot less comfortable."

"Some of what you say is correct," she admitted. "Mr. Sinclair was quite attentive to me, and I succumbed to a brief and ill-judged romance. But you are wrong about one thing: I had nothing to do with his death." She sniffled. "It came as a terrible shock to me."

"It was also convenient for you." Webb didn't take her word about being innocent in Sinclair's murder any more than he believed that she "succumbed" to affairs. "You got what you wanted from him—jewels and gifts—and you were still able to enjoy Benjamin Freese's financial support."

Dolores Tenison was silent for a few moments, working out her next lines, Webb thought. "I suppose it worked out that way," she said. "But his death was not of my doing."

"I'm sure the police will be able to determine that," Webb said. "Of course, they'll need to interview the cast and stage crew at the theater, and probably your friends and some of your other 'admirers,' but I'm confident they'll be able to sort it all out."

Tenison hesitated again, then sighed heavily. "There will be no need for that. I believe I know who killed Mr. Sinclair."

"Who?"

"Two of my younger admirers." Tenison wasn't a very good actress; she was trying to make it seem that she was reluctant to talk, but Webb had the impression that she was actually eager to tell him about Sinclair's killers—so eager, in fact, that he was increasingly suspicious of every word she said. "They confessed to me—actually, they bragged to me about it, like they were trying to prove that they would do anything for me."

"What did they confess *to?*"

"They were jealous of his relationship with me. So they went to talk to him, to tell him to stay away from me. The discussion turned into a fight, it got out of hand, and they ended up throwing him over the balcony."

"Why didn't you go to the police after they told you this?"

"How could I know they were telling the truth? They might have just been trying to capitalize on Mr. Sinclair's death to win my favor." She smiled. "Besides, they're such sweet boys. If they did do it for me, it would have been terribly ungrateful of me to turn them in to the police."

"But how did they know about you and Sinclair in the first place if it was a secret? You must have told them."

Miss Tenison hesitated, as if she'd dropped a line on stage. "Perhaps Mr. Sinclair told them," she suggested.

Webb didn't believe her. He suspected that she had encouraged them to kill Sinclair for her. "What are their names?"

She shook her head. "I won't tell you their names. I will go to the police, however, and tell them all I know."

More likely, Webb thought, she would tell them whatever story she believed would do her the most good.

As the hansom cab nudged its way slowly north through the early-evening traffic, Rebecca saw the Ninth Avenue El passing them overhead. She wished she had considered the time of day and taken the El instead. The slow progress of the cab was agonizing for her, especially since it gave her so much time to imagine all sorts of possible problems.

The nurse who'd telephoned Rebecca had failed to make it clear what the difficulty was. All Rebecca could gather was that Alice wasn't well and was asking for her sister.

Two blocks before reaching Fifty-sixth Street, the cab was again bogged down in a traffic jam, and Rebecca elected to hop out and go the rest of the way to Roosevelt Hospital on foot.

Breathing hard from what was nearly a sprint, Rebecca got the number of Melissa Ostertag's room at the hospital's admissions desk and hurried up a flight of stairs to room 214. When she reached the room, she almost collided with a horse-faced nurse in a starched white uniform who was coming through the door.

"This is a private room," the nurse said.

"My name's Rebecca Davies. My sister's in there—Alice Updegraff—and I had a telephone call that she's sick."

"No, she's not sick." The nurse took Rebecca by the arm and led her a few steps down the hallway. In a quiet voice, she explained, "I'm Nurse Wiggins; I'm the one who phoned you, and I apologize if I was unclear. Mrs. Updegraff is not really ill, but she is terribly distraught. We tried to calm her down, but—"

"Why is she upset? What happened?"

"It's Miss Ostertag. She's taken a turn for the worse. The doctors are working on her now, but it doesn't look—"

Rebecca brushed past the nurse and into Miss Ostertag's room. Everything in the private room was a sterile white, including the one iron-rail bed in which Melissa Ostertag lay motionless. Two doctors and a nurse were huddled over her, the elder doctor with a stethoscope pressed to her chest. Alice Updegraff sat stiffly on the edge of a nearby chair; her wide eyes had a look of disbelief in them.

Before Rebecca could go over to her sister, the doctor lifted the stethoscope and shook his head. "She's gone," he said. He nodded to the nurse, who pulled the sheet up over Miss Ostertag's lifeless face.

"No!" Alice shrieked.

Rebecca ran over to her and crouched next to her chair, putting her arm around her sister's shoulders.

Alice shook off Rebecca's touch. "No," she said again, this time in a faint voice. Then she began to wail like a little girl, her slim body shaking and tears streaming down her cheeks.

The doctor who'd pronounced Miss Ostertag dead stood before them. "I am so sorry," he said. "We tried everything."

"What happened?" Rebecca asked him in a hushed tone. "I thought she was recovering."

"We thought so, too," he said apologetically. "But this was a case of chronic poisoning. Over time, the arsenic must have done a fair amount of damage to her liver and kidneys—it put a strain on her heart." He hesitated. "I believe we'll find the cause of death was cardiac failure."

"No!" Alice yelled at the doctor. "You said she'd be all right. You *promised!*"

"I said we hoped—"

"You're a liar!" Alice lowered her head and her cries became so ragged that she seemed unable to catch her breath. Rebecca again put her arm around her; this time Alice buried her face in Rebecca's shoulder.

The doctor said again, "I *am* sorry. We really did do all we could." He cleared his throat. "We'll leave you alone for a few minutes before we come back for . . ."

Rebecca nodded. She was glad he hadn't said "the body." She still thought of the dead woman lying on the bed as Melissa Ostertag.

After they were alone, Alice continued to cry freely, soaking the arm of Rebecca's dress. After some time, the tears ebbed and Alice began to breathe regularly again. "She can't be dead," she said in a plaintive voice. "They said she'd be all right."

Rebecca wondered if Alice had ever been close to anyone who died before. The two of them were fortunate in that they still had their parents, and except for the occasional passing of a distant aunt or uncle, they had lost few relatives. Colden House, however, was full of women for whom hardship and death were common experiences. And the sad fact was that some of those girls didn't survive themselves. Rebecca wished that Alice had never come to the home; her sister simply wasn't prepared to see the harsh reality of what some poor women went through in their lives—and how those lives all too often ended.

CHAPTER 37

Nicholas Bostwick almost flinched when Dolores Tenison, a spotlight focused on her hourglass figure, walked onto the stage of the Empire Theatre. He recalled how insulting she had been to him the last time he'd seen her, when he and Marshall Webb had visited the actress in her dressing room. Bostwick had hoped never to see the horrid woman again—he'd even taken her picture off his wall—but Liesl Shulmerich had wanted to come to the show.

Webb had telephoned him—Bostwick's new salary had enabled him finally to get one of the instruments for his home—and told him about Sinclair's death and his suspicion that Miss Tenison was behind it. Bostwick, in turn, had relayed the information and the speculation to Liesl. He had at first been tempted to hold back anything that might reflect badly on her brother, but she had been so eager for every detail that he'd eventually told her all that he'd learned from Webb, including the fact that she'd promised to tell the police about the men who claimed to have killed him. That had raised hopes of an arrest, but it had been days now and there was no news.

This morning Liesl told him that all she really wanted to do was see the woman who had been her brother's romantic interest. So here they were, in third-row seats, watching Dolores Tenison perform in *Scenes of Spring*.

When Miss Tenison began her first song of the show, Liesl leaned toward him and whispered in his ear, "She doesn't have much of a voice, does she?"

Bostwick hesitated, enjoying the feel of Liesl's breath on his neck. Then he shook his head. And it was true that Miss Tenison didn't sound nearly as good as she had when he'd first heard her sing—but then, that was before he'd discovered her true personality.

After the show, which Bostwick found almost unbearable, Liesl leaned toward him again. "I'd like to see Miss Tension. May we go backstage?"

That wasn't a prospect that Bostwick was willing to entertain. "I don't think they let anyone back there."

"But this is the last show of the night, so we won't be disturbing her. And you told me you'd been in her dressing room once before, with that writer."

Bostwick regretted having ever mentioned that, but ever since he'd met Liesl, he'd found her so easy to talk to that he found it impossible to keep from telling her anything. "Yes, but that was Mr. Webb's doing, under the pretext of reviewing the show. I doubt that she would agree to see us." He did not want to be insulted in front of Liesl the way he had been when he'd been with Marshall Webb.

"Please. It would mean a lot to me to have a few words with her face to face."

Five minutes later, Bostwick was bribing the stage manager into asking Miss Tenison to see them. It was a dollar to relay the message, and two dollars more for him to guarantee that she would give them five minutes.

The stage manager emerged from the dressing room and held the door open for Bostwick and Liesl to step inside. When Bostwick nervously began to introduce Liesl, Miss Tenison cut him off, "I have an engagement tonight, so I'm afraid I only have a few minutes." The actress had a loose silk robe pulled around her and a glass of champagne in her hand. Behind Miss Tenison, her maid was ironing a blouse.

"I appreciate your time, Miss Tenison," Liesl said. "Your performance was so exquisite tonight that I simply *had* to come and tell you."

The actress obviously enjoyed the flattery, but Bostwick was bewildered by it. Why was Liesl acting like one of Dolores Tenison's admirers when she knew that the actress might be behind her brother's death?

"Your voice is every bit as beautiful as your face," Liesl gushed.

"Well, thank you."

"It's no wonder my brother was attracted to you."

Miss Tenison paused with her champagne glass lifted almost to her lips. "Your brother?"

"Yes. You knew him as Lyman Sinclair." Liesl quickly added, "Don't worry. He told me your relationship was a secret. I know you have a reputation to protect, and I'll continue to keep the secret. I just wanted to see the woman who had so enchanted him." She hesitated. "And there's another reason I wanted to speak with you."

Miss Tenison asked cautiously. "What's that?"

"Lyman left something for you—an emerald necklace. I found it when I was going through his effects. He had your name written on a gift card, but I suppose he didn't have a chance to give it to you before he . . . Anyway, now that I've seen you, I'd like you to have it."

Bostwick was now totally lost, so he didn't say a word.

"That is very kind of you," the actress said warmly. There was a greedy glint in her eyes. "I was exceedingly fond of your brother, and I am so sorry for your loss." She sniffled unconvincingly. "I feel the loss quite acutely myself." Quickly recovering her spirits, she added, "I would be happy to accept the necklace as something to remember him by."

"Oh, I don't have it with me," Liesl said. "My family has only recently been given access to his apartment—that's where I found it, and it's still there. We can go get it if you like, but I would hate to keep you from the engagement you mentioned."

Dolores Tenison didn't take long to say, "I suppose it won't matter if I'm a bit late. So I'd be happy to go with you. You know, your brother had excellent taste in gems, and he knew how much I love emeralds."

Bostwick decided simply to follow Liesl's lead in whatever she said. All he hoped now was that Sinclair's apartment wasn't yet rented. As he'd promised the superintendent, he'd recently got Jacob Updegraff to lift the police seal on the place.

The apartment hadn't yet been rented, but the building superintendent said he was grateful to Bostwick for getting permission to let it again. Since there was no new tenant yet and Sinclair's furniture was still in the place, the superintendent let them inside.

When the three of them were alone, Liesl asked Miss Tenison, "Were you as happy with my brother as he was to be with you?"

"Absolutely," the actress replied in a dispassionate tone. She was eyeing the apartment and walking about the parlor, as if trying to determine where the necklace was. "We had the most wonderful times together."

"And you cared for him?"

"Oh, yes, he was a fine gentleman."

"Then how could you have him murdered?"

Miss Tenison drew up short and shot a look at Liesl. "What are you talking about?"

"You already had a, uh, 'benefactor'—Benjamin Freese. Everyone knows that you're a kept woman and that he's your keeper. And you didn't want Mr. Freese to find out about you and my brother, so you had Lyman killed."

It was a long moment before Miss Tenison said, "There is no necklace, is there?"

"No."

"Then I'm leaving." She took a couple of strides toward the door.

Liesl pulled a small nickel-plated revolver from her purse. "But I do have this for you." She waved the muzzle of the weapon. "Sit down."

Bostwick was shocked. He looked from Liesl's face to the gun in her pale, thin hand and back to her face. Her expression was taut and fixed—and thoroughly determined.

Miss Tenison must have been able to tell that Liesl was serious, too, for she did as she was told and sat down in the corner chair. "You're making a mistake," she whined.

"I don't believe so," Liesl replied calmly. "And I suggest you don't make any mistakes, either. I want you to tell me exactly what happened the night my brother died. And you'd better tell the truth, because if I get the sense that you're lying, you'll be going off the balcony, too—but there won't be any question about how *you* died, because there will be a bullet hole in you." The revolver was steady and aimed directly at Dolores Tenison.

The actress stammered, then began to speak. "I really had nothing to do with it. A couple of my more ardent admirers—two sweet but impetuous young men—were trying to protect my reputation. I wanted to end my relationship with your brother. I did care for him, but I also had to consider my, uh, commitment to Mr. Freese. Your brother, for all his virtues, was rather indiscreet, and these two young men heard he'd been talking about me. They simply came here to try to convince him to leave me alone and hold his tongue."

"My brother's certainly quiet now," Liesl said softly.

"They didn't intend to kill him. There was a struggle"—the actress pointed to a couple of small scuff marks on the wall next to the china cabinet—"and it got out of hand. Your brother ended up going over the balcony."

Liesl asked, "And they did all this for you?"

"Oh, no! They might have thought that's what I wanted, but I didn't."

Bostwick spoke up. "Then why didn't you stop them?"

"How could I?"

"You were here," he answered. "Otherwise how did you know those marks are from the fight? They're barely even visible."

Dolores Tenison had no immediate answer, so she resorted to crying. But her sobs were from fear, not sorrow. "Yes, I was here. But I only came to warn your brother. You see, I suspected these men might go to see him, and I wanted to stop them from doing anything rash. But I was too late—they were already fighting, and it didn't end until . . ." She looked toward the balcony.

Liesl said, "Tell me what happened."

"I didn't see it start. By the time I came in, the three of them were grappling. Your brother was putting up quite a fight, and it got rather ferocious. I was yelling for them to stop, but they didn't. The fight continued out onto the balcony, and then they . . . they threw your brother over the railing."

"I don't believe you," Liesl said. She cocked the hammer of the weapon. "I believe you were here, but I think it was because you wanted to make sure they did what you wanted. Tell me: did you enjoy seeing them throw my brother over the balcony. Was it a show for you?"

Dolores Tenison shook her head tightly. She began crying again, and this time, Bostwick was certain, the tears were real. The actress was obviously terrified.

Bostwick looked from Liesl to the gun to Dolores Tenison. It seemed as if time had frozen. Then he glanced at the French door and realized that Miss Tenison's story didn't make sense. "I don't believe you, either," he said. "The door to the balcony wouldn't have been open on a winter night. And if Mr. Sinclair was putting up the fight you say he was, it would have probably taken both of those men to force him outside. So who opened the door for them? Was it you?" He immediately regretted expressing his thoughts aloud, because he saw Liesl's hand began to tremble. *Please don't shoot*, he silently urged her. *Please don't shoot.*

Dolores Tenison didn't reply to Bostwick's questions, but her guilty expression was answer enough.

Then Liesl began to cry. "I can't," she said. "I can't shoot you. Heaven knows you deserve it, but there might be somebody who would miss you as much as my parents and I miss my brother. I can't kill you."

Relief washed over the actress's face, and she began to compose herself. Bostwick felt a similar relief, and he was able to breathe normally again. He would have felt no sympathy for Dolores Tenison, but he would have hated for Liesl Shulmerich to go to jail for killing the actress.

"So you get to stay alive," Liesl said. Still holding the gun, she added, "But unless you go to the police and report what happened, I can't guarantee you for how long."

CHAPTER 38

Marshall Webb couldn't tell from the morning newspapers if Dolores Tenison had done as she'd promised. None of the front-page articles mentioned the actress going to the police. What they did report was that a couple of Fordham University students named Zachary Johnson and Joseph Kelty had walked into the Thirty-seventh Street station house and confessed to killing Lyman Sinclair.

Marshall Webb was skeptical of the men's claims, but according to the papers, they swore that Dolores Tenison bore no responsibility at all for what had happened. The articles portrayed Johnson and Kelty as a couple of love-struck stage-door Johnnys who wanted to rid Miss Tenison of an unwanted suitor. The two insisted that they hadn't intended to kill Sinclair, only to scare him into leaving Miss Tenison alone.

While Webb was pondering the news reports, Nicholas Bostwick telephoned with additional information. The accountant told him that Miss Tenison had confessed what had happened, but since it was a confession made at gunpoint, Bostwick couldn't very well tell that to the police. The two of them discussed it and agreed that Dolores Tenison had probably gone to speak with the two young men instead of reporting them to the police. And no doubt her reason for doing so was to make sure they were consistent in their story—a story that would keep the actress free of any blame. According to Bostwick, the only worry for Miss Tenison now was that Lyman Sinclair's sister would decide to take revenge; the accountant said he was sure that Miss Shulmerich wouldn't do such a thing, but he hoped Miss Tenison would live with that fear for some time. Webb could think of no other punishment for her, either.

It wasn't until after he hung up with Bostwick and continued through the newspapers that Webb found brief reports of two other murders. Brick Fessler and Danny Alcock, Rabbit Doyle's hired thugs, had been found dead of knife wounds under the Jefferson Street pier. There were no suspects according to the reports, and since they were described as a couple of "unemployed dockhands," Webb was sure there wouldn't be much of an investigation. With Fessler and Alcock dead, it would be virtually impossible to prove what had happened to Tom Lamonettin, the old man who'd been killed on Fire Island.

Benjamin Freese had told Webb the last time they had spoken that he would be safe because the death of a reporter would raise too many questions. The deaths of Fessler and Alcock, though, were unlikely to do so; their killings would prevent more questions than they were likely to raise.

Once again, Webb realized, the rich and powerful were trying to let others bear the consequences of their actions. Webb didn't want to let that happen this time. He decided there was one other person he should speak with.

Marshall Webb arrived at the Updegraff mansion Saturday night fully prepared to apply whatever pressure it might take to get Jacob Updegraff to speak with him.

It turned out that there was no trouble getting in to see the banker. The Updegraffs' butler went to announce him and promptly returned to report that Mr. Updegraff would see him in the library. He then escorted him to the room and opened the door for him.

Webb stepped inside to find Jacob Updegraff by himself, a cigar in his mouth, and a full wineglass on the side table next to his overstuffed chair. He also found that the library was almost identical to the one in the Davies home—in fact, it was probably the same as almost every such room in every mansion on Fifth Avenue.

Updegraff didn't stand to greet him, nor did he speak. He waved his cigar toward a chair, signaling Webb to take the seat. The butler closed the double doors, leaving the two of them alone.

"I have some questions," Webb said, no more eager to bother with courtesies than Updegraff was.

"I have one, too." Updegraff turned a bleary eye to him. "Alice left me. I want to know where she is." His tone was sad and his thick speech slurred.

Webb shrugged; he wasn't about to reveal where Alice was staying. "The men who killed that landowner for you on Fire Island are dead," he said. "It was in the newspapers."

"I read that, too. But you have it wrong: they didn't do it for me. I never even met them."

"Then why *did* they kill that old man? And how is it that you were the one who bought the island afterwards?" In case Updegraff was reluctant to talk, Webb had written a piece that tied him to the Fire Island killing; although he had no intention of showing it to anyone other than the banker, Webb was prepared to tell him that he would get it into print unless Updegraff told him the truth.

Updegraff sighed. "I was never even interested in buying that damned island."

"What *were* you interested in?"

The banker sipped from his glass and exhaled a wet spray. "The only thing I'm interested in now is getting Alice to come back to me. Her parents heard from her—she wrote to tell them that she's well. But she hasn't contacted me at all."

"Maybe once everything is cleared up, she will come back," Webb suggested.

"That's all I want." He sighed again. "And the, uh, business I was involved in has all concluded."

"What *was* that business?"

Jacob Updegraff moved his lips, but no words came out for some time. Several times he appeared on the verge of saying something before he finally spoke. "I was going to ask you to be discreet," he said. "But to tell you the truth, Mr. Webb, I really don't care anymore. I miss Alice and I want our lives to go back to normal."

"So what happened? How did it start?" Webb wanted to prod him while his guard was down.

"It started with that damned Lyman Sinclair and his Western Continental scheme. He was embezzling, and he'd taken more money from investors than the railroad was worth. And after he got himself killed, my bank was responsible for making those investments good."

"But if the railroad went bankrupt," Webb interjected, "no one was entitled to anything."

Updegraff nodded. "Exactly. I couldn't very well buy the railroad myself and suddenly declare bankruptcy, though; it would have raised too many suspicions. So I contacted Benjamin Freese—he's always looking for a deal that will make him a quick profit, and he doesn't care too much about whether the deal is legitimate."

"How could he make a profit on a bankrupt railroad?"

"I was going to give him the money to buy it, plus an extra ten thousand for his trouble. Trying to pay back Sinclair's investors would have cost me considerably more than that."

Clever scheme, thought Webb, and thoroughly despicable. It left people like Rebecca Davies taking the biggest loss for Sinclair's fraud. "What about Fire Island? How did you get involved in that?"

"Through Freese. He had a deal of his own in the works—of somewhat questionable ethics—and he needed somebody reputable to front it." Updegraff snorted. "That's what I used to be: 'reputable.' Before I got mixed up with the likes of Benjamin Freese."

"That was the Fire Island deal."

"Yes. Freese had gotten a tip through somebody in Tammany Hall that the state was about to buy the island for a quarantine station. Whoever owned that island was about to come into a lot of state money."

"Rabbit Doyle was the one who gave him the tip?" Webb had suspected Doyle and Freese were involved in something together.

"Freese never told me any names—he plays his cards pretty close to the vest." Updegraff paused for another drink. "Anyway, Ben Freese made me a counteroffer: He would buy the railroad for me and I would buy Fire Island for him. He led me to believe that we would both make a substantial profit on the island."

"Did you?"

"Not much. Freese told me he'd be taking fifty percent for himself, which I agreed to. What he didn't mention was that I wasn't getting the other fifty percent. I only got twenty-five, and the other twenty-five went to some other partners of his."

"And he didn't tell you the names?"

"No. But when I complained about the split, he told me I'd better not get too inquisitive, because his partners had had some trouble on the island. One of the landowners was killed while Freese's partners were 'convincing' him to sell." Updegraff looked at Webb, appealing to him with his eyes. "I never knew anything like that would happen, and I've been positively sick about it ever since. I wish I had never gotten involved with Benjamin Freese, and if I could change what happened, I would." He sighed. "All I want is for my life to go back to normal."

Webb believed him.

"I'm not sure I believe him," Rebecca said. She had known too many women who had returned to their husbands only to be hurt again. To Alice, she said, "It's up to you, of course, but I would be awfully wary of going back to Mr. Updegraff."

"What do you think, Mr. Webb?" Alice asked.

The three of them were in Colden House's sitting room. Webb had just come from the Updegraff home. He'd first told Rebecca what the banker had revealed of his business dealings with Benjamin Freese; then he mentioned how much he seemed to genuinely miss Alice. Since her sister had lately been mentioning that she was thinking of going back home, Rebecca suggested that Webb give her his impressions of Mr. Updegraff.

Webb answered thoughtfully, "I can't know what's in his heart, of course, but your husband seemed quite genuine when he told me how much he misses you. He also said he wants to go back to a normal life."

"I'd like to go back to the life I used to have, too," Alice said wistfully. "But I don't know if that's possible. Some things have changed."

Rebecca put her hand on Alice's arm. "It's up to you. You can stay here as long as you like. Take time to think about it." Her sister was still getting over the death of Melissa Ostertag, and Rebecca didn't want her trying to make any important decisions yet.

"I have been," Alice said. "And I think that if I do go back to my husband, there are going to be some more changes—and some conditions." She turned to Rebecca. "One of them is that I intend to help you with Colden House—and not just with money. I want to work with the women here."

Alice had already been helping. She had even insisted on making the funeral arrangements for Melissa Ostertag and had paid all the expenses. At the small service, Alice had been inspired by meeting Miss Ostertag's friend Sarah Zietlow. She told Rebecca that if someone of Miss Zietlow's limited means could pay medical bills for other women at Colden House, the Updegraff family should do its fair share, too. "I would like that, Alice," Rebecca said. "But be sure it's what you want to do."

As the sisters began to discuss it, Webb excused himself to go home, leaving them to talk in private.

CHAPTER 39

"Was Mr. Pritchard happy with your new novel?" Rebecca asked.

"He was happy I finished it," Webb replied. "I don't know if he's read it yet, but there's no reason he should—one Western is the same as any other." He shifted on the seat of the small boat. "Pritchard gave me some news about Dolores Tenison, by the way."

"What's that?"

"She's lost more than Benjamin Freese's financial support." He chuckled. "Her maid took off with all her jewels. Miss Tenison is broke. Pritchard also tells me she's having trouble attracting any new suitors—no one wants to end up the same as Lyman Sinclair." Her two witless young admirers had taken the entire blame for Lyman Sinclair's death, pleading guilty to manslaughter charges, but Dolores Tenison wasn't going to be able to enjoy the results of what they had done for her.

"I'm just glad it's all over," Rebecca said, adjusting her parasol as the boat shifted course and sunlight streamed onto her golden hair. "This is nice."

"Yes, it is." The water of Central Park's lake lapped at the sides of the gondola as Marshall Webb and Rebecca Davies slowly glided around. Spring sunshine bathed them in warmth, the scent of blooming flowers was in the air, and birds sang in the budding trees.

To Webb it seemed like ages since he and Rebecca had ice-skated on this same spot, but it had only been a few short months. So much had changed since then, though.

Thanks in part to Webb's series in *Harper's Weekly*, there was a move afoot in the state legislature to open investigations into

Tammany Hall. And, while speaking with one of the society's sachems, Webb had made a point to mention Rabbit Doyle's involvement with Benjamin Freese on the Fire Island land sale. He knew that Tammany's system of graft and corruption operated according to strict rules, and, as Webb had suspected, Doyle had broken those rules by giving Freese the tip on Fire Island. Doyle was now no longer a ward heeler, and wouldn't even have a chance of getting a sanitation job in this city. Webb regretted that he hadn't been able to bring Benjamin Freese to some kind of justice—the financier was no doubt huddled in his den, working on some new deal at this very moment—but he was determined to keep track of his activities, certain that he would find a chance to bring him to account in the future.

There'd been a change at Fluitt and Schlichting Confectioners, too. After the death of Melissa Ostertag, the Health Department pressured the candy makers into using different color additives. It took the threat of criminal manslaughter charges before they agreed to do so, but at least the girls who worked there, and those who ate their products, would be safer.

The Updegraff household wasn't the same, either. Although Jacob Updegraff's bank was on sound footing again, and Alice had returned to him, it had come at a cost. One of the conditions Alice had given her husband for her return to him was that he had to establish a trust fund that would provide the shelter with a monthly income adequate to cover all its operating expenses. She'd also insisted that she would spend at least one day a week working in Colden House.

And that meant that Webb and Rebecca could be together more often, enjoying more days like this one.